Laird of the Mist

Foery MacDonell

Moongypsy Press

Las Vegas, Nevada

Laird of the Mist

ISBN: 978-0-615-32480-7 (ebk)

ISBN: X978-1449538754

EAN-13: 978-1449538750.

Cover artist Janet Elizabeth Jones

Printed in the United States of America

Moongypsy Press, Las Vegas, Nevada

Dedication

To Sally, who got me over to Scotland when I needed it the most. I will never forget the night we met. Friends such as you are rare, indeed.

To Kevin, who came back into my life when all was lost and showed me the way. You are my real-life warrior and primarily responsible for Carrick saying to Cat, "Ye will listen this time." You are my first, last, and always.

Acknowledgements

There are so many who are, in some part, responsible for this book, I can't possibly remember you all. If I have forgotten anyone, please forgive me.

First, to my wonderful daughter, Tierney de la Lama, British Association of Teachers of Dance -Member, and United Kingdom Alliance. Your insistence on taking Highland dance lessons at age eight threw me into the Scottish world and caused me to revisit my heritage and family history. You gave me a new appreciation for what our ancestors lived and built for us. Thank you, also, for educating me on Highland dance and culture as we traveled to all those Highland games and competitions through the years, as well as your companionship and friendship. Thank you for your expertise with the Highland dance scenes in this book. Laird would never have been written without you.

Thanks to Mary Beth Klein, BATD and SDTA, of Highland X press and a two-time World Champion Highland dancer. Your wit, especially the way you re-wrote the waterfall scene that no one will ever see— ahem— kept me laughing and excited. (Note from Mary Beth upon reading this: ("Literally. Ask Kevin.")

Thank you to Fred DeMarse of the San Jose School of Highland Dance in California, Fellow of the British Association of Teachers of Dance, and the United Kingdom Alliance, Scottish Official Board of Highland Dancing (SOBHD) World-Wide Judging Panel, Certificated Teacher of the Royal Scottish County Dance Society. And to Alan Twhigg, Certificated Teacher of the Royal Scottish County Dance Society. Hearty thank yous for your help in constructing the country dance sequences. You gave me the means I needed for Cat to remember Carrick.

Special thanks to Shirley Kleiman and Vickie Eisner, my dear friends and counselors at Rehab Services to the Blind for Nevada. Shirley was a wonder! Vickie, without your assistance, I would never have begun writing again. You are a marvel and inspiration, lady!

Thank you to Amanda Scott, fabulous Highland author who really got me interested in writing this. She was my first critter in the early stages of Laird. Thanks for the great humor at all those Highland games and your encouragement! You are a great lady and I am your biggest fan!

A huge thank you to Anne MacDonald of the Glengarry Castle Hotel for your friendship and wonderful hospitality every time I visit. You always make me feel welcome and at home. It is truly a magical place and you are part of that special Highland magic. Besides, you laugh at my silly jokes!

To my dear OES sisters for their love and support. You are true sisters!

Heartfelt gratitude and love to my dearest friends, critters, and sister-authors: Diana Rubino, Tabitha Shay, Kari Thomas, and AC Katt. You are the greatest! Big thanks to Janet Elizabeth Jones, an amazing artist and web mistress. You both accommodated every crazy idea and change with grace and style!

Now read the story!!

PROLOGUE

While ye visit here at Invergarry, listen carefully and ye may hear the legend of a particular brave Laird. It isna an ancient legend, being only 250-years-old, but 'tis a fascinatin' one, and willna be put to rest.

The Laird of Beinn Fhithich, so the story goes, fought well at Culloden Moor in the '75. He watched the Sasunnach murder his wife and clan. Wi' the help of a witch, and when the mists were high, he traveled through time to find his Jenny in the future; for she had reincarnated in a new life. The legend says he brought her home to Beinn Fhithich, and together they helped their people survive the Clearances.

Ye dinna believe in reincarnation? Ye dinna think a body can travel in time? Weel, my friend, I do. For I ha' met the Laird and his Lady wife. They visit here to this verra day, when there is need upon their people. He never evicted a single family, nor did he force mass immigration to the colonies, as did many of the cruel and brutish Lairds. There are yet crofts in the glen and life at Beinn Fhithich thanks to the Laird of the Mist. I ha' seen it all wi' my own eyes and lifted a pint or two with the noble gentleman.

So, while ye're stayin' wi' us, keep yer eyes open for a braw Scot, the like ye dinna see today. He is a warrior long past, and he is even still for his family and clan. But I warn ye, mind yer words if ye speak to him, for he doesna suffer fools; nor should he, given all he has seen.

I welcome ye to Invergarry, then - the place where legends are born.

Nigel MacDonell
Innkeeper

Chapter One

Invergarry, Scotland - May 1746

Laird Carrick MacDonell had stood at the edge of the clearing for over an hour waiting for the mist of dawn to clear. He had been debating whether or not what little courage he had left would bring him to knock on the door of the little stone cottage at the other side. Covered in moss due to the density of the forest, the cottage appeared neat, with a well-tended herb garden to one side. Smoke from a fire curled its way upward as if in welcome, and the door stood slightly ajar to allow the enormous orange tabby its entrance or exit.

Carrick had come, determined in purpose, to the home of Morag, the witch of Invergarry. Odd how all the destruction and sorrows of the last months were nothing compared to what he felt standing before the witch's home. Doubt that she would help him, hope that she would. For he needed mending in spirit and soul, and it was possible that only God could provide them, and at that, only through death. It was unlikely Carrick would ever see peace again while living.

With slow steps and a deep breath for comfort, Carrick approached the door of the home with caution. Morag had healed his wounds and brought him back from near death, something he would not thank her for. had come to ask a final favor of the witch, one for which he *would* be grateful.

He raised his powerful fist to knock on the oaken door, but a tiny, gnarled face haloed in silver peeked round the side of it and her eyes widened in acknowledgment.

"Aye, I ken ye'd come soon enough, Carrick. And here ye be, just as the omens foretold." She opened the door wider and put her spiny hand upon his arm. "Come in wi' ye now and sit. I'll make ye some brew and ye can tell me yer reason for comin'."

Without a word, Carrick bent to pass under the low beam and enter the clean, warm home—redolent with the fragrance of herbs and dried flowers. It was a one room affair with a cozy stone hearth over which Morag had hung a pot of water to boil. Carrick sat silently as Morag meticulously mixed herbs from several roughly sewn sacks into cups that seemed as ancient as she.

"So, me laird, it has been near a week gone since these old eyes ha' set upon ye. And here ye are, healed and braw. I see the darkness of mourning on ye still. I s'pose 'tis why ye're here in the now and wantin' me help. Ye were always runnin' to ole Morag ever as a bairn, and here ye are again."

Carrick accepted the strange tea with a shaking hand and nodded in reply.

"Aye, Morag. 'Tis true. I am here for a purpose I am sure ye ken too well." He nodded toward a linen sack filled with stones that sat on the shelf over the hearth. "I imagine my mother and the runes ha' spoken to ye of my troubles and I need no tell the story to ye."

"Ah, Carrick," Morag soothed him as she stroked his auburn hair. "Ye ken the runes ha' rarely failed me. And poor Molly is worried sick for ye. 'Tis true I ken the tale of yer loss and yer sorrows. Now ye come to see if I can ease yer pain as I did when ye were young and I was nanny to ye all."

She gestured toward the sack of stones. "Aye, the runes ha' spoken to me, and I ken it well. How ye fought at Culloden Moor and saved many of yer clan. How the Sasunnach butchered ye all and gave no quarter. And how ye lost yer Jenny at their hands."

Morag sat next to Carrick and reached a gentle hand to his. "I am told ye sleep no more, but walk the hills all night. Ye haunt the forests in search of yerself and a meaning to yer life. Still ye find no relief for the loss of yer love. All this 'tis true, is it no?"

With a sigh that could have broken him, Carrick nodded and, taking his hand from hers, dropped his head into his hands.

"'Tis true, all of it," he whispered. "And more. I fought at Culloden, aye. I fought well, but no well enough. I saved no enough of the clan. And in the end, Jenny was taken by the Sasunnach and rudely used. She came to the moor to tend my wounds after the battle. The grass was no to be seen for the blood that day, and the stench of it thick in my throat. The filthy foul bastards took her by force as I lay in the mud nearly dead, watching them."

His jaw tightened at the memory. "I could do nothing to stop it-nothing. The cut in my shoulder was too deep and I couldna move. When they finished wi' her, they held her by the hair and put a knife across her chest. I lay helpless, watching the life flow from her." Carrick took a deep breath recalling how, at the last, Jenny had managed to put her gold wedding ring—a circle of celtic knots— into his palm and close his fingers around it. He still had the ring. He kept it safe with him always. It comforted him and kept her close.

"Her last words were 'Please, forget me never,'" he said at last. "I watched the shine of her eyes turn dull. I could bear no more and the good Lord let me pass into sleep for days on end. They brought me home and ye saved me. I didna wish to be saved. I wished to die with' Jenny on the moor. And I wish to die now."

His voice dropped to a near-whisper. "They never found her body. Buried in the mass graves, they think. No even a proper grave..." he trailed away. A single tear flowed down his cheek and onto his tattered kilt; he could not go on without his wife. He wanted to die, end it all, for days now. Had he been a more courageous man, he would have given himself the coup de grace by his own hand. Instead, he had wandered aimlessly around the estates, leaving the management of them to his younger brother, Ian.

He should have been a real Laird to those left of the clan, but the pain was too unbearable. He could not think, he could not eat, he could not sleep. He was turning into nothing, and it suited him fine.

"Aw, Carrick, ye blame yerself fer the loss lad, and it isna so." Morag petted his head. "Ye couldna help, yerself sae injured and near to death. Ye did what ye could to save yer clan and that was fine; ye saved many that day. So lad, what brings ye to Morag this day?"

Carrick ran his long, broad fingers through his thick hair; hair that fell loose on his back and had not been cared for in some time. He took a final sip from the cup and set it on the table, then rose and turned to the one window in the room.

"I thank ye, Morag, for yer generous words. Yer kindness is more than I deserve." He turned slightly to face her. "The truth is that I didna do enough for any of them. Yer words canna change it. It is true. I wish to die, Morag. 'Tis best for the clan if Ian is made Laird by my death. He is nearly Laird now. I am a coward and so I come to ye to ask for one favor. Ye raised me and loved me well, Morag. Ye can grant me one last wish—to mix a potion and let me join my Jenny. I canna go on wi'out her. I simply canna."

The wizened witch stretched out her twisted hand and laid it tenderly on Carrick's arm.

"Nay, me lad," she softly said. "'Tisna the answer. Ye ken 'tis sin to take yer life by yer own hand. I willna be party to such; I never ha' and I never will. There is an answer to yer pain, lad. Strange it may sound, but 'tis true. 'Tis possible ye may be one o' the lucky ones who can do it. For I ken yer Jenny yet lives and ye needna die to be wi' her."

"Morag, ye were ever the wise one, and a fair

healer ye are. I ha' always trusted ye in such things. All of us have," Carrick said gently. "How can ye be sure of such a thing? How can it be possible? God knows, I want to believe ye, I do. But for all yer magic, a person canna live again after death."

"Aye, they can and do, Carrick," she replied with a tender smile. "The one who made us all made us to live yet again and again until we ha' finished wi' what He meant to teach us. Believe me when I tell ye that she is reborn in a future time and place. Trust this one small thing, for what ha' ye to lose?"

"Morag, dear Morag," Carrick humored her. "Ye're of an age and I fear for yer mind. Ye canna truly believe this? That Jenny lives in future times? If this is true as ye say," he challenged her, "then tell me where she lives. How do I go to her?"

"Carrick, lad, I am no addled. I saw this morning." She turned away and picked up the bag of Runes. "The Runes spoke to me and I saw again in the pool, ye ken the seeing pool? I saw yer Jenny alive and fit, and it may be possible for ye to go to her."

"What did ye see Morag?" Carrick wanted to believe his old nursemaid. Heaven knew her magic had always been potent, always healing and more. Could he believe her now, or was she just losing her wits to her age? On the chance that she could still be as powerful as she once was, Carrick sighed and said, "tell me now what ye ken. No more of yer riddles! Tell me all and tell me now."

"Aye, I'll tell ye, but ye may no like the tellin' of

it." Morag set the bag back on its shelf.

"Like it or no isna the issue Morag." His blue eyes crackled with fire. "I will ha' the story and ha' it all. Then we will see if ye're addled or no."

Morag looked down at her aged hands and up again to meet Carrick's gaze, steel for steel.

"She lives in another time and place. In what ye would call the future. She is reborn there-she lives there-and it may be wi' the help of the stones and something of Jenny's, ye can travel to her there."

"Again wi' the future?" Carrick laughed. "Ye crone, ye dear old crone, ye're too old. Surely ye're confused in this seeing. 'Tis impossible to do as ye say. Ye gave me false hope for a time and it was for naught. Be kind to me Morag, and fix the potion so that I may leave this earth and join Jenny in death."

"Fool 'tis what ye are, " Morag retorted angrily. "Ye're a bloody fool. Ye dinna believe me? Come ye then to the pool and see fer yerself, ye silly man. Ye ha' no understanding of the way the power works. All ye understand is battle and brawn, ye thick-headed sot. Come ye to the pool and see for yerself then."

Carrick drew himself to his full height and smiled for the first time since Jenny's death. "Fine then, old woman. Let's on to the pool, where I am certain we shall see nothing but water from the spring."

"Aw, ye were ever a foolish lad," Morag laughed, as she wrapped her shawl about her shoulders and walked through the door. "Come ye, lad. For if ye can see the meanings in the pool, ye shall be able to travel to yer Jenny."

Having nothing to lose and only more to gain, Carrick followed the witch to a small, crystal-still pond in a tiny, well-hidden clearing. It almost appeared to be dusk, so thickly surrounded by trees as it was.

Morag approached the pool reverently and slowly, then knelt upon the mossy bank and dipped a finger into it, causing a ripple to ride away toward the other side.

"Life is a circle, Carrick," she mused. "We make these ripples and they meet wi' each and the other. They never end. Kneel and look, lad. Look deeply and ye shall see yer beloved."

Carrick did as he was told and sat for a time gazing into the pool. "I see nothing, crone. Ye make a fool of me," he sighed, beginning to rise on one leg.

"Sit ye down now!" Morag cried out to him. "Laird or no, do as I say in this, for ye shall suffer all the more if ye dinna. Now sit ye down and gaze - look wi' yer heart and no yer bloody eyes!"

With a sullen demeanor, Carrick settled back down onto the moss and stared deeply into the pool.

"That's the way, lad," Morag encouraged. "Still ye that mess of yer brain and think of yer Jenny. Feel yer love for her wi' yer heart and feel it deep as ye look. Keep ye lookin' now, and dinna stop."

Carrick sat silently and as still as he could.

He tried desperately to erase his thoughts; the very thoughts that had haunted him and turned him into the ghost of Invergarry, rather than its Laird.

Memories of battle screams, heard above even the skirl of the great Highland pipes, overwhelmed him. Watching in frustration as clan after clan was massacred on the moor; blood soaking his kilt and boots, dripping from his hair, his chin and nose. Tired and starving, the clans fought on and became no match for the English.

He remembered being cut by sword again and yet again, and falling into the mud and filth, unable to rise. And Jenny, sweet Jenny, who had insisted on being near to nurse the wounded. Her hand stroking his face, smiling encouragement into his eyes, telling him he would be well, that he must live, for she was with child. Memories of her silken hair falling onto his face mixing with blood, her tears and her touch, until the Sasunnach dragged her from him and...

"Carrick," Morag whispered. "D'ye see? She is there! In the pool! Look ye now."

Carrick blinked back the mist in his eyes and looked deep, deep into the very depths of the water, still as stone, clear as wind.

"Jenny," he barely spoke the name, no longer in doubt of Morag's awesome magic. "Jenny. Ye're alive! Where are ye *mo cridhe*? Tell me, please. I am lost without ye. Tell me so I may come to ye now..."

"Carrick!" the image in the pool cried in delight. "Where are ye husband? Come to me, for I am also lost. My life is nothing here. I am in a strange time and an odd place. I ha' been reborn into a new time. I am in a place so odd I canna tell ye how it is. The year is 2010 and the town is Destin, in a place called Florida. 'Tis America. Come to me Carrick, ye must. For I canna be much longer without ye, my heart, *mo leannan...*"

Her image slowly dissolved as she spoke the words and the pool returned to its clear calm as though nothing had ever happened.

Chapter Two

Destin, Florida - 2010

Caitriona MacPhail woke in a pool of sweat, the sheets sticky and twisted, even though the breeze through the bedroom window was cool and refreshing. Reaching for the lamp on the side table, Caitriona slowly sat up and tried to regain her bearings. The dream had been more than a dream. It had been so real, so vivid, she could hardly distinguish between it and the reality of the room she awakened to. As the light cast its beam about the room, Caitriona, whom everyone called Cat for short, rose and slowly walked to the top of the staircase. All was quiet in the old Victorian mansion that had been her family home since before she was born, and was now hers. She checked in on her grandfather MacPhail, peacefully asleep.

"At least someone can sleep," she sighed to herself, as she made her way down the stairs to the kitchen, where her owl-eyed Maine Coon cat, Guinness, was waiting for her.

"So there you are." She reached down to pet his long, brown tabby fur. He cooed in satisfaction and settled on a chair to watch her make a cup of tea. A hot cup would help soothe her nerves and get her back to sleep. The dreams were always the same theme and, lately, becoming more frequent and intense.

Always she was herself, but in another time, in what she knew to be Scotland from the clothing, landscape, and language. She looked the same, but her name was Jenny. Amazing that she could recall it.

An enormous Scotsman was always present in some way; dark auburn hair, flashing blue eyes, a ready smile, and determined mind. He loved her passionately, and she returned the love in kind. She knew he was her lover and husband. She knew she could not ever live without him, had not ever lived without him, for she had known him since childhood and their souls were joined.

In some dreams she could see their wedding (must be an influence from the many Highland games she played her fiddle at, she analyzed). A joyous event for the Laird and his Lady. A multitude of kin and clan who attended, and she knew their faces - every one of them.

Other dreams were of lovemaking so genuine that she could have sworn he was in her bed when she woke - reaching out for him in the expectation that he would be at her side.

All of the dreams had been wondrous and she had actually looked forward to them. But this last dream was the one which finally disturbed her, made her tremble with trepidation and fear, caused tears to come as though she had experienced a loss so terrible that she would never recover.

She sat at the kitchen table waiting for the tea to brew, reviewing the dream. The Scotsman had been looking at her in astonishment, calling her name, his joy in seeing her, begging her to tell him where she was. How he needed her. He must come to her, he had cried. And she had replied, telling him she was here - how could he not know where she was?

She reached over and stroked Guinness, emotion welling inside her. She was losing her mind! It was so real, so true. It was a knowing in her soul that this was the truth of her life, and the sorrow was not a dream.

She was being ridiculous, she admonished herself. It was just a stupid dream. She always had these dumb dreams just before a games! It was probably just nerves. She always was the one for stage fright.

She poured her tea and sat sipping it slowly, reviewing her life and accomplishments. Born into a wealthy family, she had never lacked for anything. When Cat was orphaned along with her younger sister, Olivia, at the age of twelve, her father's parents had taken over the raising of them. A happy family they were, despite the loss. Now her sister had her own career as an artist and traveled all over the world.

Grandmother MacPhail had died several years before, but her influence was still felt in Cat's life. Her grandma had been a concert violinist and raised Cat the same. Now Cat traveled the world and played classical music with the greatest orchestras. Playing fiddle at the local Jighland games was her therapy.

Grandda Hamish MacPhail, a retired doctor

born in Scotland and proud of his heritage, lived with Cat and it was a happy partnership. Dr. MacPhail was spry and mischievous for his sixty-five years, and teased everyone endlessly with his thick Scottish brogue.

Not a bad life. Full of friends, family, and accomplishment. She did not miss a lover, had had few, but with no real regret. Her career made romance difficult and she needed to be independent to travel and record. And tomorrow was the Emerald Coast/ Ft. Walton Beach Highland Games at which she was always expected to perform the traditional Scottish tunes.

"Well, Guinness." She picked up the enormous cat. "Off to bed with us."

Cat set the cup in the sink and made her way back up the stairs. Sleepiness began to settle as she lay back into her pillow. Listening to the contented purring of her companion she began to drift off, and through the ensuing fog she vaguely heard her lips whisper the name "Carrick."

"So then, Morag," Carrick began, feeling foolish. "I am here as ye demanded wi' Jenny's locket. What next?"

"Patience, lad," Morag whispered. "I havna done casting the circle. A moment more and then the moon is high as well. Ye step into the center when I tell ye, and I will do the rest. The magic is high tonight, 'deed it 'tis."

She was drawing a circle in the dirt with a long willow stick, a perfect circle in the center of the clearing near the sacred gazing pool. A thick mist began to rise about them—a dense fog that brought a chill to his spine.

Morag set particular stones around the edge at intervals. What they were, Carrick had no idea. The whole thing was most peculiar, but his desperate state left no room for argument or question.

"Speak to me, Carrick, what ye must do and the terms of the travel now, before ye begin," demanded the old woman. "I must be certain ye dinna fail to understand the dangers."

"God's teeth, Morag." Carrick sighed impatiently. "Is this really necessary? I ken it well, ye told it so many times."

"Do it ye clot, or I willna help ye further."

"So be it then." He folded his massive arms across his chest, skewing his plaid as he did. "I must make Jenny remember me within six moons or I will return to my own time alone. Each time I kiss her wi' the locket on my person, a memory will come to her. The locket must be wi' me at all times, for in it is the magic of her memories of me. If she does remember me fully, then we are free to stay in her time or come home as we please. The locket is the link to my own time, and if she doesna remember me, it will return me home. Are ye happy now, ye hag?"

"Aye, that will do." Morag smiled. Looking up at the full moon, an aura of mist around it, she seemed well-pleased, indeed. "One last thing. I ha' seen this place to where ye travel. It is full of strange things ye will no recognize or understand. Dinna let them steal yer mind from yer purpose, aye?"

Carrick nodded his agreement. "Aye. So ye told me."

"'Tis time then, Laird Carrick. Ye may enter the circle. Hold the locket in yer right hand—ye do ken yer right hand d'ye not?"

"Get on wi' it ye witch," he bellowed through the chilling fog. He could no longer see her. "I'm no a bloody idiot. I want to be on my way. No more of yer teases and twitches."

"Aye, aye," she chuckled, walking the rim of the circle. "Close yer eyes then, Carrick, and dinna open them. See yer Jenny as ye saw her in the pool and think only of her as ye hold the locket tight. I will speak the spell the now."

Carrick stood rock still, the mist enveloping him to the bone as Morag circled him round and round, chanting in ancient Gaelic; words he could not understand, words which had no meaning for him.

Carrick did as he was bid, holding the locket tightly in his hand for fear of it being lost in whatever should happen. What would happen? Silly old woman; probably nothing and best just to humor her. But what if this did work, what if he was truly about to travel some 260 years into the future and actually be with Jenny? The possibility raised insecurities foreign to him. She had looked exactly the same in the seeing pool; hair, eyes, her smile, even the sound of her voice. But there was little hope she would recognize him and he must prepare himself for that.

If she never remembered him, would she be attracted to him in any conceivable way? Who knew what women wanted in the future? Surely not warriors? Surely in 260 years society was more civilized, and women did not have a need to be protector as now.

Perhaps a warrior would be reviled in her eyes; he had killed, aye, but only in defense of self, family, and country. Would that be considered a noble thing where he was going, or would he be an outcast with blood on his hands? He would tread carefully there and assess the climate when he arrived—if he arrived.

A sudden beating of the bodhran in his head, not in his ear, stopped his thoughts. A rhythmic beating that pulsed with his blood and made his stomach whirl. Now a stream of brilliant colors in his vision that flashed in time with the bodhran and Morag's ever diminishing chant. Flashes of memories with Jenny, their marriage, their lovemaking in the heather, and racing naked through the streams together. Her voice calling to him, "Carrick, I am here. You are almost home. Try just a bit harder.....come to me, *mo cridhe...*"

Sounds like gypsy campfire music, tambourines, mournful fiddles and pipes, and dancing flooded his brain, and he felt the intensity of the sensual music in every part of his being. So intense it was, that he thought he would be sick. But instead, he lost all awareness and fell to the ground in a helpless heap, holding Jenny's locket tightly in his fist.

Chapter Three

"Another lovely games, eh lass?" Hamish MacPhail commented, as Cat pulled her Mercedes into the driveway.

"Aye, grandda," Cat agreed, imitating his lilting Scottish accent. "'Twas indeed. Duncan said it was the best attendance in years."

No wonder," he proudly replied as he let himself out of the car, "what with a world class fiddler on the bill."

"Oh, grandddda!" Cat laughed, taking his arm as they started through the front door where Guinness was waiting for them. The brown tabby cocked his head sideways and let out a happy, "hello!"

"I will never get used to that cat saying 'hello,'" Hamish marveled. "It's unnatural."

"Perfectly natural for a Maine Coon, grandda." Cat smiled as she bent to pet him. "He's happy to see us."

"And happy I am to be home and off to bed, m'darlin'." Her grandfather kissed her cheek. "Good night to ye and yer witch-cat."

"And a good sleep to you, grandda," Cat replied, locking the door behind them. "We'll have a nice, relaxing day tomorrow on the beach."

"Aye, lass, that we will," he agreed with a yawn, stepping around Guinness who had been observing silently. "Well, m'darlin', may the fairies bless yer sleep."

"And yours as well, granddda." Cat gave him a quick kiss on the cheek. "Off with you now." She smiled as she waved and went in back to the kitchen to make some tea, Guinness coming in her wake.

"Do you feel it too, Guinness?" she asked the cat. Her arms were tingling lightly, as though electricity swam through the air around her. An intense flash of lightening ran up her spine, causing her to sit abruptly at the table.

What is wrong with me? She tried to shake the sensations off, but instead, a maze of colors revolved in her vision nearly obscuring it.

She must be coming down with something, she decided, then prayed she wasn't. She had a full schedule leading up to recording her new album.

"Jenny?" a male voice whispered in the distance. "Are ye there? Come to me."

Cat fervently denied the experience, summoning her will to dismiss it. Slowly, it faded and left a slight headache in its wake.

She stood carefully, gripping the table's edge, and shook it off. She seemed to be recovered and let go of the table. *I'm still standing.* She let out a held breath in relief.

A walk on the beach would do her good, she decided. It was a lovely night with a full moon high in the sky that sent floating beams through the kitchen window. Cat could never resist such a night. She slipped quietly out the door and down the deck steps to the world-renown, fine white sand—so white and so fine, that it resembled powdered sugar and stuck to her bare feet.

Always curious, Guinness followed close behind her, talking softly all the way.

"Aww..." came a deep moan from somewhere near the southern corner of the house. "Oh, good God bless me," the voice groaned in pain. "'Tis true, what the witch said. 'Tis true!"

What? Cat said to herself as she walked cautiously toward the source. Then aloud, "What in the hell?"

There, in a messy, tousled heap, lay a disheveled and enormous man curled into as tight a ball as someone so large could do. His hands were wrapped around his head and his eyes were wide and staring.

"Jenny!" he cried, as he began to uncurl and stumble to his feet. "Blessed be all the Saints, 'tis you!"

"Here, let me help you." Cat bent over and grasped his upper arm in an attempt to help him stand. "Oh God!" She laughed as they both fell back over onto the sand. She hadn't anticipated how truly large this man was, and the fact that she was considerably smaller.

"Aye!" laughed Carrick. "I'm a bit much for ye. But then I always was, aye, Jenny? "nd ye look exactly the same as when I saw ye last. I would ha' kent ye anywhere."

"Jenny?" Cat grew serious, recognizing the name from her dreams. It made her cautious, yet curious. "Who is this Jenny you are talking about? My name is Caitriona and you somehow got yourself here to my house." She looked him up and down carefully now that he was standing-somewhat wobbly-but standing nevertheless.

She noticed his kilt, done in the old style, wrapped about the waist, belted, and the rest thrown over his shoulder. She noticed he wore no clan badge, and his tartan looked a bit weary at that.

Good Lord, he was the most stunning man she had ever seen. In fact, he was breathtaking. From his long dark auburn hair tied with leather in a que at the back of his neck, to his massively broad shoulders and chest - a well-muscled chest that she could get a peek of through his loosely fitted shirt. Just looking at him made her dizzy. And he had an uncanny resemblance to the man in her mysterious, recurring dreams.

Wonder what he kisses like/. Damn, random thoughts. Stop this. This man is a complete stranger. He could be dangerous. And anyway, he clearly needs assistance.

"You must be one of the reenactors from the Highland games," she ventured. "Are you lost? Perhaps I can help you get back to your hotel or - you aren't drunk are you?"

"Me? Drunk?" Carrick took immediate offense. "No bloody likely! I gave the stuff up long ago when it nearly killed me wi' wanting it so. Jenny, losing ye drove me mad. And what in heaven is a re-en-act-or?"

Suddenly, Carrick remembered that Cat had no idea who he was. She had forgotten her life with him and was no longer the Jenny he knew. He would have to proceed very carefully. Especially if he was to get her to kiss him, and recover her memories.

"Oh, come on now." Cat raised an eyebrow and crossed her arms. "Dressed like that? It's obvious you attend Highland games all the time. And you're wearing an ancient style kilt. Mostly only reenactors wear those."

"My kilt isna ancient. I've had it only a few years." He was insulted. "Worn a bit, aye, but certainly no ancient. And what in hell do ye mean 'games?' We havena' had a games in the highlands for many a year, I assure ye. Would ye mind if I just sit for a bit, lass? My head is beginning to pound as if I was hit wi' a sword."

"Oh!" The light dawned on Cat. "Then you must be a reenact or. That's it! You must have been hit on the head during an exhibition. Do you know your name?"

"Of course, I know my bloody name," Carrick bellowed. "I am no a bloody fool! I was educated in France, ye silly woman!"And ye ken it well, ye potty lass."

Cat started to approach him, ready to check his head for bumps and bruises.

"How would I possibly know your name, or where you were educated? I've never seen you before in my life! You really are becoming annoying. You must have had one hell of a hit. So what is it?"

"What is what?"

Imitating him as best she could she retorted, "Yer bloody name that I am supposed to know so damn well."

"Stop that!" he roared, as Cat began to run her fingers through his hair, looking for the telltale bump that caused his memory loss. Hopefully, it would be temporary. Granddda ought to look at him. She would wake him in a bit for that.

"I have to check your head for bumps and see how seriously you are injured," Cat explained. "Just calm down and cooperate, will you?"

"'Tis Carrick MacDonell."

"Carrick MacDonell is it? Nice name. I like it; the way it rolls off the end of your tongue." Cat made a mistake in saying the word tongue, as she immediately returned to wondering about his kisses. *Oh God...*

"It's *Laird* Carrick MacDonell, actually," Carrick replied, calmer now and remaining still as she probed his head. "Ye have a nice touch. Gentle and kind, but then..."

"Oh?" Cat interrupted haughtily, hands on her hips. "So you're a Laird now too, are you? Boy, you people really get into your role-playing. I've watched you guys, the way you think you are actually Mary Stuart or a peasant. Bet that accent is fake too, and you're really from Brooklyn!" Cat spat the words at him, but her mind was racing. Carrick? That was the name of the man in those vivid dreams she had been plagued with. Strange...

"What the - look here, lass." Carrick was growing irritated again. "I came here to find ye. Don't ye remember me at all? I was yer husband and ye were killed by the Sasunnach at Culloden Moor. It's that reincarnation thing the witch always talks about—being reborn in—what's the year now?"

"Oh, that really does it!" Cat lost her temper. "Reincarnation, Culloden Moor! Next you'll be telling me you fought next to Bonnie Prince Charlie!"

"Well, I nearly did. He was close by. I did meet him a few times."

"Oh for heaven's sake." Cat shook her head. "Ok, come on. Let's get you into the house. I don't suppose you recall where you are staying, do you? And it's too late to be running to hospitals. Come along into the house now, and my grandfather will examine you."

Guinness followed Carrick into the kitchen, rubbing his long body against Carrick's leg and cooing loudly.

"What type of creature is that?" Carrick stepped

back, alarmed at the enormity of the cat. "Ye keep wild beasts in yer home?"

"Of course not," Cat retorted as she picked up the giant fur ball and rubbed his tufted ears. "It's a Maine Coon cat, and his name is Guinness."

"I dinna care what ye call him." Carrick took another step back, "Just keep it away from me, if ye dinna mind."

"Very well." Cat set Guinness down and gave him a reassuring pat.

Carrick, keeping a wary eye on Guinness, suddenly became disoriented by the bright electric lights overhead and the whirring of the ceiling fan.

"What the devil is that contraption?" Carrick ducked down, terrified of the spinning blades. "It's bloody dangerous to ha' a thing like that hanging where it can sever a person's head. And what keeps it moving so?"

"It's a fan. Don't be ridiculous. It's to cool the room." Here she was, playing along with him again. Didn't this guy ever quit? "It runs on electricity. You should know that! Stop playing around and be serious. If you really don't understand, maybe you *should* go to the hospital."

"There ye threaten me wi' hospital again!" Carrick began to stand upright, still keeping an eye on the fan. "I'll no go to hospital. A body goes there to die, no heal."

"You might very well need a hospital. You may be better off in a hospital. Oh forget it," Cat snapped.

"That would be a bloody heartless thing to do!"

"Hey, I am through humoring you for tonight. You can sit on the sofa and my grandfather can look you over. Then we'll get you back to wherever it is you belong."

"Fine enough." Carrick smiled, adjusting the plaid over his shoulder. "But why have yer grandda look me over?"

"Because he's a doctor, that's why," Cat shot at him as she led him into the living room. "And you need one badly!" Then, mentally measuring his height against the furniture, she murmured, "Geez, I hope you can fit on the sofa!"

"I dinna need a doctor," Carrick firmly denied. "Those charlatans with their leeches and bleeding? I'll no ha' it. There is nothing wrong with me."

"Oh no?" Cat questioned, fire in her eyes. "Well, I think you do, and a doctor you shall have. My grandfather is no charlatan, and doesn't use leeches and bleeding. That's ancient medicine. Listen, do you really have to take this role-playing quite so far? Now just sit down and try to make yourself comfortable. Leeches, my ass."

"Ye want me to sit on this? How can a body sit on such a wee thing as this?" he asked, eyeing the sofa dubiously. Deciding to be tactful, he said, "Thank ye, lass, for yer fine hospitality."

Carrick reached out his hand to her. Cat tentatively reached out to shake it, a bit nervous at the thought of touching this strange person. Seeing her discomfort and realizing his mistake, Carrack quickly withdrew his hand and softened his smile.

"You're welcome," Cat snapped. "Now stay put and don't move until my grandfather comes down to look at you. And you had better get your story straight before he comes. He can see right through anyone. He can give you the medical attention you need, and I can get some sleep. I have to be up at dawn tomorrow and I have no more time for this foolishness."

"Well then, *mo cridhe.*" Carrick smiled gently and looked deeply into Cat's eyes, green as Scotland's mountains. "Ye should ha' no problem with the dawn. Ye ever were a delight in the morning."

"Oh hell and damnation." Cat started toward the staircase. "Just go sit down and wait for grandda. Damn," Cat solidly cursed her way up the stairs to wake her grandfather and explain.

"Aw, Jenny." Carrick chuckled, "Ye were ever the challenge. Ye havena changed a bit!"

Chapter Four

"What in heaven's name is he still doing here?" Cat stood rigidly in the deck's doorway, outraged at the sight of her grandfather enjoying what appeared to be an amiable breakfast with Carrick. "What the hell is going on here?"

"Now Caitriona..." Her grandfather began to rise from his chair. "Just calm yerself, lass. That is no way to speak about our guest."

"Our guest?" Cat snapped with a backward step. "Guest! You must be joking! And I suppose you fixed him breakfast, too?"A

Hamish MacPhail put a friendly hand on Carrick's shoulder and leaned to whisper in his ear. "I told ye she'd be furious. Back in a minute. Enjoy yer food, lad."

Carrick smiled and nodded as Hamish made his way to Cat, stretching an arm around her waist.

"Aye, I gave him food. The poor man was starving near to death. We can be hospitable, Cat, surely. After all, he is a MacDonald, as are we. Come now," he said, leading her back into the house. "Let's have a little talk."

"But..." Cat began as Hamish pulled out a kitchen chair for her. "I don't understand, granddda. What is going on? Is he injured or not?"

"Now Caitriona," he answered, as he sat at the table with her. "Ye need to calm yerself and listen. No, he isna injured at all. He is a healthy, braw man with nowhere to go."

Cat's eyes widened in disbelief. "Nowhere to go? Surely he has friends or someone in the area. He's a reenactor from the games. You can check with the Caledonian Society or Clan Donald and find out who he is. And I don't buy the amnesia bit, either."

Hamish reached for her hand and let out a sigh. "Nay, Cat, he hasna got the amnesia. And he hasna a soul in this time or place, I assure ye. He is a good and decent sort. I spent all the night talking with him. Ye must trust me in this. I intend to help him. "

Cat stood up abruptly. "Help him? Help him go home, yes. And what do you mean, in this time and place?"

Hamish steeled himself. He knew his fiery granddaughter well. "He is a time-traveler, Cat. He came here to find ye."

"He's a what?" Cat laughed. "You are as daft as he is! There is no such thing as time-travel."

"Aye, Cat." Hamish grew serious. "There is

such a thing. 'Tis a tricky business, granted, but 'tis true. I knew a traveler when I was a young man back home. In my town, we all knew it was a reality. And that is how Carrick came to us."

"Right, and he traveled here to find me?" Cat smirked at him. "So you're telling me he is a kind of time-traveling stalker, are you? Granddda, you are a doctor, a man of science. You know better. This is ridiculous nonsense."

"I'm afraid not, Cat," Hamish answered emphatically. "I would ask ye to hear his story before ye pass judgment. 'Tis all I ask, Cat. 'Tis a remarkable tale."

"I'll just bet it is. Fine." Cat wanted an end to this insanity. "If I listen to what he has to say, can we then be rid of him? I don't plan to harbor a mad man forever."

"I'll make no bargains with ye, lass." Hamish smiled patiently. "This is my home as well, and he has no place to go. I'll no toss him out in a strange time. He'd no survive a week."

Exasperated, Cat started toward the door. "I give up." She raised her hands in defeat. "Fine. Let's get this over with. But I warn you, if you insist on keeping this stray fruitcake, I may go stay with Olivia until he's gone. Got that?"

"Fair enough," Hamish answered as he followed her. He couldn't wait for her to hear the whole story, he thought with a secret smile.

"So you lost your pregnant wife at Culloden, then went to your local witch and she told you I was the reincarnation of – Jenny, was it? Then she did a kind of spell and sent you through time to us here in 2010 Florida?" Cat recounted, glaring across the table at Carrick.

Carrick leaned forward a bit and stared back at her. "Aye, right so far, lass."

Cat set down her coffee with a bang. "And you expect that, in time, I will somehow recall you and this past life, fall into your arms, and live happily ever after?" Cat's head was beginning to pound in rhythm to the surf breaking behind her.

She turned on Hamish. "I think I have the full picture now. I'm off to Olivia's. You two nutters try to stay out of trouble while I go book my flight." Cat began to rise when Carrick reached out and gently grabbed her hand.

"Cat," he spoke with a confident calm as their eyes met. "'Tis true, all of it. Ye're truly Jenny in every way. Ye will remember, I ken it. Just give it a wee bit of time. It will come back to ye."

Damn those beautiful eyes, she thought. The most intoxicating eyes she had ever seen. They were deep and full of passion as he spoke. And his touch - oh Lord - it sent a subtle electricity to every part of her body. It was thrilling and terrifying all at once, and part of her wanted more.

Was it really so unreasonable a request? Give it a wee bit of time? But he was a crazy man, she reminded herself. Who listens to a lunatic? Maybe give it a day or two to be certain, the other part of her piped up; the surprising part that suddenly wanted to believe in all of this, wanted it to be true. And most of all, suddenly wanted to be loved with the fierceness that drove and possessed him.

"All right." Cat relented a little. "I'll give you a day or two for your memory to come back." She turned to Hamish. "But you promise to help find where he belongs, okay?"

She realized Carrick was still holding her hand and slowly pulled it away. She felt an instant loss when contact broke.

"As ye say, Cat," Hamish agreed with a smile. He had noticed the energy between Carrick and his granddaughter when he had taken her hand. A powerful connection which left him in no doubt as to the validity of Carrick's tale. "But he is exactly where he belongs," he murmured to himself.

Cat had spent most of the day in her third floor studio reviewing selections to record for her upcoming CD. She had two weeks before she would become immersed in its production. Playing various Scottish tunes to finalize her decisions, she lowered the violin in satisfaction. It would be a departure from classical music; a new avenue to explore and she was enjoying it.

Hamish had taken Carrick off for the day to shop and orient him to the 21st century. She watched through the window long enough to see her grandfather explaining the car to Carrick, his obvious enthusiasm for the Mercedes as he got into it, and his electric smile as Hamish drove them away. Cat had known many who had a passion for cars, but this was extraordinary. You would think he had never seen one before...

"Cat, darlin'" Hamish's voice rang through the house. "Do ye come down and join us. 'Tis nearly dinner time and I want to treat us tonight."

"Coming grandda," she called down to him. She placed the violin in its case with great care and closed the lid securely. Guinness loved to play with the strings, brushing his fat paws over them creating dissonant music.

Cat stopped abruptly at the last stair before the foyer, her eyes riveted on the figure with his back to her. She barely recognized Carrick without his kilt. He was exquisite in a pair of tight fitting jeans and shirt accentuating the lines of his muscular frame. No man had ever looked that good in a pair of jeans, she thought as her gaze lifted to his thick hair tied down his back. Thank God his back was turned so he couldn't see her expression. It had to be one of open lust and appreciation.

"Aye, Cat, there ye are." Hamish had seen the fire in her eyes, but kept his counsel. "Shall we go to dinner? Ye must be hungry by now, squirreled away in yer studio all day."

Cat quickly composed herself and took the last steps down the stairs and across the foyer. "Sure grandda," she smiled, in control now. "I'm ready. You two must have had a good time shopping. New clothes, Carrick?" She turned to him at last.

"Aye, they are," Carrick answered, waving toward some bags on the sofa. "Yer grandda was kind enough to procure some breeches and shirts while my kilt is attended to."

"I see." She wondered what had become of the tattered tartan. "Who is attending to it?"

"Dropped at the cleaners," Hamish hastily interrupted. "Shall we go then?" He nudged Cat toward the door. "We can tell ye all at Magnolia's."

Chapter Five

"D'ye mind if I sit wi' ye a bit?" Carrick stood behind Cat, his voice striking against the symphony of the waves.

"No, not at all." Cat surprised herself as she smoothed the blanket beside her in invitation. "Sit if you like."

"I didna wish to interrupt yer thoughts." He sat at the edge of the small blanket so as not to seem threatening. "But I did wish to thank ye for yer fine hospitality. Tis verra generous of ye."

Cat wrapped her arms around her knees and rocked softly. "You're welcome," she answered, her former agitation with him soothed by the companionable dinner and the beauty of the shore and stars. "Carrick," she began, still looking out to sea. "Did Jenny really play the violin?"

"Oh aye," he said with tender remembrance. "A fine fiddler she was, indeed. Accomplished in the classics as well. When I heard ye playing today, 'twas as though she were..." He broke off the thought. He was learning to be careful in making comparisons.

"I'm not Jenny," Cat said quietly, placing her hand over his. "I'm not." More gently, "I may look like her, we may have had things in common, but it's just coincidence, Carrick. Nothing more."

"Perhaps." He nodded. "I never believed in coincidence. I have seen too much to begin now."

"Have you? It seems that grandda gave you quite an intense tour of our century today," Cat said, without a trace of her usual sarcasm. "What do you like best so far? Grandda talked so much over dinner, I had no chance to ask."

"Hmmm..." Carrick reflected on the extraordinary day. "I s'pose it must be the car - no - it needs must be the, uh, TV, is it?"

"The TV?" She smiled. "I suppose I can understand that."

"And the aquarium with the lovely trained fishes jumping over poles, although I did enjoy the Indian Temple Mound. It reminded me of mounds in Scotland. But then there was...."

"I get the general idea." Cat laughed. "You enjoyed it all, I guess?"

"Aye, so I did." Carrick laughed with her. "So many things to see and learn. Aye. 'Twas a good day." He sat silent, reflecting on the wonders he had seen.

Cat was silent too, letting the breeze and Carrick's masculine presence wash over her. She was definitely softening toward him, and she liked the feel of his hand under hers. It was comforting, and she began to imagine what it would be like to feel his hands touching her elsewhere.

"It must have been terrible for you." Cat attempted to divert her thoughts, but didn't take her hand away from his. She had heard a bit about Jenny's murder over dinner, and compassion welled in her throat. "Losing your wife, I mean."

"Aye." Gently, he pulled his hand away from hers. He had been holding Jenny's locket since he sat down. "I have this. It was hers." He closed it tenderly in her hand, and placed a light kiss on the back of her knuckles. It occurred to him that showing her the wedding ring, which he always carried, might be too much for her.

The kiss put a rippling shiver through her and, fascinated, she began to examine the locket closely. It was warm in her palm, and seemed to be growing steadily warmer.

"It's lovely." Cat couldn't take her eyes from it. "Such fine work..." Her voice trailed into silence. She was feeling as warm as the locket, and her vision was fading at the edges. She must have had more wine than she thought.

"Cat." She could vaguely hear Carrick through a developing fog in her head. "Are ye well?" He reached an arm around to steady her. "Ye dinna look aright."

Her stomach lurched and dropped as she saw herself in a Highland wedding dress; a flowing tartan skirt and silk bodice. Her hair was wreathed in roses and sprigs of heather, and her heart overflowed with more love than she could ever have imagined possible. Carrick was standing next to her, dressed in his finest kilt, his clan tartan draped over his shoulder and held in place with an enormous jeweled brooch. He was beaming with joy at her and saying something...

"Caitriona?" Carrick's voice grew stronger in her ears. "Cat, can ye hear me? Come, lass, say something, I beg ye."

Carrick's deep and urgent voice reached her and, at last, she surfaced back to normality.

"I'm all right," she murmured hesitantly. "I - I think I'm fine." She stared at Carrick, trying to focus on his face through the mist in her mind. "I had the strangest vision." She shook her head to clear it.

It suddenly occurred to Carrick that the locket had been the cause of her distress, and he quickly took it from her hand. He had innocently kissed her hand with them both holding the locket. Surely this had brought memories to her as Morag had promised. "What did ye see?" he asked anxiously.

Cat lay back on the blanket to steady herself. "I saw a wedding. You were there. I think you were the groom." *I must be losing my mind.* The vision had been identical to her haunting dreams. But dreams don't come when you are wide awake. Do they?

"Is there more?" Carrick felt a surge of hope and elation, but dared not show it lest he frighten Cat.

"Not really." She contemplated, frowning

in frustration. "I was in a tartan skirt—a wedding gown—with flowers in my hair. Roses and heather. It was so intense, I could actually smell the roses. I felt - I felt - like I have never felt before."

Carrick knew the roses and heather. He had given them to Jenny the day before in the garden for her bridal wreath. "My favorite flowers are thistles," she had teased him. "But they're too prickly to devise a wreath. Perhaps," she cast him a sly look, "ye're too prickly to be a husband."

"And perhaps my prick is exactly what ye need." He had pulled her into his arms and kissed the breath out of her.

"Why would I have visions of you?" Cat was saying, pulling him back to the present. "None of this makes any sense."

"Aye," he said, "it makes perfect sense. Ye are remembering."

"That must be it," Cat humored him. "I hold Jenny's locket and suddenly I am having her memories in my head."

"So the witch told me it would." Carrick nodded. "And they are yer memories..."

"From when I was Jenny." Cat sat up in protest. "Don't be absurd. Do you really think I would believe that crap? Do you really think I am that..."

Carrick abruptly pulled her to him and kissed her with a pent-up fury that stole her resolve. Never had she been kissed like this. His lips were hot against hers and his muscular arms cocooned her to his chest. She didn't bother resisting. She was melting like the Wicked Witch of the West. As his kiss deepened and explored her mouth, every muscle turned into wet rags, and she was defenseless against a flood of feelings for Carrick that came like a tidal wave.

Carrick ended the kiss and brushed lighter ones over her forehead and eyes, then pressed her close to him. He sat silent, holding her, stroking her hair, and soothed, "'Tis fine, *mo cridhe*. Dinna fash," he whispered. "All will be well."

"Carrick," Cat began softly, still in his arms. "I want to believe you. I do. But I just don't believe in time-travel and reincarnation. I want to, but.."

"Perhaps ye should take the leap," he said, touching her cheek.

"What leap is that?" Cat looked up into his sparkling eyes.

"Ye know…" He smiled back. "The leap of faith."

"Perhaps," Cat said and fainted straight away.

"Okay, okay," Cat called out at the incessant knocking on her bedroom door. "Come in and stop that banging."

In a swirl of blonde hair and open arms, Olivia

flew through the door and hugged her sister tightly. "I'm so happy to see you Cat," she cried.

"Olivia!" Cat was thrilled. "I thought you were in Edinburgh exhibiting your paintings?"

Olivia pushed Cat away a little to look at her. "I was," she laughed. "And before you ask, they all sold. I even got a commission from the National Trust to do a painting of the Battle of Culloden." She had been talking so fast, she paused for a breath. "You forgot I was going to Highland dance for Lydia's ball tonight? Bad Cat, you are. And speaking of bad, I arrive and what do I find? You've taken in a gorgeous Highlander! Good for you, Cat."

"Oh damn. I completely forgot about the ball. There's just been so much going on." Cat rubbed her eyes. She never forgot important dates. "What are we supposed to do with Carrick while we are at Lydia's?"

"Don't worry," Olivia was quick to respond. "Grandda took him to rent a Prince Charlie jacket and a kilt. They'll be back soon. It'll be fun having him along."

"Oh great...wonderful," Cat said tersely. "We get to bring a homeless person to a formal Scottish ball. You know we're just helping him out for a few days."

"I heard the whole thing." Olivia put up a hand to stop her. "It's a great story and he's terrific. Maybe he can give me input for my Culloden painting. He was there, you know. And besides, he's sexy as hell." She gave Cat a cheeky look.

"He wasn't at Culloden! He's just lost and confused." Cat yawned. What time was it? How did she get to her bedroom? "Funny. I don't remember coming up here last night."

"No wonder." Olivia squeezed Cat's hand. "Carrick said you fainted on the beach. He brought you up. Grandda said you just needed to sleep, that you've been wearing yourself out with the new CD."

Cat looked down at her clothing. It was the same she had been wearing the night before. Embarrassed, she ventured, "I fainted?"

Olivia bounced to her feet. "I guess so. You really need to learn to take breaks from your work," she admonished. "Maybe take a break with that handsome Scotsman."

"Oh God." Cat sighed with a hand to her head. "Olivia, nothing happened and nothing *will* happen."

"That's not how I see it," she stated, her exuberance for a good romance clearly showing. "I heard he kissed you."

"Oh that." Cat blushed. "Just a momentary lapse, I suppose. Nothing serious. He told you about that? Oh God..."

"Yes, he told us. A lapse. Really? Then why did you faint?" Olivia questioned. "It must have been one hell of a kiss."

"Olivia." Cat was firm. "He thinks I am the reincarnation of his dead wife. He thinks he traveled through time to find me. Oh, don't look at me that way. You can't really believe that's true?"

"Why not?" Olivia sat back down on the bed. "He also said Jenny's sister and grandda had the same names as us - Hamish and Olivia. What a coincidence, huh? Grandda and I don't remember anything, but we're open to the idea, at least." She brushed the thought aside.

"And besides, true love can do anything. It's obvious he has it for you. You should hear the way he talks about you. Wish someone felt that way about me. And," her voice turned mock-spooky, "he traveled through the mists of time to find you. Hey, he's your Laird of the mist. That's what I'll call him."

"You and your artist's temperament," Cat teased her. "Hopeless romantic, you are."

Olivia nodded at that. "So I am, and I like me just fine, thank you."

"You talked with him about me?" Cat suddenly realized Olivia must have been home for a while. "When did you get in? And you talked with him about me??"

"Last night." Olivia was up and pacing the room again, picking up perfume bottles and setting them down. She had always been a bit fidgety. "And we talked about everything for a couple of hours after they put you to bed. It was fascinating."

"I'll just bet," Cat said under her breath.

"So what did happen on the beach?" Olivia was

back at her side, anxious to hear it all.

"If I tell you, you promise not to jump to conclusions, or anything foolish like that?"

"I swear." Olivia raised a hand as an oath. "Go on. Tell me everything. Don't leave anything out."

"We were just talking…"

"Oh sure," Olivia interrupted. "Just talking. Uh huh."

"Are you going to let me tell you," Cat frowned, "or are you going to interject every other sentence?"

Olivia sat back and pointed to her tightly shut lips. She waved at Cat to continue.

"So, we were just sitting out there, talking," Cat began again, giving her sister a stern look. "He was showing me a locket that had belonged to Jenny. You know who Jenny is-er-was?"

Olivia nodded vigorously.

"I was holding it, admiring it. And suddenly, I just started feeling really warm all over." Cat wrapped her arms about herself, remembering the odd sensations. "Then I started feeling funny and seeing things."

"What did you see? Oh sorry." Olivia put her head down. "Go on."

Cat blew out a breath. "It was so intense, Olivia. As though it was really happening to me. Not like I was watching, but I was her. In her body.

"I was in a Highland wedding dress, and I was the bride. I could smell the flowers in my hair and Carrick was standing there. He was the groom..." It was all coming back to her, nearly as strong as the vision had been the night before.

"After it stopped," Cat's eyes were far away, "I was a bit shaken and we just sort of - he held me and kissed me. I guess I fainted after that." Cat shuddered slightly, recalling how oddly wonderful it had been.

"Wow!" Olivia said finally. "Cat, that's incredible! Carrick told us the witch said you would remember if he kissed you while he was holding the locket. Don't you see?"

"See what?" Cat asked irritably. "See that he's a nut case? See that I just kissed a lunatic?"

"No Cat," Olivia reached for her sister's hand. "Don't you see? You love each other and always have. What the witch said was absolutely true."

Chapter Six

"She'll be fine, lad," Hamish reassured him yet again. "She just needed a bit of rest."

"Aye," Carrick responded, his mind still on Cat's sleeping form when they had laid her on her bed. "I'm certain ye are right."

Carrick stared out the window of the vintage Jaguar roadster Hamish pampered. Just yesterday Carrick had seen cars for the first time and became enthralled with their speed and power. Today, however, his wonder was shadowed by his sense of responsibility for Cat's distress.

"Ye'll enjoy Lydia's ball tonight." Hamish tried to distract him. "She gives a good party, aye."

Carrick shifted in his seat to look at Hamish. "A charity party, ye say?"

"Oh aye, for the sick bairns, ye ken." Hamish stopped at a red light. "She's a great one for charity, is our Lydia. And she is anxious to meet ye, coming as she does, from near Invergarry."

"Invergarry," Carrick repeated. He wondered

how his brother was faring as laird. "A fine place to call home. Although my grandda came from Glencoe originally."

"Glencoe?" Hamish drove through the clear intersection. "Yer grandfather? Surely he was no at the massacre?"

"Aye, he was, indeed," Carrick answered. "Infamous to this day, is it?"

"Very much so." Hamish sighed sadly. "A horror for all time. Killing innocent MacDonalds just to set an example. A sad day in our history, to be sure."

"Verra true," Carrick agreed. "My grandda spoke little of it. He escaped through the glen with his mother when he was sixteen. Many died on the way. But his second cousin, Chief Ranald MacDonell at Invergarry, took pity on him and his mother. The Chief gave him some lands and a home. My family still owns Beinn Fhithich."

"Raven Mountain?" Hamish translated.

"Aye. Our farm." Carrick smiled at memory of the place.

"What do ye farm there?" Hamish asked.

"Cattle and barley. We brew a fine whisky." Carrick wondered how Ian was managing. It was a vast stedding and required careful management and much labor. "Tis a bonny spot with a view of Loch Oich. Do ye ken the place?'

"I know the area," Hamish said, nodding. "I grew up in Kingussie, near Loch Lagen. I had an uncle near Loch Oich." Hamish did not mention that Carrick's cousin's home, Castle Invergarry, had been burned, then bombed to ruins by Cumberland after the 1745 rising. It would do no good to tell him now.

"You know Lydia has always fancied grandda," Olivia explained, as Cat pulled the Mercedes into the long drive leading to Lydia's brightly lit mansion. "I'm sure her need for him to be here early was just one of her ruses. And he did bring my dance costumes."

"I suppose," Cat agreed, as they rounded the bend and pulled into the line of arriving cars. "But I still think it was rude for them to go ahead of us. We should have arrived together."

"Now Cat," Olivia teased her sister. "Are you saying we need an escort? You? The independent, modern woman?"

Caught out," Cat smiled in chagrin. "Well, no. I just think they could have waited for us. Simple courtesy is all."

"Good evening, Miss Caitriona," the kilted valet greeted Cat as he opened her door. "I hope you are well. And you as well, Miss Olivia."

"Thank you, Gerald," Cat responded, gathering her long skirts and accepting his proffered hand.

"Have a lovely evening." He smiled as Cat and Olivia made their way up the steps to the portico filled with faint fiddle music and illuminated by sconces.

"There you two are!" cried a silver-haired, statuesque woman as she grabbed each woman's hand. "I thought you'd never arrive!"

Lydia ushered them into the entry, filled with people. "I have been so enjoying your Carrick, Cat. What a catch that one is!"

Cat pulled Lydia up short. "He's not my anything, Lydia," she corrected. "He's just a houseguest for a few days. Surely grandda explained..."

"Oh yes!" Lydia's eyes sparkled. "He explained it all. A handsome Highlander from another time come to find you. How romantic that must be for you, Cat!"

Olivia started to giggle.

"Don't you start!" She pointed at Olivia. Then to Lydia, "This has gone too far, Lydia. It's not the least bit romantic..."

"Ah," Lydia interrupted as they entered the enormous ballroom. "There's your grandda and Carrick. Why don't you go over and join them. I'll see you in a bit." And with that, Lydia whisked away, leaving Cat starring directly into Carrick's eyes from across the room.

Cat's stomach lurched as Carrick began to make a path toward her. Panicked, she grabbed Olivia's hand for comfort. "He's coming over," she whispered.

"Of course he is," Olivia whispered back. "Do you expect him to stay across the room all night?"

Before she could reply, Carrick was in front of her, gently lifting her hand and bowing over it.

"Good evening, Caitriona," he smiled. "And a good evening to ye as well, Miss Olivia." He gave a slight bow in her direction.

Olivia smiled at him, but her eyes were fixed on Cat, who was flushed all over. Was her sister actually trembling?

"Thank you, Carrick," Cat managed, slowly retrieving her hand. "Are you enjoying the ball so far?"

"Aye, I am." Carrick offered his arm as escort. "May I see to ye ladies' refreshment?" He began to lead Cat toward the vast array of food and drink displayed in the adjoining room. Cat shot a reproving look at Olivia, who smiled broadly.

"Hey..." Olivia leaned to whisper. "Don't look

at me like that. You're the one who wanted an escort." Turning to Carrick, she said, "If you two will excuse me, I'm off to find where and when Lydia wants me to dance. Have fun," she trilled as she glided off into the crowd.

"Olivia dances?" Carrick asked, handing Cat a glass of wine.

"Yes," Cat said, careful not to spill on her white gown. "She is a former World Champion Highland Dancer. Five years ago, I think."

"Lassies Highland dance now?" Carrick nearly sputtered. "They compete, do they?"

"Of course they do...oh…" Cat suddenly realized. "That's right. In your time, women don't do Highland dancing. Well, they do now and have ever since Jenny Douglas broke with tradition and won a competition in the late 1800's. You don't often see men do it nowadays."

"Truly?" Carrick shook his head. "Who would-ha' thought? Well, here's to the lassies then." Carrick smiled and raised his glass to her.

"To the lassies," Cat agreed, and touched her glass to his. "Shall we go out to the terrace?" she suggested. "It's a bit warm in here."

"Aye." Carrick raised his arm in invitation and Cat laid her own upon his. "A bit of air wouldna be amiss," he agreed and led her through the open French doors to the terrace overlooking the shore.

"Ye are particular beautiful this night, Caitriona," Carrick said softly, placing his glass on a nearby table. "I mean, ye are always a beauty, but..."

"I knew what you meant." Cat smiled. How could she not smile? He was stunning in his Prince Charlie jacket and kilt, his hair tied back and those eyes—those sparkling blue eyes filled with his entire soul.

"You look especially fine yourself, Carrick," Cat returned the compliment, as Carrick took the glass from her nervous hand. "Modern dress suits you well."

Was she beginning to believe his story? Every time he touched her, it was as though her very being rose to scream, "home, familiar, déjà-vu."

"Your Miss Lydia decorates a ballroom most interesting." Carrick broke the silence. "Such a collection of swords and targes, I rarely have seen."

"Lydia does like to collect antique Scottish weapons." Cat nodded toward the ballroom. "I never quite understood her fascination with them. Especially the targes. But it does have a unique effect."

"Quite so." Carrick laughed. "Like an armory, to my thinking."

"They're playing a strathspey." She changed the subject as the fiddler struck up again.

"Aye, so they are." He bent his head lower to her face. "Would ye care to dance?"

"I'm not much of a dancer..." she began, as Carrick brushed his lips against hers, and she lost her voice and all thought.

"We shall have to remedy that," he whispered, as he drew back to look at her again, a tender smile lit his eyes.

"We shall?" Cat was numb.

"Aye," he answered, pulling her closer. "Come along and I will show ye."

He led the dazed Cat into the ballroom, where they stood watching the others moving through the intricate steps of a strathspey to the tune of The Miller's Daughter.

"These arena steps I ken," Carrick reflected, as the dance ended. "Mayhap I spoke hastily."

"Not a problem." Cat squeezed his hand. "I can't do it either."

"Oh, I can dance," he said, more confident. "I danced at Court many a time. I won the competitions as well. These steps are just verra different from..."

"From your time?" Cat shook her head. "Isn't everything?" Don't let the sarcasm show, she reproved herself as the strains of St. Bernard's Waltz began to play. The lilting fiddle washed over her, making her feet want to move.

"Well, this is one dance I do know. Are you dancing?" she asked.

"Are ye asking?" he replied with a grin.

"I am asking," she answered with a mock curtsy.

"Then I am dancing. I warn ye though, I dinna ken the dance," he answered, bowing in return. "But for ye I shall try, if ye are inclined to show me."

"All right then." Cat reached for his hand. "Come along and do as I say." She led him onto the dance floor and put her left hand on his shoulder, assuming a waltz position. Carrick pulled her into his arms and mirrored her, his back to the center of the circle of couples.

"It's a simple waltz," she said quietly, as the music began to swell. "It goes like this. Step with your left foot, close with your right foot." Carrick did as she instructed.

"Now again, step left foot, close right foot, step left foot, close right foot and do a light stamp. Then lightly stamp your left foot." Cat led and Carrick followed. "That's very good!" She was amazed at how such a large man could be so graceful.

"Now to the opposite side, but only twice and don't stamp. That's right," she continued. "And step back left, step back right." They were moving towards the center.

"Step towards me on your left foot, now with your right and turn me under your arm. Now we waltz around." Cat went under Carrick's upraised arm and he grasped her around the waist, twirling her around in a gliding spin.

"Perfect!" She beamed up at him. "You did it perfectly! Now we start again!"

"I like this dance." Carrick was proud of himself as he waltzed with Cat around the floor with the other couples.

"Ye do it verra well Caitriona, and ye are a fair good teacher as well."

"Why thank you, Carrick." She blushed slightly at the compliment. "You are an excellent dancer and student."

He moved with the grace of a jaguar; sinew and strength, elegant and commanding. Cat felt safe in his arms, protected and precious. His hold on her was firm, yet tender, as they swirled about, never breaking their gaze from each other's eyes. It was all too comfortable, too familiar, and she swore she could faint from the joy that was, inexplicably, welling from deep within her.

"Carrick?" she began as they danced. "Do you miss your home?"

"Beinn Fhithich?" he asked, his eyes suddenly wistful. "Aye, verra much. 'Tis a lovely place. Aye, I miss it."

"Beinn Fhithich? What does that mean?" she queried, genuinely interested for the first time.

"Raven Mountain," he replied, twirling her

under his arm. "Named so after my cousin's castle at Invergarry, Cragan an Fhithich, which means..."

"...rock of the raven," Cat finished. How had she known that? Where had that come from?

"Aye, it does." Carrick looked at her quizzically. "Do ye ken the Gaelic, Caitriona?"

"AUh, no, no I don't," Cat stuttered. "I must have heard it somewhere, I guess. Maybe when I was in Glencoe a long time ago."

"Oh aye, that must be it." Carrick didn't believe her. She had gone white when the translation came out of her mouth. Maybe she was remembering the place? It had been her home when she was Jenny, after all. "Any road, I should like to show it to ye one day, Cat. If ye would care to go."

"I think I would enjoy that." Cat smiled to cover her unease. "And your family? Are they there, too?"

"My mum and brother are there." Carrick led her back towards the center, his feet nimble and soft. "My brother Ian is laird by now, I s'pose." His eyes were suddenly far away.

"Why would he be laird now?" Cat asked, alert again. "You're still alive and dancing with me. You can go home anytime you like."

"Nay, Cat." Carrick bowed to her as the waltz ended. "I canna. I dinna ken how to go home to 1746."

"There you are." Olivia sat down on the bench next to Cat, the ocean breeze raising escaped tendrils from her hair's Highland bun. "I saw you dancing with Carrick, and then you disappeared."

"I'm sorry," Cat answered vaguely. "It was getting too close in there. I needed some air."

"Well you two certainly make a nice pair," Olivia commented enthusiastically. "And he dances like a dream."

"Thank you, Miss Olivia," Carrick said from behind her. "Had I kent ye were here, I wouldha' brought ye a drink as well." He handed Cat a glass of champagne, which she received gratefully.

"That's okay, Carrick." Olivia stood up and adjusted her dance kilt, a lovely blue Royal MacRae of Conchra tartan. "I have to go dance anyway. Not a good thing to dance with liquids in you."

"Aye, I s'pose not." He couldn't take his eyes off her kilt. "Ye wear the kilt when ye dance now times? I canna believe it." He shook his head in astonishment. "Lassies do Highland dance and they wear the kilt to boot."

"It must be a bit much for you." Olivia laughed.

"A bit," he agreed. "But I do admit ye look well in the kilt, Olivia. May I ask which dances ye will perform?"

"I think I will start with the Sword, then maybe the Fling, then we'll see what I am up to after that," she replied, straightening her velvet vest. "Am I all straight, Cat?"

Cat looked her up and down critically. "You're fine, sweetie. Go knock them dead."

"I'll try!" She laughed, turning to Carrick. "Do you know these dances, Carrick?"

"I ken the Sword and the Fling, aye," he answered. "But I am no certain it is the same today as when I danced it last."

"Well, come watch and let me know." She started toward the door into the ballroom. "Coming Cat?"

"Yes, of course." Cat rose to follow and found Carrick's hand once again under her arm. It was a touch she had come to anticipate and enjoy throughout the evening. Carrick led her into the ballroom where everyone had assembled around the perimeter.

"Honored guests," Hamish MacPhail began, a microphone in his hand. He was in the center of the room, about to introduce Olivia. "I am privileged to be with ye tonight, and even more so to introduce to ye my lovely granddaughter, Olivia MacPhail, the 2005 World Champion of Highland Dance."

Olivia came out from behind him, a dancing sword in each hand, carried with the points toward the ceiling. As Olivia ceremonially placed the swords in a cross on the floor in front of her, Hamish explained the dance.

"Olivia will now perform the Ghillie Calum, or the Sword Dance," Hamish explained. "It is an ancient dance. Legend has it that the best dancer would perform it on the eve of battle. If the dancer didn't touch the blade, it was an omen that the battle would be won. If the blades were touched, well...no so good." Hamish laughed.

"Let us see what kind of fortune Olivia can bring to us tonight."

Hamish stepped to the side as the piper adjusted his bagpipes. Olivia took position in front of the swords, hands on her hips, and bowed from the waist.

"She's verra good," Carrick commented to Cat, not taking his eyes from the dance. "So much better than the way we dance it. Verra precise, this dance."

"Oh?" Cat looked at him. "More precise? In what way?"

"The hi-cuts are verra sharp, and the angles of the legs are verra defined," he critiqued. "The leaps are so high and confident. A stronger dance in evra way. No just thrown together, ye ken?"

"I think I understand," Cat answered, leaning toward him. "And you do this dance yourself?"

"No as well as yer wee sister," he smiled. "And the steps are..."

"Different?" Cat filled in his sentence as Olivia completed the dance and bowed to the crowd.

"pplause and whistles followed, as she grasped the microphone from Hamish's hand.

"And now," Olivia began, looking straight at Carrick, "we have a special guest tonight all the way from Scotland." She breathed a little hard from exertion. "Carrick." She beckoned to him. "Come and join me in the Fling. Laird Carrick MacDonell, everyone."

The applause began again as Carrick looked at Cat in astonishment. What do I do? his expression asked.

"Go, Carrick." Cat squeezed his hand. "Enjoy it," she encouraged.

"But I canna..." Panic shone in his eyes.

"Yes, you can," Cat gently nudged him. "Go on. Impress me," she teased.

"Oh verra well then," he relented, and started toward Olivia.

As the applause grew louder with cheers of approval, Carrick noticed a Culloden targe on the wall nearby. With a deft hand, he removed it and set it on the floor in front of him, next to Olivia.

Olivia recognized his intention to dance on the targe in the ancient style of the Fling, and raised an eyebrow in question. Carrick bowed to Olivia, took his position with her, and they bowed together.

As the piper began, each dancer did their own variation of the Fling. Olivia was a strong, nimble dancer, but Carrick's footwork was extremely intricate and unique. He performed the Fling on the targe, managing to avoid the center spike while remaining within the confines of the shield.

Cat was transfixed by Carrick. She couldn't believe he was actually dancing on the targe! She had thought it was merely legend that the Fling had been danced this way, but he was doing it with skill and incredible precision. And although his Fling was entirely different from Olivia's, it was stunningly familiar. So familiar, her blood surged wildly hot and cold simultaneously.

She knew the steps he was executing. She knew every muscle movement and gesture. It was as ingrained in her as if she had danced it a thousand times herself. Her muscles tensed in tandem with Carrick's as he danced the complicated choreography, each tendon strained and relaxed according to the step. Her vision began to overlap with a background of ancient stone architecture and long, oaken tables filled with guests.

She saw Molly, Carrick's mother, smiling at her from across the hall as Carrick, now in his great kilt and lace jabot and cuffs, danced with ease for the assembly.

She heard Ian whisper in her ear, "Aye lass, he is the best of us," as the memories of her life as Lady Jenny MacDonell flooded her senses and consumed her. It's true, she knew it now. It was all true. She remembered having been Jenny as if it were only a day ago. She wasn't crazy, and neither was Carrick. Her hauntingly vivid dreams had all been true. Recollections of a former life and love.

It was part of a magical, creative universe that joined them together when all was thought lost. And here he was, come back to her, to find her, to love her. The ecstasy of it overwhelmed her near to tears.

"Caitriona?" Carrick had finished the dance to much acclaim and was standing at her side. "Come, lass." He slipped his arm around her and led her out onto the terrace. She numbly obeyed, legs weak with... fear? Joy?

"Cat?" he said again, turning her into his arms, concerned by her expression. "Are ye well, lass?"

A glow filled Cat like an internal lantern. It suffused her body and face as she reached up and put her arms around him, a vibrant smile in her eyes as she met his gaze.

"It's true, isn't it?" she began. "All of it...it's true."

"Aye, Caitriona," Carrick responded softly in surprise. "'Tis true."

"Welcome home, Carrick." She tightened her embrace. "My beloved husband. I dreamed of you so often! I am overjoyed that you found me, *mo leannan*," she said as she kissed him with the most explosive release of passion the universe could ever know.

Chapter Seven

Carrick kissed Caitriona with equal fervor and a tenderness that permeated her every sense. He couldn't believe she remembered. He had nearly abandoned hope, deciding it would be enough to be a peripheral part of her life. Content to be near her, he had resigned himself. And from nowhere, this! His heart was close to exploding with the unexpected rapture of it.

"Caitriona." Carrick gently lifted his lips from hers. "Do ye truly recall? Everything?"

"Yes, Carrick," she answered, tears glittering in her eyes. "I am so sorry about the way I treated you..."

"No apologies, *mo cridhe.*" He touched her cheek. "'Tis God's own mystery, this life. But I am relieved and joyful ye remember. I have missed ye more than I can explain."

"And I, you." Cat laid her head on his chest. She suddenly couldn't get close enough to him. "I remembered every single thing when you danced the Fling. I remember helping you choreograph those steps. I remember dancing it with you. It all came back!"

"Truly?" He pushed her away a little to look at her. "You devised most of that dance. I performed it for the first time..."

"When your cousin hosted Prince Charlie at the castle, just before Culloden," Cat finished for him. "Yes, I remember it. And I remember your mother, Molly, and your brother, Ian. While you were dancing, it was if they were right there in the room with us."

"They loved ye, Cat, nearly as much as I. They, too, were devastated by yer death," Carrick reflected, instantly somber. "They are all gone now, I s'pose."

Suddenly sad, Cat dropped her hands from Carrick's shoulders. "I'm so sorry. Of course, they would ne gone now. I supposed we are going to have to tell you everything that has happened to Scotland since Culloden."

"Aye, ye must," Carrick agreed. "Although yer grandda did speak some of it to me. There will be time for that." Trying to cheer them both he said, "For the now, let's take joy in our reunion and share our happiness, shall we?"

"There you are, bad Cat!" Olivia teased as she joined them from the ballroom followed closely by Hamish. "You missed my Seann Triubhas..." Olivia broke off as Hamish put his hand on her arm to stop her.

"Caitriona," Hamish began. "What is it, lass? You seem..."

Cat smiled through her tears, a smile that lit the

night. “Oh yes, grandda,” she beamed. She inserted herself under Carrick’s arm and reached a hand to her grandfather, who took it and squeezed with affection. “I remembered! Everything. Well, nearly everything. There are some big holes in my memory. But enough to know I was, indeed, Lady Jenny MacDonell. I remembered when Carrick was dancing the Fling!”

Olivia’s eyes widened in stunned acclimation. “You remember being Jenny? Oh my God! I never knew the Fling could have such an effect!” she laughed happily. “Is this real?”

“Of course it is,” Hamish replied, tightening his hold on Cat’s hand. “I knew ye would recall in time,” Hamish assured her. “Such a miracle this is!” Extending the other hand to Carrick with a warm, knowing expression. “Congratulations to ye, Carrick.” He shook his hand. “Welcome to the family.”

“Thank ye, sir.” Carrick accepted the welcome. “I am most honored and verra happy to be part of such a fine clan.”

‘About time, too,” Olivia exclaimed. “Everyone could see it but you, Cat. Oh hell.” She sighed and went to her sister, hugging her tightly. “I am so thrilled! This is so great, I can hardly believe it! Welcome, brother Carrick! So when’s the wedding?” Olivia blurted, leaving the question hanging between three other startled souls.

Silence reigned among the four as Carrick reached into his sporran and retrieved something, tightly hiding it in his hand.

"Olivia," Cat broke the silence. "That is not necessary."

"Aye, Cat." Carrick turned her to face him. "I'm afraid yer wee sister is correct. We are no married in yer time."

"But Carrick…" Cat began.

"'Tis true Cat," he answered, taking her hand and quieting her. "It is a situation we shall have to remedy immediately." Carrick looked to Hamish. "With yer permission, sir?"

Hamish, who had been following the conversation closely, nodded his approval.

"Caitriona MacPhail," Carrick bent his head to her. "I have nothing to give ye in yer time, save my heart, my soul, my loyalty, my protection, and my verra breath. Will ye take me as yer husband? I swear I will never fail ye, should ye answer aye."

Tears welled again at the unexpected proposal. "yes!" Cat glowed. "Oh yes, Carrick. I will. Forever!"

Carrick opened his free hand and revealed a beautiful golden ring, a circle of celtic knots that appeared to be very old.

"My ring!" Cat exclaimed, putting her hands to her mouth, tears flowing freely. "I gave it to you when I was dying..."

"...at Culloden, aye," he finished for her. Gently, so gently, Carrick took her hand in his and placed the ring on her finger. "I have carried it with me since that day. It kept me safe, and comforted me that I would find ye."

Cat put her face into her hands and sobbed. "Oh my..." she cried, as Carrick helped her to sit. All was quiet while Cat spent her emotions. No one said a word. It was all too awesome to witness, incredible and beautiful. It filled them with wonder at the miracle of life and creation. They were speechless in the certain knowledge that life does go on, that there is no death, and that love can last forever.

"I'm sorry," Cat said at last, recovering herself. "It's just so amazing." She looked up at them. "And I am so very happy!" She smiled to reassure them.

"'Tis fine," Hamish assured her, clearing his own throat of emotion. "We are as happy as ye, and we wish ye both the joy ye have waited so long to have."

"Absolutely!" Olivia hugged her grandfather. "Well said grandda. This calls for champagne! Be right back." And she went off to find some as she wiped away her own tears.

Ian MacDonell sat at his brother's desk staring between the fire in the grate and the letter he held in his hand. He read it for the hundredth time, still stunned in disbelief at its message.

He had found the note on his night table several days before. Awakened by the early cry of ravens, it was the first thing he saw that morning.

"My brother Ian," it said in Carrick's elegant hand. "I am off to bring Jenny home, for I have reason to believe she yet lives. I appoint you Laird in my absence. You have my blessing. Carrick, Laird MacDonell, Beinn Fhithich."

"Damn." Ian breathed in frustration as he sipped his whisky.

"I heard that," Molly said from the doorway. "Still fixed on Carrick, are ye?" she asked, seating herself in an opposite chair as she reached for the whisky decanter. "Ye'll torture yerself for no good reason, lad. Carrick does as he must, and so will you. He has always done his best for ye, Ian. He sent ye away to France to be educated, rather than fight in the bloody rising. 'Twas a good decision. Dinna doubt him now."

Ian laid the note on the desk with a heavy sigh. "Aye, Carrick has always been wise. But how can he believe Jenny lives? We all know she is long dead. He seeks a ghost."

"Nay, Ian," Molly admonished her younger son. "Carrick is no addled. He wouldna have left had he no sound information otherwise. We must trust his judgment in this."

"I s'pose," Ian replied, taking another sip of the soothing amber liquid. "But I canna help wondering why he didna tell us more. Where he was going, what news he had, ye ken?"

"Oh aye, I wish he had," Molly answered. "Yer brother was always a private one. We havena choice but to respect it and get on with things until he returns."

"Do ye truly believe he will?"

"Of course he will." Molly reached out and patted his hand. "He knows of the troubles, surely.

He wouldna leave us to fend alone could he help it. Aye, he will come home to us. And ye must do yer verra best as Laird until he does."

"Aye, then." Ian nodded. "I shall. I had word today Cumberland's troops are spreading out from Inverness. Likely they will be on our doorstep soon."

"Then we shall have to prepare ourselves, shan't we?" Molly stood and drained her whisky. "We will begin in the morning. Now, ye need to sleep so ye can have yer strength for the task."

"Aye, mother," Ian agreed, as Molly bent to hug him. "I will be to bed soon."

"Good night then," Molly said softly, as she left the study with a strong sense of foreboding.

Chapter Eight

"Pillaged and burnt 29 May, 1746," Carrick read the plaque which stood in front of the ruined Invergarry Castle. It was now fenced completely around with no way to enter and investigate.

Having deposited Guinness, the cat, with the animal-loving Lydia and closing up the house, they had come to Invergarry to be wed a few days after the ball.

"I left here 21 May, 1746." Carrick counted aloud. "That means..."

"Today is 27 May. Day after tomorrow is the anniversary," Hamish figured aloud. He and Olivia had joined them.

"Well," Carrick reasoned, "if I am correct, in my time, it will happen tomorrow. And there is no a thing I can do. Do ye ken what happened to the family?"

"No." Hamish shook his head. "But I'm sure we can find the answer."

"It's okay, Carrick." Cat put her hand on his shoulder. "You couldn't have done anything if you had been there. We can go to Beinn Fhithich though, and see what there is of that."

"Aye, so we shall." He took her hand as they began walking back to the nearby hotel where they were staying. "A lovely old manse this," he gestured toward the Glengarry Castle Hotel, once a Victorian mansion.

"And a great choice for your wedding," Olivia chirped, trying to cheer everyone as usual.

"I'll fetch the car," Hamish offered and strode ahead down the long, tree-lined drive, Olivia in tow.

"You're still looking a bit green, Carrick," Cat observed. "Is it from the plane, or seeing the castle?"

"Aye." Carrick stopped and looked sheepishly at her. "The plane was a bit of a turn. I'll never understand how such a great metal beast remains in the air. But truth is, the castle was more of a fright."

"I can imagine." Cat nodded. "You must be worried to death about Molly and Ian."

"Verra much." He took a deep breath and started walking again. "Nothing I can do in the here and now, so best to get on with it."

"In ye go." Hamish pulled the rented Mercedes next to them. "Are ye up to the trip, Carrick?"

"Oh aye, I think so," he answered, climbing into the back seat with Cat. "Let us see what remains."

"It looks great!" Olivia exclaimed as they rounded the bend to find the looming great house of Beinn Fhithich.

"No burnt nor bombed at least," Carrick agreed, as the car pulled to a stop in front. "Vacant though, it appears."

"Great!" Olivia lept from the car. "Then we can explore."

"Be careful, Olivia," Cat warned, as they walked up the front stone steps to the door. "We don't know how bad it is inside. It looks like it has been abandoned for some time."

Carrick pushed carefully on the wooden door. "'Tis empty," he said, stepping into the hall. "Full of dirt, but no much else."

"Oh my!" Cat took a breath as she entered the large sitting room to the right. "I remember this room so well. When I last saw it, there were tapestries and lovely chairs."

"Aye, Cat." Carrick put his arm around her. "You recall correctly. Welcome home, such as it may be."

"Aye." Hamish cleared his throat. "Welcome home to ye both," he said, handing Cat a packet of papers.

"What is this?" Cat took the packet and turned it over to open it. Pulling out the papers, her face lit and a smile flooded her expression. "Oh, grandda!" She threw her arms around him. "How can I thank you?"

"What is it?" Olivia interrupted. "What's going on?"

"Grandda has bought the house and land for us—a wedding gift!" She handed the papers to Carrick who looked them over.

"'Tis verra generous of ye, sir." He was astonished at the gift. "But I canna accept such a..."

"Aye ye can, and ye will," Hamish reprimanded. "It is my wish that my great-grandchildren be born in my home country. And it is the least I can do for my Caitriona's happiness."

"Well then, Carrick shook his hand in gratitude, "we most gratefully accept yer kind gift and will do our best to give ye yer wish."

"Do I have any say in this?" Cat broke in, laughing.

"Of course ye do, lass," Hamish apologized. "I only assumed..."

"And you assumed correctly," Cat teased him. "It is a wonderful gift, grandda. Thank you with all of my heart."

"Don't thank me too soon," he chided. "Ye have yer work cut out for ye by the look of it," waving a hand around the place, which would need a great deal of restoration.

"Hard work I can do." Carrick beamed proudly. "This once was fine, arable land and rich in cattle. No reason it canna be again. Let's see how much will be needed."

They explored every inch of the mansion, making mental notes of what would have to be done. Parts of the house had been restored at some point. It was entirely possible that the structure had seen some damage in the Culloden aftermath, but even those restorations needed repair. When they finished their inspection, Carrick grew somber.

"I have put it off long enough," he said quietly. "It is time to see their graves."

"Yes." Cat took his hand tenderly. "Yes, we should do that."

Carrick led them up to the top of the hill behind the house, a beautiful view down the glen and beyond it, Loch Oich. A spectacular resting place for those lost loved ones. Picking a handful of wildflowers growing at the edge of the path, Cat nodded to Olivia to do the same.

Carrick stopped abruptly and surveyed the stone markers, a puzzled look on his face.

"I dinna understand," he murmured. "Where are they?"

Cat quickly read the names on the stones and shook her head. "Molly and Ian. They aren't here. What could have happened to them?"

"I dinna ken, but there must be an answer and I intend to find it."

"Carrick?" Cat knocked lightly on the door of his hotel room. It was past midnight and she had not been able to sleep thinking of Molly and Ian. She needed the comfort of Carrick, even though she had said she would not make love with him until after the wedding. Somehow the tradition of waiting appealed to her. But it suddenly seemed right to be with him after the events of the day.

"Are you there?" she asked, not certain he had heard. Perhaps he was asleep.

As she was about to turn back to her own room, the door creaked open, a soft light spilling into the hall, illuminating the spiral staircase behind her.

"Caitriona?" Carrick opened the door wider for her. "Ye must get yer rest for the ceremony in the morn. What are ye about this hour?" He was clad in only his great kilt, hastily wrapped and draped around his body with clearly nothing underneath. The sight of him stole the breath.

"I - I couldn't sleep," she stuttered.

"Ye'd best come in then." He pulled her into the room. "Ye canna stand there in your dressing gown for all to see."

"Who will see?" She laughed lightly. "The wee ghosties?"

"Dinna mock the ghosties, Cat," he chided. "Ye shouldna be in my room until after we are wed the morrow, lass. What will they think of us?"

"Carrick." Cat sat in an antique chair. "I explained to you. In this time, no one thinks badly of an engaged couple sleeping together."

"Aye, so ye said." Carrick sat on the bed. "Still..."

"Nevermind all of that," Cat interrupted. "What are we to do about Molly and Ian?"

"Ye ken yer grandda has asked the historical people to have a look in their records," he answered calmly. "So we wait. No much else, aye?"

"I suppose." Cat looked into her hands. "I just hope they can find something soon."

"And I." Carrick rose and pulled her into his arms. "But we already ken they are gone, so it willna make much difference. I'd just like to ken that they were put to rest properly, aye?"

"Of course," she said, looking up into his soft blue eyes. His touch and presence distracted her thoughts and teased at her sensually, causing her concerns to momentarily flee. "I do love you so," she said, her blood racing at his touch.

In response, Carrick bent to kiss her, his hands smoothing her long hair down her back. "Ye could kill me with wanting ye so," he whispered.

Cat tentatively slipped her hand up his naked thigh under his kilt. His hard flesh twitched in response to her touch and he pulled back.

"Nay, Cat, ye musn't" he admonished her.

The mist in her body was rapidly overtaking her. "Oh yes," she said between kisses over his chest. "I'm afraid we must," she insisted, gently pulling the tartan from his shoulder to expose his bare torso, a long newly-healed, pink scar down one shoulder.

Tenderly, she ran her finger, trailed by her tongue, down the scar. "Culloden." she said, recognizing it.

Carrick nodded and lifted her into his sinewy arms. "Are ye sure?" He carried her toward the inviting, high bed.

"More than anything in my life," Cat assured him, and closed her eyes. She wanted to savor every moment now, let it fill her, invade her, and flood her with the passion she could no longer suppress. She had waited too long for this blessed reunion with her soul mate; she would have every bit of it.

As if she were a precious gem, Carrick laid

her on the bed and began to kiss her everywhere. He explored and found the laces of her gown. Deftly, he untied them to reveal the firm and awakened treasures beneath.

Cat moaned ferally as his tongue touched each mound, yearning for his attention. She ran her fingers up the hollow of his thigh where the muscles met and twined.

The mist between her own thighs thickened and spread a flaming glow throughout her awakened body. Her hands traveled farther onto his buttocks, encouraging him with her caresses.

He was a considerate, generous lover and Cat reciprocated. With sure hands and tongues, they rediscovered each other's secrets and memories sprang anew.

Separated by war, death, and time, they renewed their love in physical union; explosive as the cannons which had denied them.

"Two hundred years is a verra long time to wait," Carrick managed between expended breaths. "Let us no wait so long again, aye?" he said.

Contented, Cat curled round him in agreement. His love had found the keys to her soul.

Chapter Nine

Olivia carefully made her way to the landing outside her room and felt the wall for the light switch. She had awakened before dawn, as she usually did when she traveled to Scotland. Funny, she didn't get jet lag coming to Scotland, she got it when she returned to the States, where she would sleep for a couple of days to catch up.

In the darkness of the hour, she had the castle all to herself. Not a single person was about and it gave her a sense of peace. It would be a fine thing to sketch the sunrise, she thought, as she secured her pad under her arm.

Finally, she found the switch and turned on the light, casting away the gloom. She nimbly made her way down the long staircase to the ground floor and turned the lights on in the hallway. Switching off the stair's light behind her, she ventured on into the large entry hall and made her way to the oak door that was the castle's entrance. A printed sign on the door read, "Please bolt the door when you return. Door is not self-locking."

She found the iron bolt and pulled it across to open the door. A real bolted door, she smiled to herself, enjoying the antiquity of the place. The age and mood of the Victorian castle engulfed her as she stepped out onto the stone steps, shivering slightly in the mist that greeted her.

Olivia sketched for a few minutes as she watched the sun rise over the loch. The cold began to permeate, and regretfully, she stepped back inside the door, bolting it as the sign requested. Not ready to go back to her room, she sank comfortably into an overstuffed wing chair and sketched a bit more.

The silence was broken by a strange sound, as though someone was walking through the room. Light footsteps alerted her and she looked up from her pad.

Standing across the room was a tall man dressed in a Clan Donell kilt, matching hose, a plaid draped over his shoulder, and a dirk at his waist. He

stared silently at her with a smug smile, his brown hair flowing down his collar.

"Who are you?" Olivia whispered to him. "Why have you come?"

The apparition nodded to her in a courtly gesture and slowly faded away.

Olivia shook off the vision she had just witnessed and hastily began drawing him on her pad while she could still recall his features. Perhaps one of the castle staff would know who he was.

"Good morning, grandda." Cat kissed her grandfather's cheek before sitting at the elegantly laid table. "Did you sleep well?"

"Aye, Caitriona," Hamish answered with an affectionate smile. "And a good day to ye too," he greeted Carrick, who seated himself in one of the burgundy striped chairs. The dining room was warm and welcoming. Crisp, white tablecloths, Victorian wallpaper, and a fireplace gave the ambience of a home.

"A fine view of the loch." Carrick nodded toward the windows. "A verra comfortable manse, this," he commented, sipping the strong coffee that had been poured for him.

"I thought no one would ever get up!" Olivia plopped into her chair and grabbed a scone. "I'm starving."

"How long have you been awake?" Cat asked, hiding a yawn behind her hand.

"I got up to watch the sunrise." She laid her sketch pad on the table and poured herself some tea. "You won't believe what I saw."

"What did ye see?" Carrick asked, since Hamish and Cat were busy with their toast.

"Well..." Olivia was clearly excited. "I was

sitting alone in the foyer, and all of a sudden, a ghost appeared. Honest, I'm not kidding," she said to Cat, who was giving her a skeptical look from across the table.

"Okay, Olivia," Cat patronized her. "If you say so."

"Hey, I even drew him," Olivia protested, opening her sketchbook to the drawing. "See for yourself." She handed the portrait to Cat.

"Nice drawing," Cat said, examining it closely. "No one I recognize." She handed the pad to Carrick. "Anyone you know?' she said, half joking.

Carrick took the pad and studied the drawing intently. "Aye," he said finally. "I know him. He's my cousin John."

"You're serious?" Cat was taken aback. "You mean John MacDonell, Chief of Glengarry from your time?"

"Oh aye," Carrick nodded, still looking at the drawing. "Ye should remember him, Cat."

"I only met him a few times, and my memories are still coming back slowly." She looked over at the drawing again. "He's the one who let his first wife starve to death, isn't he?"

"He did? Wow! This is great!" Olivia was beaming. "I really did see a ghost."

"Of course ye did." Hamish squeezed her hand. "The place is full of them."

"And a right fair image of him, too, Olivia," Carrick complimented her. "Ye have him dead on. I wonder why he appeared to ye as he did."

"Thanks, Carrick." She grinned, retrieving the pad. "It was quite an experience. But he just kind of glowered at me. Didn't feel like talking, I guess."

"And you talk too much," Cat teased her. "He probably couldn't get a word in."

Everyone laughed at that, enjoying the companionable breakfast.

"Olivia's artistic skill reminds me." Hamish grew serious. "Ye have yer birth certificate, Carrick? The Priest will need it this afternoon."

Carrick nodded and swallowed his egg. "Aye, I do," he answered. "'Tis safe in the room."

"Good." Hamish sat back in his chair. "Our Olivia is a brilliant forger, what with the help of a computer. Put her art to good use, I say. Ye do remember," he continued, "ye must go to Inverness and obtain a passport. We were lucky to get ye into the country, but ye shall no leave again without it."

"I understand." Carrick smiled at the memory of Olivia creating a birth certificate for him. They had used Cat's, for she had been born in Scotland. Being that she was only one year younger than Carrick, the documents would have been contemporary in format.

The new birth certificate read *Carrick Alasdair MacDonell,* and listed his birth date as February 8, 1983, instead of February 8, 1721.

"Look!" Cat pointed toward the window. "There's a deer underneath the apple tree where we are going to have the ceremony!"

"A good omen, to be sure." Carrick kissed her hand.

"It certainly is," Hamish agreed as they watched the graceful animal graze.

"So grandda." Olivia nudged him. "What's in that long box you brought on the plane? When will you stop being so mysterious?"

"In good time, Olivia." He smiled at her. "Everything in good time."

They spent the rest of the morning exploring the expansive grounds of Glengarry Castle Hotel. The four of them walked down to the dock and enjoyed the music of the loch lapping against the shore. Then they wandered through the dense forest which skirted the grounds, stopping to examine particular plants, or listen to a bird singing in a fir tree.

The wedding was set for one o'clock, so after a quick lunch, Olivia joined Cat in her room to help her dress.

"This is a gorgeous ensemble, Cat." Olivia held

the green velvet stays up to herself, admiring it in the mirror. "Not white though." Laying the stays aside, she picked up and shook out the full skirt.

"No," Cat answered brushing her long hair over her shoulder. "I wanted something more to Carrick's time. White wasn't a wedding color then. Besides, I look good in that shade of green. And I love the arisaidh in the Donell tartan."

"Yes, you look gorgeous in that color," Olivia agreed, helping Cat into the full skirt, and stays, then lacing up the back. "It fits you perfectly. And it's just right with your eyes and the flowers."

Cat swirled the arisaidh over her shoulders and pinned it in the front with a Donell clan brooch, with its single raven in the center. It formed a cape-like effect. The blues, greens, and reds of the intricate Donell tartan gleamed against the green of the stays and skirt.

Cat had wanted it simple. An elegant Highland outfit, unbound hair, and a bouquet of freshly picked heather, foxglove, thyme, and hawthorne blossoms from near the castle. Olivia wove some delicate heather into Cat's hair. When she finished helping her adjust the plaid on Cat's shoulder, she stood back to view her sister.

"You are so beautiful." Olivia's eyes were misting. "You have a kind of glow about you."

"Thank you, Olivia." Cat hugged her, her own eyes a bit dewy. "It's time to go," she said, breaking the embrace at the knock on the door.

"As the door opened, Hamish caught sight of Cat in her gown. With a proud smile, he extended his arm to her. "Ye're a lovely bride, Caitriona." He struggled to keep his emotions in check. "I;m happy I'm giving ye to the right man," he said, leading her down the stairs and through to the terraced lawns beyond. There, under the apple tree where they had seen the deer, Carrick waited for her with the Reverend Watson.

Hamish had arranged for the priest to come from St. John's, an Episcopal church in Ballachulish, near Glencoe. Carrick was a Glencoe descendant. He and his family were Episcopalian, as was Cat.

As they neared the tree, Cat caught her breath. Carrick was in his great kilt and lace-trimmed shirt, his auburn hair tied back with a velvet ribbon. His eyes lit as Hamish placed Cat's hand into his.

"Go, lass," Hamish whispered as he kissed her. "Be happy always."

"I will," Cat replied as she fit her hand into Carrick's and turned to face him, a gentle smile in her eyes.

"We are gathered to witness the marriage of Caitriona Eilean MacPhail to Carrick Alasdair MacDonell," the priest began. With most of the formalities complete, the priest took the end of his stole and wrapped it loosely around Cat and Carrick's joined hands.

"I bless this marriage and the fruit of it," he said solemnly. "And I pronounce ye husband and wife."

He removed the stole and nodded to Carrick.

Deliberately, Carrick swept Cat into his arms and kissed her fervently. She put her arms around his neck and kissed him in equal measure.

"Ahem..." Hamish interrupted the kiss, lest it last all day. "I have a gift for ye, Carrick."

Reluctantly, Carrick broke from Cat and turned to Hamish. "Aye?" he said quizzically. "A gift? But I have nothing to give ye in return."

"My Caitriona's joy is all the gift needed," Hamish said as he opened the long, mysterious box lying nearby.

He withdrew an old basket-hilted sword and extended it to Carrick with both hands.

"I present ye with the family sword," Hamish began. "To welcome ye to the family, and in faith that ye will use it to protect Caitriona."

Moved by the gesture, Carrick bowed his head to Hamish. "I gratefully accept both honors," he said humbly. "I will protect her forever, I assure ye," he vowed as a large, jet-black raven landed on the branch above his head. Carrick gave a slight shudder at the bird and said, "May it no come to the sword."

"What's with the raven?" Olivia whispered as Carrick kissed Cat again.

"An omen of war," Hamish whispered back. "Not good."

"Oh! But..."Olivia began.

"Shhhh..." Hamish quieted her.

Carrick ended the quick kiss and raised the sword with respect to Cat. "I have a wee gift for ye, Caitriona," he said and handed the sword to Hamish. "If you would, sir," he said, removing a small package from his sporran.

"This is rightfully yers," he explained as she took it. "It will serve to remind ye that I will keep ye safe and provide for ye always."

Cat's eyes widened as she removed the locket from the paper wrapping.

"My locket," she murmured. "I had forgotten," she said as she held it out for all to see. "Thank you so much!" she said, holding it up to her neck and turning for Carrick to fasten it. It was the perfect way to end the ceremony.

Reverend Watson bid then all a joyful farewell and left them under the tree to enjoy the champagne the hotel had provided.

"Much joy and many bairns," Hamish toasted them, and they all raised their glasses together. They stood, laughing, talking, and sipping the champagne for a while, not wanting to end the moment.

Suddenly woozy, Cat groped for the chair behind her and quickly sat. A fine mist rose from the ground around her, causing her to shiver involuntarily.

"What is it, Cat?" Carrick took the glass from her and bent over in concern.

"Probably just too much champagne and excitement." She smiled up at him, her arms around her stomach. "I'll be fine in a minute."

"Aye, probably so." Hamish placed his hand on her cheek. "No fever. Just sit and rest a bit, Cat," he advised, and backed up a bit to allow her some space.

Carrick and Olivia did the same, not taking their eyes from Cat, who was now bending over in half, gripping her head with both hands. The mist grew into a dense fog, nearly obscuring her from view.

"Oh my God," she cried, trying to see them through the mist. "The music is deafening and it's making my head explode!"

"What music?" Olivia asked, looking around for its possible source. .

"Can't you hear it?" Cat's eyes were streaming tears of pain. "It's the worst pain I've ever..."

With that partial declaration, Cat faded and disappeared completely from sight, leaving the mist to slowly evaporate.

"Caitriona!" Carrick yelled and raced to the empty chair. "Where is she?" He waved his hands to clear the remaining mist, then turned to the astonished pair behind him. "What has happened?" He was frantic, feeling every bit of the chair with both hands, as if he could conjure her back.

Olivia, stunned, stood stone still and silent, letting the champagne flow sideways from her glass onto the lawn.

Hamish was white and looked strangely frail. He could not move or speak a word.

"God's damnation!" Carrick raged as he lifted the locket from the empty chair, holding it at arm's length as if it were a venomous snake. Realization dawned as he wrapped his fist around it. "That cursed locket," he swore. "It's taken her back to 1746!"

The statement shook Hamish from his shock. "Oh dear Lord," he said, terror shaking his voice as he trembled. "Tomorrow is the day Cumberland attacks the castle and fires all the crofts in the glen!"

"The witch's words were true," Carrick said, his head in his hands. "I shouldha thought…" He raised his face to look at Hamish. They had come into the sitting room to discuss the situation and plan what to do.

"It's not your fault, Carrick," Olivia assured him, putting a sympathetic hand on his shoulder.

"No, it's not," Hamish agreed. "The witch led ye to believe the locket would allow *ye* to travel. She didn't say it would affect Cat."

"True." Carrick nodded. "But it doesna make it less so. We must go to her as soon as we can manage it."

"How are we supposed to do that?" Olivia stood up and began to pace. "We don't know how the thing works. And you said the witch used special chants and stones and stuff."

"Aye, she did," he answered, his face tense recalling the strange ritual. "Do ye no have witches in yer time?" he directed to Hamish, who appeared deep in thought.

"There are witches in our time," Hamish began slowly. "I knew a pair of sisters in my home, Kingussie. They were verra adept."

"Then we must go to them," Carrick decided firmly. "Mayhap they will ken the words to send us."

"That is a possibility," Hamish agreed, uncertainly. "If they are still there. It has been many years since I last saw them, mind."

"Well, let's get going then," Olivia demanded. "Let's pack and get to Kingussie." Olivia started walking toward the door. "We need to find these witches and get to Cat right away. I'm going to change and pack," she said over her shoulder as she left the room.

"We will need a plan," Carrick said as he rose to follow.

"Aye we do," Hamish agreed, joining him. "We can devise it on the way to Kingussie. We'd best hurry." His voice was grave. "Our Cat has stepped into verra dangerous times."

"Ohhh," Cat groaned, her hand on her face to shield her eyes from the afternoon sun. "My head..."

"'Twill be fine, lass," a raspy voice said from above where she lay. "I'll fix ye some willow tea to stop the ache. Let's get ye up slowly, aye?"

Cat opened her eyes to see an old, familiar face framed in wild grey hair looking back at her, eyes full of kindness and concern.

"Morag?" Cat ventured, recalling the witch. "Is that you?"

"Aye, Jenny." She laughed. "So ye do remember me," Morag said, helping Cat to shakily stand. "I dinna expect ye to come. I thought Carrick would be wi' ye by now, in yer own time."

"He was." She was still a bit unsteady as they made their way from the edge of the pool. "I think I was sent back somehow...oh..." She suddenly remembered, putting her hand to her throat. "The locket."

"The locket sent ye?" Morag shook her head in wonder. "The spell was nae to bring *ye* back, only Carrick. Here we are." She led Cat into the cottage and bade her sit at the table. "I'll brew ye some willow while ye tell me all."

Cat sat sipping the tea, and told Morag everything that had occurred since Carrick's arrival in her time. Morag listened with intense interest to every word. By the time Cat finished the tale, her headache was gone.

"'Tis clear there are things we must do," Morag said, finally. "First, we must get ye to the big house. They can properly care for ye there."

"To Molly and Ian?" she questioned. It was all surreal to her. How did this happen? Here she was in Carrick's time and he was stuck in...

"Aye, lass." Morag nodded. "I will take ye there the now. But first," she said, taking an end of Cat's arisaidh, "we must hide this away. Tartan is outlawed since the rising. Ye would suffer severe penalty should it be found."

"But the Act of Proscription doesn't happen until August," Cat argued, unpinning it from her gown. "No one will care until then."

"Mayhap so, lass," Morag admonished. "But word has come that Cumberland has banned it the now and ye dinna wish to beg the issue, aye?" Morag carefully folded the arisaidh and hid it away.

"I ken ye are Caitriona," she went on. "But the others, they ken ye as Jenny. Ye must answer to it now. And ye need to speak like a Highland lass. Do ye ken the way?"

"Aye, I do," she answered, smiling. "I ken it well. I will practice yer advice, Morag." She grabbed the ends of the shawl Morag placed around her shoulders.

"I hope Carrick finds a way to come soon," she said. She was both sad and worried sick. She knew what history had in store for them all.

"As do I, lass," Morag answered gently, leading her toward the door. "I ken the lad well, and he will move the heavens to find ye. Ye'll see."

"Morag," Cat ventured. "There are things I must tell ye as we go along. Things of the future."

"If ye must," Morag answered as they walked through the forest.

"I must." Cat felt a responsibility to warn her. Morag would believe her, after all. "'Tis for the safety and protection of ye all."

"I ken, lass." Morag smiled at her. "I ken it will be bad. The runes ha' told me so. I will hear ye and help where I can."

"The first thing is that we must get away from here." Cat was urgent in this. "We must find a place in the hills to hide for a time. Cumberland's troops will be here tomorrow or the day after. They will murder, burn, and pillage the entire glen."

Morag stopped in her tracks and looked at Cat. "Ye ken this for certain, do ye?"

Aye, I do," Cat answered, grasping the old woman's hand in hers. "They will burn and pillage the castle tomorrow."

"Ye have seen this in yer time?"

"I have seen the history of it in my time, aye," Cat assured her. "And I have seen the ruins of the castle myself this verra day before I..."

"I will help ye." Morag nodded in understanding. "We will tell them ye met wi' soldiers coming here."

"A good plan," Cat answered as they arrived at the door to the great house where Morag knocked and gave Cat a conspiratorial look.

"Good day to ye, Anne," Morag said to the young woman who answered. "I ha' brought Lady MacDonell home. Would ye be so kind as to tell the Laird and Lady Molly we are arrived?"

Anne instantly recognized Cat and threw her arms around her in greeting.

"Oh my!" she squealed. "We thought ye dead! Come through, come." She pulled Cat by the hands into the sitting room. "I'll fetch Ian and Molly. Don't ye dare move!" She hurried out of the room, barely containing her excitement.

"Quite a welcome," Cat said to Morag as they stood waiting for Molly. "And aye, I do remember her."

Before Morag could answer, an ebullient Molly flew through the door and stopped dead to look at Cat.

"Oh, my good Lord! Jenny MacHendrie, ye are

alive!" she cried, reaching to enfold Cat in her arms. "I didnat believe it when Carrick said ye were alive and he was gone to find ye. Oh, thank God!" She tightened her embrace.

Tears welled in Cat's eyes as she recognized this loving mother-in-law. Memories poured in of the love and friendship they had shared. She felt the kindness and generosity Molly had shown her, and the family she had in this home.

Before Cat could respond, Ian arrived, a stunned look on his face. "Jenny?" he said hesitantly. "Where have ye been all these days? I canna believe it!" He hugged her hard, then stepped back to wait for her answer.

"I was taken to Edinburgh," she sputtered, creating a story. "Ye ken my grandda there? The doctor? And my wee sister?" Jenny had had a younger sister, also called Olivia. Her grandfather, Hamish MacAllan, had been a doctor. They moved to Edinburgh some years before after her mother abandoned the family and the wee Olivia. Would they still be alive too? she wondered. She must find them once this crisis was over.

"I will tell ye the tale later," Cat continued quickly, trying to distract them from the subject. Remembering the task at hand, she said, "I am so verra happy to be home, but I have urgent news, and we must act quickly."

"But where is Carrick?" Molly wiped tears from her face. "Is he no with ye?" she asked.

"He will be along in a day or so," Cat lied cautiously. "He sent me ahead to - uh - to warn ye all that the soldiers will be here soon. We must prepare and hide immediately." Cat let out an anxious breath. *Pray God they believe me.*

"Aye, I ken," Ian answered, his demeanor turning grave. "I had word of them coming just the other day. We have already begun to prepare," he assured Cat.

"Good," Cat nodded. "There is no time to spare. Ye must send the servants home. Then we must take what we can and go into the hills."

"We have hidden the valuables and weapons in the cellar in the barn. My father put one there with a false floor after the '15," he explained. "Anne is the only servant here as she has nowhere to go. There's a wee herdsman's shelter deep in the woods. The soldiers wouldna find it, even if they cared to go that far, aye?"

"We were about to go when ye arrived," Molly added. "'Tis good ye came when ye did." Molly turned to Morag. "Ye're coming as well, Morag? Ye canna stay in the glade."

"Aye," Morag answered. "Let's be quick to the task," she said as the tension rose.

Come quick Carrick. The glen needs ye as never before.

Carrick, who had insisted on learning to drive early in the trip, pulled the Mercedes to a stop. It had not taken long to find the stone cottage that belonged to the Henderson sisters. Carrick, Hamish, and Olivia had stopped for food at a pub in Kingussie and inquired about them.

The cheerful proprietor had been a boyhood friend of Hamish, and though it had been a few years, recognized him instantly.

Armed with directions, they set off down a winding, forested road to find the home of the witches of Kingussie.

Hamish led the way to the door and knocked loudly. Relieved to have found the place, he waited for an answer.

"Aye?" A tiny, blue-eyed face looked out at him. "What d'ye want?" she asked impatiently.

"Mistress Henderson," Hamish said, politely bowing to her. "I am Hamish MacPhail. Perhaps ye remember me?"

"Hamish MacPhail," she repeated, searching her memory. "Oh aye," she smiled, recognizing him and opening the door wider. "'Tis been many a year. Do ye come through." She gestured in invitation. "

Margaret," she called over her shoulder, "we have guests." Then to Hamish, "Sit ye down and tell me why ye've come after so long an absence."

"Thank ye kindly." Hamish stood before the sofa and put a hand on Olivia's shoulder. "First, may I introduce ye to my granddaughter, Olivia MacPhail? And this is my grandson-in-law, Carrick Laird MacDonell."

"*Laird* MacDonell?" Her eyes went wide at that. "Oh my, please accept our hospitality. And ye too, Miss Olivia."

"Did I hear ye right, Mary?" Another tiny lady stepped into the room. They looked like aging faery twins, both with speckled hair and bright blue eyes.

Ye heard," Mary acknowledged her sister. "'Tis Hamish MacPhail and his granddaughter, Olivia," she made the introductions. "And this is Laird MacDonell." She nodded toward Carrick.

Margaret looked each one over closely and said, "Ye must stay to tea. I'll fetch it right away," and was out of the room before anyone could reply.

"Do ye sit," she invited again. "And tell me the reason for yer visit."

Hamish began to tell Mary the tale of what had brought them to this point, interspersed with remarks from Carrick and Olivia. Margaret had joined them with scones and tea, and sat listening all the while with rapt interest.

When Hamish finished the story, Margaret spoke up for the first time. "A fascinating tale, to be sure. But what has it to do wi' us?" she asked suspiciously."Well, ye see," Hamish began gingerly. "I recall ye have the - er - gift and we were hoping ye could help us."

"Help ye how?" Mary broke in. "And who says we ha' the gift? Ye believe that old gossip?"

"I believe it," Hamish said flatly. "All of Kingussie kens it. 'Tis no a secret."

"No," Mary sighed and sat back in her chair. "I s'pose it isna at that. Still..."

"I traveled here wi' the help of the gift," Carrick spoke up. "I ken it can be done. I am proof of it."

"He speaks true. And we did help a traveler once. He wanted to go to the future." Margaret nodded, putting a hand on her sister's arm. "But that was long ago and we never kent if our efforts were in vain."

"He just," Mary began with an airy wave of her hand, "disappeared."

"Then surely it must have worked." Carrick leaned forward in earnest. "Are ye willing to try again?"

"Oh my goodness," Mary exclaimed. "That is much to ask. I dinna ken if we could, if we still have the strength of the gift."

"It canna hurt to try." Margaret was enjoying the thought of adventure. "If my wee sister doesna wish to help ye, I will," Margaret stated emphatically.

"Oh, all right then," Mary relented. "Tomorrow night is full moon. We can try then. We need time to set things in order."

"Come back tomorrow at eight o'clock in the evening." Margaret smiled at them. "And we shall make the attempt."

Carrick let out a long sigh of relief. If all went well, he would be reunited with Cat tomorrow. Hopefully, it would be in time to prevent any harm coming to her.

Chapter Ten

"I am too going with you!" Olivia blocked Hamish's path in the middle of the sidewalk. They had come to Inverness the night before to purchase needed items for their journey through time.

"No, ye are not," Hamish argued back, trying to step around her. "Come now, lass, let me pass. We must be on getting these things."

"Why won't you let me go?" Olivia was furious with him. "She's my sister, you know. I'm not a child. I am twenty-one-years-old and you're being ridiculous!"

"I explained it to ye before." Hamish sighed in exasperation. "'Tis too dangerous for ye. I couldna bear to loose ye."

"Nor I you," she responded, softening her voice. "But you're sixty-five. You're too old to be galavanting through time. What if the soldiers get you? You're too old to wield a sword!"

"She has a point," Carrick said from behind them. He had come out of a shop where Hamish had been purchasing coins and jewelry to use as currency. "Perhaps ye should reconsider," he added. "Mayhap the family should stay together in this, aye?"

"Yes!" Olivia cried, grabbing Carrick's arm in agreement. "All for one, you know? "nyway, you can't stop me. I'm going." Olivia stood her ground.

"Aye well…" Hamish shook his head in resignation. "I see I'm outnumbered. Ye must take care, mind? And stay out of trouble, ye wee sprite. Agreed?"

"Agreed." Olivia hugged him. "I'll be careful, I promise. Now what else is on that list of yours?" She took the paper from his hand and looked it over carefully.

"Neurofen?" She frowned. "What's that?"

"Ibuprofen with codeine." Hamish looked over her shoulder at the list. "For fever, aches, pains, and the like. I havena time for proper medical supplies, so I must do what I can at the chemist." Hamish was mightily concerned about the lack of effective medicines in the 1700's.

"Let's get on with it then," Olivia urged. "It's nearly noon and we still have a lot to do," she said as she resumed walking down the street, Hamish and Carrick trailing behind.

They walked along the River Ness, stopping in shops as necessary. As they progressed under Friar's Bridge, Carrick suddenly stopped.

"Ye must excuse me," he said softly, his eyes on

a high steeple down the way. He strode determinedly ahead of them and they struggled to keep up. As they neared the lovely Old High Church, Carrick disappeared into the narthex, leaving them standing in the surrounding cemetery..

"What is he doing?" Olivia asked Hamish softly.

"I am no certain, Olivia," Hamish answered. "I suspect he means to pray. Perhaps we should join him, aye?"

"I suppose you're right," Olivia agreed as they entered. They stood in the narthex for a moment to adjust their eyes and finally located Carrick. He was kneeling at the Altar of the Holy Family, his head bowed deep in prayer.

Silently, Hamish directed Olivia to a pew and they settled on the kneeler in front of them. Both began their private prayers for their journey to come and Cat's protection.

Olivia, who had never been religious, found solace in the serenity of the place. The fragrance of sweet incense permeated her senses and calmed her.

They prayed for a long while, each sitting back into the pew in silent contemplation until the other was finished.

Carrick, who had been immersed in his own meditation, ended at last and came to join them.

"Come," he said with a new confidence. "With

the blessings of the saints, let us be on our way to her."

"I canna find Anne," Cat raced into the hall where Ian was holding a bundle of blankets. They had taken Molly and Morag to the herdsman's shelter the night before. Cat, Anne and Ian had returned to the house to gather a few last items. "She was in the kitchen no twenty minutes ago."

A shadow crossed Ian's face at the news. They had heard cannon fire in the glen an hour earlier; the soldiers could arrive at any time. Besides, Anne was barely seventeen and a tiny thing at that. "Ye looked in the yard, aye?"

"I did," Cat answered. "And she isna there, nor in the house."

"We must find her." Ian laid the blankets on the floor. "Let's check the barn once more. Mayhap she went to be certain that last goat went." They had released all the livestock during the night, except for a stubborn goat that would not budge from his comfortable surroundings. Anne had done everything to coax him out to no avail.

"I canna believe she would risk herself for a silly goat," Cat said as they hurried toward the barn. "'Tis no rational..."

A piercing scream rent the air, stopping them in their stride. Loud sobs and more screams emanated from behind the barn, and Cat knew it was Anne. *Oh, my God. The soldiers are here at Beinn Fhithich.*

Ian's eyes held the same recognition as he urged her, "Get ye to the smokehouse."

The screams stopped abruptly and did not begin again. Cat's legs would not respond, and she stood staring at him in horror. "Jenny!" He pushed at her. "Go!"

"Lady MacDonell," an English accent haughtily addressed her, as she turned to go. "And the Laird himself." The sneer was audible in his tone.

A tall, dark-haired soldier in his redcoat stepped from the barn's shadows not ten feet from them. How had she not noticed him?

Cat and Ian stood frozen, not daring to breathe. The soldier approached, blood speckled on his face and a dripping sword in his hand.

"Do you think to escape me again, Lady MacDonell?" he asked as he came closer to Cat.

"Now do not pretend you don't remember me. After all, we did share such a lovely moment until your late husband interfered." He was within inches of her with his arrogant smile.

His features familiar, Cat searched her memory and retrieved it. She began to tremble as she recalled him, a Captain Caldwell Camden. *Lord* Caldwell Camden. An English Lord with a proclivity for rape and murder. She had met him in earlier days, before Prestonpans, before Culloden.

Oh, dear Lord, she recalled. She had met him at Invergarry castle. Laird John had never been openly Jacobite, playing both sides with aplomb. Lord Camden had been a guest there, though a secretly unwelcome one.

After failed attempts to seduce Cat that evening, Carrick caught him ravaging Cat's unwilling mouth. They had been bitter enemies since, as he had remained in the area to spy on Laird John, among other Highland Lairds.

"Ah, I see that you do remember," he said, triumphant at the sight of Cat's revulsion. "Shall we go on where we left off at the castle?" He put his filthy hand around Cat's throat and pulled her lips to his. His putrid breath stung her eyes and she choked as his tongue dug into her.

"Leave her, ye bloody Sasunnach bastard!" Ian roared, a piece of fallen branch in his hand. With a swift arc from an arm accustomed to a sword, Ian brought the branch down on top of the captain's head, which caused Cat to bite a piece of his lip in two. In response to the useless blow, Camden drew back and slapped Cat full-strength across the face—so hard that she flew several feet before hitting the rocky ground.

"You sorry, pathetic piece of Highland shite," Camden began slowly, his attention diverted to Ian and the blood that splattered as he spoke. "I'll see you dead in hell..."

"Captain," a lieutenant, with a corporal by his side, interrupted him. "All is in readiness, sir," he reported.

"Very well, Lieutenant," Camden answered, his eyes still fixed on Ian. "Hold this man," he ordered them. The two soldiers did as they were told and held Ian painfully in their grip, his arms forced behind his back. His vain struggle no match for the powerful men.

"I should kill you." He spat blood in Ian's face. "You should have gone to Culloden with your dead brother. I would, however, rather see you suffer for a time before I return and send you to join him. You shall never protect that God damned Scottish bitch again. Turn him round," he commanded his men.

Cat was half-aware as she saw the men obey and hold Ian still. Camden took a dagger from his waist and bent to the back of Ian's legs.

"This will remind you not to ally yourself with whores," he swore, as he leaned and deftly sliced the backs of Ian's ankles. Overcome with pain and unable to stand, Ian fell to the ground and lost consciousness.

"Ian," Cat tried to cry out to him, but her voice was gone. Her last memory as she sank into unreality was the smoke of the burning barn and the cry of ravens overhead.

"'Tis different than Morag's way," Carrick

commented to Hamish and Olivia as they stood in the glade behind the witchs' cottage. They had arrived punctually and were watching the sisters prepare the spot. "They are drawing something on the ground," he said.

"Aye." Hamish nodded. He had some knowledge of the ancient ways, having had a grandmother who practiced them. "A five-pointed star—a pentacle. It symbolizes the four elements plus the fifth for spirit."

"What does it do?" Olivia asked, fascinated with the proceedings before her.

"Aye well," Hamish began, watching a thick mist begin to crawl across the ground around them. "I believe they will use it to summon the elementals from the four directions, then cast a circle to bind them and protect us."

"It is time." Margaret came to them, a sword in her hand. "Do step ye into the star. Ye each stand on a separate star point, aye?"

Cautiously, the three did as she asked.

"What now?" Carrick asked, holding tightly to the canvas bag full of items they had deemed necessary for the coming trials. Olivia and Hamish each carried their own full bags.

"Ye do nothing," Mary replied solemnly as she handed each a sprig of pungent rosemary for protection. "Be ye still and concentrate on yer lady," she told Carrick. "We shall do the rest."

The three were silent as the Henderson sisters began a low, melodic chant. Carrick felt the hair rise on his arms in response to the fog that gathered and swirled. It was similar to the sensations he felt when Morag sent him to Cat.

Olivia, dressed in the old-style gown she had worn for Cat's wedding, began to feel nauseous and eerily chilled. She watched closely as Margaret used the sword to draw a circle around the perimeter of the star, closing the travelers within it.

Strange, ancient music engulfed the three; the skirl of bagpipes rising, accompanied by the beating of bodhrans that pulsed with the blood in their ears. The intensity of it so painful, Olivia nearly cried out.

Hamish and Carrick noticed her distress and took her hand on either side. They held hands, squeezing tightly as the music and chants blended into one cacophony of vibration and rendered them unconscious.

Carrick roused himself slowly, mentally checking every muscle and bone for signs of injury. The only aftereffect he felt was a slight ache in his head. Definitely not as bad as the last time he traveled, he thought. If he had, indeed, traveled successfully.

He raised himself on one arm and gazed about him. There was the pool, the seeing pool, a few feet away. And there, on the other side, was a prone Olivia;

Hamish next to her.

He was home! he thought as he got to his feet. They'd done it! All that remained was to be certain they had come to the correct date, then on to find Cat. The thought of seeing her soon made his heart dance. Best get everyone moving. He urged himself on to where the others were waking.

"Did we make it?" a groggy Olivia asked, as she shakily got to her knees, careful not to trip on her skirts.

"We are in the proper place, aye," Carrick answered as he extended a helping hand to her. "No certain of the date yet. Here," he said as she got to her feet. "Let's help yer grandda."

Hamish stood with their assistance and shook his head. "That was quite the experience," he reflected, smoothing his rumpled jacket. "Are ye both all right?"

"Aye," Carrick answered, gathering their bags and readying himself to leave the pool. "I am thinking we will go to the witch's cottage. If all is well there, we can go on to Beinn Fhithich."

"Sounds good to me," Olivia agreed, putting the bag over her shoulder. "Let's move our assess then."

"Olivia." Hamish grabbed her arm. "Need I remind ye of what Carrick and I counseled ye? Ye must speak like a Highland lady, no a twenty-first century tart. Aye, lass?"

Embarrassed, Olivia bowed her head and looked at Hamish. "Aye, grandda."

"And what else, ye elf?" Hamish wanted to be certain Olivia would not give them away.

"You and I are Jenny's grandda and sister come from Edinburgh." She had memorized the story they would tell and the identities they would assume.

Carrick had told Hamish of Jenny's grandfather and sister, who had the same first names. He told them how Jenny's grandfather had taken her three years-younger sister to Edinburgh with him after Jenny's mother abandoned the family. Jenny stayed with her father, William MacHendrie, in the Highlands, and had not seen her sister since the latter was a tiny child.

Hamish checked with the clan genealogist and discovered they died in 1745. That they were buried in Edinburgh was the only information they could gather. If Cat remembered them, she would be devastated, Carrick thought. He would tread carefully on the subject when the time came. For now, there were greater issues at stake.

As they found Morag's cottage empty, but familiar things in place, they assumed they were in the correct time and walked on to Beinn Fhithich.

Carrick felt increasing unease in every step and his stomach surged when, through the moon's full light, he saw smoke rising from the direction of the great house.

"Christ's blood," he swore as he ran up the hill.

"Hurry," he called back to Hamish and Olivia, who had also noticed the smoke. "As fast as ye can."

Carrick ran to the top of the hill, his blood pulsing like ancient war drums and dove under a thick gorse hedge.

"Cursed *whin*," he swore at the bushes as the thorny spines dug into him. His keen eyes surveyed the area around the house for traces of soldiers. In the light of the burning barn, it appeared they had gone. Olivia and Hamish joined him, more wary of the thorns than Carrick had been.

"I think the sasunnach have gone," Carrick whispered to them. "Ye stay put while I go and look," he told them, crawling back from the hedge, a bloody tear in his shirt from the plants.

"Aye," Hamish whispered. "We will stay," he agreed. Olivia was quiet with terror and merely nodded.

With precision and stealth, Carrick made his way toward the house. He hid behind vegetation and rocks as he went, his arm aching for a sword and his hand twitching for a pistol.

"Cat!" He bolted from the shadows toward her. She had recovered enough to attend to Ian, who was still face down on the bloody ground.

"Carrick?" Cat rose to meet him. "Thank God ye've come!" she cried, throwing her arms around him. "Oh, thank God," she sobbed into his shoulder.

Carrick held her tight for a moment, then drew back in alarm to look at her. "Ye are bloody, Cat. Where are ye hurt?"

"Not me," she said with urgency. "Ian. We have to help Ian. Did grandda come with ye?"

"Aye, Caitriona, I'm here," Hamish said as he and Olivia stepped forward. "Let me take a wee look at him." Hamish knelt beside Ian and began to triage him. Cat had done a fine job using torn strips of wool about his ankles to staunch the bleeding. But the wounds were deep and would need great care if he was to survive.

"Who did this to ye?" Carrick saw her horribly swollen eye first thing. Anger swelled in him like the fires of hell.

"Captain Camden hit me, then cut Ian's ankles." Cat could barely say the soldier's name.

"Caldwell Camden?" Carrick repeated. "The one from the castle who tried to take ye?"

"Aye, Carrick, 'twas he," Cat answered, her mind on what her grandfather was doing with Ian. "Please, let's discuss it later. We must tend to Ian. Please."

"Just so," Carrick answered her with an arm around her waist and drew her back to him to await Hamish's verdict.

Hamish pulled a stethoscope from his canvas bag and listened. "His heart is strong," he announced with relief.

"But Anne," Cat interrupted urgently. "I think Camden murdered her by the barn. You must see to her."

"I'll go," Hamish volunteered. "Just keep him warm. He's stable for now," he instructed as he left in haste.

Hamish was gone only a few minutes. He answered Carrick's questioning expression with a slight shake of his head. "No," he answered softly. "She's gone."

"She's dead?' Cat began to tremble again. "Oh God, no!' Tears ran fresh down her face as she tried to pull herself together.

"Nothing ye can do for her, lass," Carrick said, sorrow welling within him for the lost girl. "Ian needs us now."

Cat nodded and drew herself up. "Ye're right. What do we do, grandda?"

"Carrick, help me get him into the house. He's lost a great deal of blood and I will need to stitch him. Cat and Olivia, go and set water to boil and find some linen." Hamish quickly directed them, so as not to call attention to Anne. He had, in fact, been so intent on Ian and Anne, that he finally noticed Cat's swollen face. "Caitriona - your face..."

"I'm fine, grandda." Cat had forgotten her own pain. Resolutely taking Olivia by the hand, she started toward the house. "No need to worry about me, just take care of Ian." Then to Carrick, "What about the barn?"

"Let it burn," he answered, looking at the sky. "The walls are stone and it's going to rain any road."

Cat nodded in answer and tugged Olivia along with her.

"Where d'ye want to put him?" Carrick asked as they carried Ian into the hall.

"Have ye a large table?" Hamish asked.

"This way." Carrick nodded, leading them into the dining room. Light from the moon and fire lit the room in gloomy amber. All was intact, though. The soldiers had not touched a thing.

As they lay Ian on the table, Cat rushed in with linen, followed by Olivia with lit oil lamps.

"It will be a few minutes for the water," Cat said, placing the cloths on the table. "They ransacked the kitchen, but everything else looks fine," she reported. "It's as if something distracted them in the kitchen...oh…," Cat's heart sank. "Anne," she said, tears welling anew.

"Aye, Cat." Carrick looked up from adjusting a blanket around Ian's torso. "She's gone, may she be at peace."

"Oh." The shock of it caused Cat's heart to pound vehemently.

"Where is Molly?" Carrick was concerned by his mother's absence.

"Safe in the herdsman's shelter with Morag," she answered him, setting candles on the sideboard to increase the light.

"Good." Carrick was relieved. "We will go to them in the morning."

"Here, grandda." Olivia set a tray with two large bowls of steaming water on the sideboard. "What next?" She was still shaken.

Hamish began to thoroughly wash his hands. "Find some alcohol, aye?" he told her. "And more lamps if ye can."

"Right," she said and hurried from the room.

"I'll need ye to hold him should he wake," Hamish instructed Carrick. "I have the ether, but will use it only if I must." Then to Cat, "Carrick will assist me, lass. Go see to yer sister and then perhaps put a fire in the sitting room. He'll need warmth when I'm finished."

"Aye." Cat stood for a moment watching her grandfather's gentle hand wash the dried blood from Ian's legs.

"Go, lass," he urged. "Finish the tasks and take yer sister to sit away from here. The shock has got her."

Silently, Cat nodded to Hamish and Carrick and went to find Olivia, as she murmured prayers of gratitude and desperation.

"I did my best." Hamish sank into the soft chair, clearly exhausted. "Now we will have to wait and keep a close eye on him. He'll need watching through the night, aye?"

"It's fine, grandda," Olivia answered softly as she sat down next to Ian's inert figure on the sofa. "I'll stay with him."

"Thank ye, lad." Hamish gratefully received a glass of whisky from Carrick. "I gave him an injection of penicillin for infection and laudanum for pain. I pray they will do. The penicillin is veterinary medicine."

"Why veterinary?" Cat asked between sips of her own whisky. It warmed her and soothed the pain in her face.

"I havena license to prescribe since I retired," Hamish regretfully sighed. "So I bought veterinary from a feed shop. 'Twas the best I could do in so short a time."

"I'm sure it will be fine, grandda," Cat assured him with a pat on his arm.

"How did ye light the fire so quick, ye wee pixie?" Hamish looked at Olivia suspiciously. He had prohibited them from bringing twenty-first century items unless deemed absolutely necessary for emergencies.

"I - uh - I brought a couple of lighters." Olivia looked sheepish. "I'm sorry, grandda. I just thought they might be important. I'll keep them hidden, I promise."

"Aye, well," Hamish relented. "It seems ye were right in this case. Do keep them hidden away unless I tell ye, right?"

"Right," Olivia answered. "I just thought it couldn't do much harm if we are only here a short while."

"It seems we will be here a long while," Hamish said thoughtfully. "We canna leave while wee Ian is so poorly, and as I told ye before, there is no guarantee we can go back. Ye must learn to do things in the fashion they do now, ye hear?"

"I hear." Olivia nodded. "I'll try."

"Fine then." Hamish relaxed a bit and looked up at Carrick. "Thank ye for yer fine assistance, Carrick. Ye did a right fair job."

"I never saw such a thing," Carrick spoke up from his place next to Cat. "Injections? The fine stitching? Ye saved my brother and I am most grateful to ye. Will he walk d'ye think?"

"'Tis possible. They did not sever his Achilles, so he should. It will be slow for him for a time, at least," Hamish answered, looking at Cat's still swollen face. "Caitriona, I must tend to ye now."

"I'm really fine, grandda," she protested. "I washed it clean and the whisky is helping the pain."

"Oh, aye," Carrick reproved her. "Why was your face bloody then, when I first saw ye?"

"Oh that," she sputtered. She knew Carrick would be even more furious when she told him, but how could she not? "Camden - he - he tried to take up where he left off that night at the castle," she explained.

"He tried to force his mouth on ye?" Carrick began to rise from his chair.

"Sit down, Carrick," she said firmly. "He did. Ian hit him on the head with a tree branch and I bit his lip verra badly. 'Tis where the blood came from."

"Ye bit him and tasted his blood?" Hamish was instantly alarmed. "Nay, lass. Ye must have antibiotic immediately."

"'Tis nothing." Cat tried to wave him off.

"Oh aye, nothing." Hamish was indignant. "A soldier's blood full of God-knows-what infections? Nay, lass, ye shall have the injection if Carrick has to hold ye down."

"Aye, Cat, I will." Carrick stood staunchly before her, arms folded across his chest. "Do what yer grandda tells ye."

"Fine," she said hotly. "Go ahead. Ye know how I hate those damned needles. Just do it quick," she spat, rolling up her sleeve.

Hamish retrieved his bag and began rubbing her arm with the alcohol swabs he had brought. He filled the syringe and injected the penicillin.

"No so bad, was it?" Hamish smiled at her softly. "Much ado, aye?"

"Only because of yer gentle touch, grandda." She hugged his neck. "Ye should get some rest now."

"I'll no argue with ye, Cat.," Hamish yawned. "But first, I need to examine ye a wee bit. Look straight at me, Cat."

Hamish picked up a nearby candle and shined it in her eyes. He set it down and felt around her face and head. Cat knew better than to argue at this point and sat still for him.

"No concussion, nothing broken," he said at last. "I was worried as ye said ye lost consciousness."

"I did," Cat answered him, sitting back in the chair. "But I didna think it was for long."

"Well, other than the nasty bruises and swelling, ye seem to be fine." Hamish stood and smiled at her. "We'll keep a watch on ye all the same, aye?"

"Aye, that's fine. Come then." She rose and entwined her arm in his. "Let me take ye upstairs and show ye where to sleep. Be right back," she said to

Carrick and Olivia as they left

Olivia was still sitting by Ian's side sipping her whisky from time to time. *He has a beautiful face.*. She reached over and gently touched his auburn curls, thick yet soft.

A scattering of freckles dotted his face. Faery kisses, she recalled from childhood. She had had a few freckles on her nose as a child. When teased by her school friend, Emilia, her grandma told her that each freckle was where a faery had kissed her. Emilia, who had no freckles, began to cry. "Why don't the faeries ever kiss me?" she whined. The faeries must truly love Ian, she smiled to herself, hoping they were watching over him now.

"How are ye feeling, Olivia?" Carrick broke her reverie. "Are ye up to the task, or would ye like some sleep?" He sat down next to her and refilled her glass from the decanter.

"I'm fine, thank you, Carrick." She took a sip. "This must be terrible for you, finding your brother like this."

"It is no easy, true," he agreed, warming his glass between his hands. "I ha' always tried to protect him, but I failed him now."

"Cat's always trying to protect me, too." She touched his arm in sympathy. "But I mostly wish she wouldn't. She can't protect me all the time, you know.

She has to live her own life, and I'll bet Ian feels the same about you."

"Mayhap." He nodded, thinking it over. "I hope he lives long enough for me to ask him."

"He will," Cat reassured him from the door. "He'll be fine. Grandda is an excellent surgeon, even under these circumstances. I have complete faith in him. At least I got him to bed, thank heavens." She sat with the others and stretched out her legs.

"If ye two will excuse me." Carrick rose and reached for an oil lamp. "I must go look for Anne. Hamish found her behind the barn, aye?"

"I'm going with ye." Cat jumped to her feet.

"Cat." He grabbed her shoulders. "Ye should stay with Olivia. What I find mayna be pleasant for ye."

"She was my responsibility," Cat argued. "I'm going with ye."

"Well, if you're going out there..." Olivia grabbed her bag and dug through it. "You should take my flashlight, not a lamp. Here, I'm glad I thought to bring it. Don't have a lot of batteries, though." She extended it to Carrick. "And don't tell grandda!"

"Olivia." Cat sighed in exasperation. "Please dinna tell me ye brought yer iPod?"

"Well, I..."

'No." Cat put up a hand to stop her, momentarily allowing her Highland accent to slip. "I don't want to hear it. And if you *did* bring it, you'd best not let grandda catch you or he will redden your bum, you brat."

"Okay." Olivia blushed, recalling the spankings she deservedly received as a child. "Here, Carrick." She was still holding the flashlight out to him. "Take this at least."

Carrick set down the lamp and took the flashlight. He had been enamored with it from the first, wearing out several sets of batteries before he was satisfied.

"Thank ye, Olivia," he said. "Verra helpful."

"Just sit there, aye?" Cat commanded her sister, recovering her speech. "We dinna ken how dangerous it may be, so dinna go wandering. Just sit until we return."

"Oh, aye," Olivia replicated Cat's accent, remembering that she was supposed to speak in the same manner. "I shan't leave Ian."

"Good lass," Carrick said over his shoulder as he led Cat out, flashlight showing the way.

"I wish ye hadna come." Carrick tightened his hold on Cat's arm. "'Tis no place for ye, Cat."

"I've seen blood before," she replied.

They had gone halfway round what was left of the scorched barn. The rain had come and the fire extinguished, leaving a charred ruin; roof open to the sky. As they reached the back corner, Carrick put out a hand to stop Cat.

"Stay," he ordered. "I see her. I'll go." Carrick made his way to Anne's limp form laying a few feet away.

"Oh, my God." Cat stood behind him, holding her stomach. "Oh, Anne," she whispered at the sight of the lifeless girl drenched in blood and rain. Her throat had been cleanly and deeply cut, and her clothes torn into ragged pieces.

"I told ye to stay." Carrick turned to Cat, who was doing her best not to vomit. "I do wish ye'd listen, Caitriona."

"I'm sorry," she managed. "I didna ken...I didna imagine."

"Ye're in my time now," he admonished her. "Ye dinna see much of this in yers, I ken. This land has been at war since its beginning and 'tis a tragedy that we ha' seen too much of it. Now go to yer sister. I will take care of the body and we shall have a proper burial in the morn, aye?"

"Aye," Cat answered quietly. "I'm so sorry," she said to "Anne's grey corpse. "I'm so terribly sorry." With a remorseful look at Carrick, Cat turned away and headed back to the house. She was the reason for Anne's hideous death. She was the reason they were all here in this brutal time. Would this nightmare ever end? And, more importantly, could she ever forgive herself?

"Are ye awake, Cat?" Carrick whispered, as he pulled her closer to him in the warm bed. "I thought I heard ye say something."

Cat turned in his arms, careful not to brush her bruises against the pillow. "Aye, Carrick. I canna sleep. And ye?"

"No. My mind willna stop. And I find I have a thing I must say to ye." He released her and sat with the headboard against his back. "I pray ye willna take offense."

"Go on." Cat rose up on her elbow. "I'm listening."

"I am concerned for ye." He stared across the room at the banked embers in the grate. "Ye dinna ken how it is here, in this time. Ye dinna ken the dangers. Ye must do as I tell ye. 'Tis for yer own well-being, aye?"

Cat thought a moment. She was so used to doing everything on her own, without anyone's approval or permission. But hadn't she learned a valuable lesson tonight?

"I suppose yer right," she admitted. "I am sorry. I am so used to doing things for myself and alone. I didna mean to be reckless. I will listen to ye, I promise."

Carrick sighed and pulled her into his arms

again. "In the morn, I wish to hear the story of how ye came here and the events this night. But for the now, believe me when I tell ye that I dinna think ye reckless. In yer time ye have no the dangers as here. Ye are as independent as a cat, as ye are aptly named. I ask ye for yer trust, Caitriona, and to remember ye are no alone anymore, aye?"

Cat's heart melted at the words of her protector, warrior, and partner.

"Aye, Carrick. I am no alone," she answered, snuggling deeper into him. "And neither are ye."

Low moans of pain woke Olivia in the chair where she slept. Where am I? she thought, as she rose through the fog in her brain. "Carrick," the moan called and instantly brought her awake. That's right, she remembered. Ian.

"It's okay." She leaned over to look at him. "I'm here," she whispered, not certain he could hear, but offering comfort. She touched his damp forehead and smoothed the hair from his brow. He must have broken a fever, she decided. A good sign. She lightly drew her fingers down his cheek, unable to resist touching him.

Without warning, Ian's hand gripped her wrist, and his eyes opened to assess her.

"Who are ye?" he rasped. "What are ye doing?"

Struck dumb, Olivia stared back at the yellow eyes piercing her in suspicion. As quickly as they had opened, they shut again and grimaced with a great groan. Ian released her arm and put both his hands to his face. "Christ's blood," he swore. "God help me."

"Here, drink this." Olivia lept to his side with the laudanum Hamish had found in the panty's medical supplies. He had left it should Ian awake and need it. "It will help the pain, I promise," she assured him, as she lifted his head to help him. "It'll be better in a minute."

Ian drank it down without argument. Sinking back into the pillow, he examined her critically.

"Have ye poisoned me, lass?" His eyes were gleaming with wariness.

"No!" Olivia cried, kneeling on the floor beside him. "Why would I do that? It's only laudanum and besides, I have been sitting here with you all night. You've been through a really bad time."

"Aye, I can feel it." He grimaced again and shifted his body on the sofa. "Who in creation are ye, and why are ye here?"

"I'm Cat - er- Jenny's sister." She caught herself quickly. "My name is Olivia and I'm taking care of you just now."

"Olivia? Hmpf." He still didn't trust her. Suddenly remembering, he tried to rise. "And where is Jenny? Damnation!" He lay back down in pain.

"I think you'd better just stay still for a while."

Olivia pulled the blanket farther up around him. "And Jenny's fine. She's upstairs in bed with Carrick."

"Carrick is home?" Ian's eyes were tightly shut now, but news of Carrick made his face glow. "Is he truly come home?"

"Yes, Ian." Olivia touched his hair again. She couldn't help herself. He brought such tender feelings out of her. "He really is. He arrived here earlier tonight along with me and my grandda."

"Your grandda is here as well? I thought ye were in Edinburgh long past. I barely remember the two of ye."

"Uh - yeah - we were," Olivia stuttered, trying to recall their story—trying to recall Ian. After all, Carrick suspected she was the reincarnation of Jenny's lost sister. But no memories sprang forth.

"Grandda is a doctor and he stitched you up," she went on. "He gave you some injections and - oh shit!" Olivia let the words slip out before she realized it. She was an idiot, she reprimanded herself. She had to be more careful.

"Do they speak that way in Edinburgh now?" Ian asked, looking at her through half-closed eyes. "Lassies are allowed to curse? And what's an in-jection?" he asked.

"No, lassies are no allowed to curse." Olivia did her best to recover her Highland accent. "I shouldna ha' said it. 'Twas wrong of me. I'm sorry," she said, reaching for his hand that draped the edge of the sofa.

"Dinna fash, Ian. All is well."

"Olivia. I like the sound of it." Ian was sinking from the laudanum. "Olivia?" He squeezed her hand.

"Aye, Ian? What is it?" She squeezed back. Her soul thrilled with knowing he would live.

"I dinna care who ye truly are, be ye faery or real," he murmured. "Dinna go away, aye? Ye are the most beautiful lass I ha' ever seen." He smiled as he faded back into a deep sleep.

Chapter Eleven

"The grave is ready," Carrick said, closing the doors to the dining room behind him. "Do ye need help?" he asked Morag and Molly, who were busy washing Anne's body on the table. He had gone to the shelter at sunrise and brought the women home. "I can ask Cat to come," he said, forgetting to call her Jenny.

"Nay." Molly smiled at him. "No, I wouldna' ask her after all she has seen. Leave her be. We can manage."

"Aye, then. I'll just be..."

"Here, Molly." The doors opened and Cat stepped in carrying what appeared to be sheets. "I found them just where ye said." She put the bundle on the sideboard and stepped closer to the table. "May I help ye?"

"Nay, Cat." Carrick came quickly to her side and took her arm.

"Cat?" Molly looked up from washing the body's hair. "Why do ye keep calling her Cat?"

"Caitriona is her second name, mother," he covered himself. "She has used two of her nine lives. One last night, and one at Culloden. I find it fitting these days, aye?"

Cat raised a brow at him as if to say, good save!

Morag, who knew Cat's true identity, shot Carrick an approving smile.

"I suppose," Molly answered. "Cat it will be then." She gave him a mother's indulgent smile.

"Cat." He touched her cheek. "'Tis no necessary. Come away."

"Nay, Carrick." Cat smiled up at him. "I must do this. She was my responsibility, ye ken? 'Tis the least I can do. Go now. Be with Ian," she urged.

"The lass can stay." Morag looked squarely at him. "If she feels the need, then ye must respect it, aye?"

Carrick nodded mutely, then to Cat, "Ye certain?"

"Aye, I am." She hugged him. "Go now, please?"

"All right then." He shrugged. "I will be wi' Ian when yer ready."

Cat went behind him and gently closed the doors.

"Tell me what to do," she said quietly. "Let me help ye put her to rest."

They laid Anne's broken body, shrouded in linen, in a small wagon. Olivia covered it in wildflowers, fragrant and vivid.

Hamish stayed behind with Ian, and with Carrick pulling the wagon, the five of them made their way up the hill to the family cemetery. It was the same cemetery Cat and Olivia had visited in their own time. Funny, Cat reflected, there had been no marker with Anne's name on it then. How could that be? she wondered sadly.

The small cortege arrived at the grave side in somber mood. No bagpipes would play this day to mourn her, for they had been proscripted. Not officially for a few months yet, but they dared not. The best they could manage was Cat's fiddle and Olivia's voice.

Cat had found her fiddle—Jenny's fiddle—in the bedroom armoire along with Jenny's clothes. Untouched as she had left them before Culloden. She would play *Amazing Grace*, a song which would not be written until 1779, and by an Englishman at that.

They circled round the open grave and Carrick bowed his head. He made the sign of the cross and the others followed.

"Our Father, Who art in Heaven," he began, leading them. "Hallowed be Thy name." Together they said *The Lord's Prayer* and stood silently for a few moments.

"We come to lay to rest Anne MacHenry, a fine lass ruthlessly murdered in youth and without provocation." He cleared his throat and went on. "She was devoted helper and friend to us all. May God bless her rest and give her peace wi' His Saints."

Tenderly, and with tears welling, Cat assisted Carrick in lowering the body into the grave. When it was done, they each gathered a handful of soil and lovingly sprinkled it into the grave.

Cat retrieved her fiddle and nodded to Olivia. She slowly began the first notes of *Amazing Grace;* Olivia's trained soprano crafting each note with care. Morag and Molly held each other close. The mournful music filled them with the grace that had sustained and uplifted them with courage through so many turbulent years.

May it finally be over, Cat prayed fervently to herself. But she knew it was not to end. Not in this lifetime, at least.

"Hamish MacAllan," Molly addressed him from the doorway, watching Ian sleep comfortably. She had not had time to speak with Hamish, what with Ian's injuries and Anne's funeral. "It is good to see ye after so many years." She seated herself in a chair next to him, careful not to wake Ian.

"Aye, Molly," Hamish smiled back at her. "'Tis good to be home," he agreed, although he was thinking of his own time and how it felt to be back in

Scotland—1746 or... "I do regret the circumstances, however."

"Verra unfortunate," she agreed. "I thank ye for all ye've done for Ian. Ye saved him and I am verra grateful to ye."

"He's a fine lad." Hamish glanced at the sleeping young man. "He's strong. He'll be fine, Molly. Have no doubt."

"He is." She looked at Ian with affection. "No better son a mother could wish for." Maternal pride shone on her face. "And it is good of ye to heal Jenny - Cat, I suppose she wishes to be called, and bring her home to us. How did she come to ye?"

Hamish thought for a moment. He had the clear impression Molly was testing him. Good job he had prepared for this.

"She was brought to my door by some clansmen," he answered, as though recalling a true event. "They said she had awakened enough to tell them my name and where I was. It was a shock, I assure ye."

"I imagine it was, indeed." Molly patted his hand. There was something in her eyes when she looked at him. A strange mix of tenderness and, perhaps, suspicion? "Well, in any event, it is good to see ye safe, and our Cat alive and well. Will ye have a bite, Hamish?" she asked, rising to leave.

"If it willna trouble ye, thank ye, Molly." He rose to stretch his legs and gave her a courteous bow.

"I'll send something in for ye then." She turned

to leave. "We will have ourselves an interesting conversation later, aye?" She looked at him over her shoulder.

"Certainly." Hamish nodded, a twinge of anxiety rising. A most interesting conversation that would be.

Cat found him in the barn, sitting on an upturned bucket among the burnt timbers and planks. He looked a million miles away in thought, and she stood back, silently observing him. It had to be wrenching, to come back to this loss; his brother injured, one of his people murdered, his country in turmoil.

Carrick knew what was to come. Hamish knew his history well and had tutored him in it. He knew it would be worse before it would be better—that Scotland was about to change, never again to be as he had known it. That had to hang heavily on him. She shifted her feet in the ashes, making a soft *woosh.*

"Cat, are ye there?' he looked up to see her in the shadows. "Do ye come and sit," he beckoned, pulling another bucket to his side. "I would have a word wi' ye."

Cat walked over to him, stepping gingerly over fallen roof timbers and scorched farm implements. As she drew closer to him, she could see ashes in his hair. Soot coated his hands and clung to his face. He had clearly been working here for a while.

"Aye, Carrick.What is it?" She sat next to him and waited.

"I ken ye were sent here by the locket." He rubbed his hands together and looked into them. "When ye arrived, tell, me how it was."

Cat spent a good five minutes recounting all that had led up to her encounter with the vile Camden. As she told the tale, anxiety rose in her and she searched frantically for the source.

"Carrick," she said, her voice shaky. "I have a thing to say to ye. I need ye to listen to it all before ye react, aye?"

Comprehending that something was troubling her, Carrick merely nodded and remained still.

"Before ye came to me," she said tentatively. "Before I kent about ye and remembered, there was a man." She saw the blood begin to rise in him and put a calming hand to him.

"Nay, Carrick." She wanted to stop his thoughts in the wrong direction. "'Twas no like that. He was a verra famous composer and a colleague. I worked wi' him. I didna date him. Ye ken the word 'date,' do ye no?"

Slowly, waiting for her to finish before he judged, he nodded his head. "Aye, courting? Ye were no courting each other?"

"That's right." She smiled to reassure him. "I didna even like the man," she continued. "He was arrogant, brilliant, but arrogant. Smug, and self-absorbed. But he wanted me and I didna want him at all." Cat took a breath to relieve the troubled memory.

"I rebuffed him time and again. Still he wouldna stop his attentions. In my time, it is called stalking. He meant to make me his and wouldna stop. I had to go to the courts and obtain a restraining order to keep him away. Do ye understand so far?"

"Aye, I think so," he answered, checking his growing emotions. "Did he harm ye, Cat?"

She shook her head and looked him squarely in the eye. "Nay Carrick, I promise ye. He never touched me, never. And I hadna seen nor heard of him for over a year when ye came to me. But Carrick, I think - I am fairly certain - well, we all ken about reincarnation, do we no?"

"Aye, Cat, we are proof of it," he agreed.

"Then ye'll no think me mad when I tell ye, I think Camden is that man reincarnated. I am fair certain of it now."

Carrick stood up abruptly and began to pace in the debris. He put a hand to his hair and ran his fingers through it, dislodging ashes that had accumulated.

"But he is alive in yer time," Carrick said, trying to reason it. Only the dead could reincarnate as far as he understood. "*Is* he alive in yer time, Cat?"

Cat remained seated and shifted her legs. "Nay, he's dead," she answered him, her face drawn. "He took his own life in London where he was working. Over a year ago now, I think. It was a scandal in the music world, the way he stalked me. His suicide was no a shock."

"Then it is possible, I suppose," he answered, thinking through the ramifications. "That means..."

"That Camden will come back as he swore he would. And it would explain his fascination wi' me as well," Cat finished for him. "Aye. He thinks ye dead at Culloden, ye ken? If he finds ye alive, he will kill ye."

Carrick sat down on his bucket and let out a long breath. "Well then," he said, deciding the issue. "We must be verra wary of him in future, aye? And I must be more vigilant protecting ye."

Cat smiled into his worried eyes and reached for his blackened hand. "I'm sorry I had to tell ye, Carrick. But I thought it best ye knew."

"Good job that ye did," he answered and leaned to kiss her. "Dinna fash, Cat." His touch released the tension in her. "We'll no let him near ye again, aye?"

"Aye," she answered, fully confident in him. "Well now," she stood and surveyed the rubble. "What next? Tell me what to do."

Carrick rose and shook off the conversation. He went into a stall and began to kick at the fire's wreckage.

"What are ye looking for?" she asked. "Did ye loose something?"

"Are," he answered, picking up a shovel and scrapping away the muck. "The door to the cellar. It's here somewhere."

"Oh that." Cat remembered Ian had secreted the valuables there. It should be fine, shouldn't it? The fire only got the roof."

"Aye, it should." He found the edge of the door, crafted so that it made a barely perceptible seam with the other planks. "Let's find out." He raised the door, sending ashes and other mess dancing into the sunbeams. "Ye coming?" He gestured to her.

"Of course," she answered, and lifted her skirts to follow.

He lit the steep stairs into the cellar with Olivia's flashlight. He had kept it well-hidden in his jacket. Carrick went down first, then shone the light on the stairs for Cat.

"What a smell!" She sniffed as she stepped onto the stone floor. "It smells of mildew and rot. I do hope your valuables arena the type to be affected." She was tempted to pinch her nose against the odor.

"Oh, aye." Carrick flashed the light about the small room. The shelves were full of family silver; tea services, bowls, turines, goblets, trays, and candlesticks. Among the silver were leather-bound books, crystal, porcelain, and an armory of various weapons. Several casks lined one wall, whisky she presumed.

Along another wall were two large trunks.

Carrick went to one of the trunks and stopped in front of it, feeling along behind the shelf above it.

"Here now," he said, retrieving a key that was fastened by hook to the back of the wall. It had been hidden behind the books where Cat would not have seen it.

"What is it ye're looking for?" she asked in awe. It was like stepping into Aladdin's cave. Full of glorious treasure. She could not recall ever seeing the place when she had been Jenny.

"We'll need money to rebuild and restock." He bent to unlock the trunk. As it sprang open, he gestured. "Ye see?"

Cat had never seen so many banknotes and coins in one place. "Oh my!" She knelt beside him to get a closer look. "Why do ye no keep it in a bank?" She ran her hand across the top of the neat piles.

"No in these times, Cat." He took a small leather bag from his jacket and put one stack of notes into it. "Jacobite accounts have been seized by the sasunnach for some time, aye? 'Tis safer here." He stood and helped her rise.

"I never kent about this, did I?" She rubbed her arms against the damp cold.

"Nay," he said thoughtfully, reaching for the flashlight. "I didna want to endanger ye wi' the knowledge, ye ken?"

Cat nodded. He was always protecting everyone around him, but never himself. Even with knowledge.

"Carrick." She looked up at him in the gloom. "Where is it ye will go to buy these things?"

"Inverness, after I ha' spoken wi' Geordie, our Factor, and ha' seen to things here," he said flatly.

"I want to go wi' ye," she said. "Ye canna stop me in this. Aye," she rebutted his raised brow. "I ken - it's dangerous. I went wi' ye to Culloden before and other dangerous places."

"Oh, aye," he argued. "Only after ye beat me wi' yer words and ye see the result? Ye dead and me having to find ye?"

Cat was suddenly ashamed of herself and turned from him. "I ken it well. Was I truly as shrewish as I recall? I'm so sorry, I didna realize it. I couldna bear being without ye." She turned back to face him. "But this time, I promise I will do as ye say, aye? I do recall how to use a dirk and a pistol. Ye taught me well."

"Nay, Caitriona." He put his arms around her and held her close. "Ye were never a shrew. But ye did wear me down on the point. Fine then," he said. "Ye can help with the inventory and then we go. But mind ye, Cat." He touched her cheek. "Ye *will* listen this time."

"Carrick! Jenny!" Ian was sitting up weakly on the sofa, Olivia beside him. She had run out to tell Cat and Carrick that Ian had awakened asking for them; then she ran straight back to him.

"Ian." Carrick pulled a chair beside him and heartily shook his shoulder. "It does me good to see ye awake."

"It does me good to see ye both home," Ian replied with a grin. "I thought ye gone for good."

"And Jenny, it's twice I thought ye dead," Ian shook his head in wonder. "Yer sister tells me Carrick calls ye Cat now because of yer nine lives. I will call ye Cat as well, I think."

"'Tis fine, Ian." Cat laughed with him. "I hope to use no more lives, if ye dinna mind."

"It's great -er - wonderful." Olivia's eyes danced with happiness. "The family is reunited. And grandda said Ian is going to be fine."

"Well…" Ian hesitated. "We dinna ken how soon I will walk, Olivia. He said I'll live, aye. But it could take time..."

"Oh, aye. Ye will be up and around soon!" Olivia grabbed his hand and squeezed it. "I will help ye when ye're ready. I promise."

"There ye have it then." Carrick laughed. "Ye

have yer own nurse. How could ye no walk soon with such a motivation?"

"Carrick." Ian grew serious. "Have ye spoken on matters wi' Geordie? We did the best we could while ye were away. I hope ye find it all to yer satisfaction."

"No yet." Carrick rose to give Molly his chair. She had come in with a tray of soup and bread. She set the tray on the table and seated herself.

"I will speak wi' him soon,' Carrick continued. "I'm certain ye did a fine job, Ian, or I'd no have asked ye to do it. We will speak more of it later, when ye're rested. There will be much to do and I will depend on ye, aye?"

"Oh, aye, whatever ye need, Carrick!" His brother's approval caused Ian to glow. "I willna let ye down," he said, proud of his brother's confidence in him.

"I wouldna think otherwise," Carrick answered firmly.

"Do ye yer business then." Molly waved at Carrick. "Ian must eat." She stood to shoo Carrick and Cat from the room. "Ye come back after his rest, aye?"

Olivia rose to follow. "Nay, Olivia, stay," Ian protested. Olivia looked at Molly who nodded imperceptibly.

"Only if it willna tire ye." She smiled at him. "I'd be happy to."

Cat glanced back at Olivia. Olivia was illuminated by Ian's insistence that she stay. Ian, in turn, seemed enthralled by her sister. If Cat was not mistaken, something was brewing there. Pray God Olivia, always a bit flirtatious, would be careful with Ian, who was clearly enamored with her. Best keep a keen watch on them...and speak to Carrick.

Chapter Twelve

"It's good to have ye back." A stocky, grizzled man rose and extended his hand to Carrick as they entered the study. "I'm happy to see ye well, lass." He nodded to Cat.

"And ye, Geordie." Carrick shook the older man's hand with a congenial slap on his back. "Sit ye down and tell me how it goes. Are ye well? No trouble from the sasunnach, I hope."

"Nay." Geordie reseated himself. "After firing the castle, they seemed to lose interest in much of this glen."

Cat made herself silently comfortable a few feet away, as memories of this stoic old friend swept her. Geordie had been at Beinn Fhithich since before Carrick was born. A boyhood friend of Laird Hugh, Carrick's father, Geordie had seen his share of sorrows and remained a cheerful, if reclusive, man. Nine years before, he lost his beloved wife and teenaged daughter to a fever which swept the glen. Alone since then, Geordie expressed his loss in hard work and fierce loyalty to Beinn Fhithich.

"I heard tell though," Geordie's voice reached Cat through her meanderings, "other parts of the glen are in ruin—burnt by the Butcher Cumberland. And

Laird John arrested and taken off to London to boot. The Bonny Prince was given refuge at the castle during his escape. It seems Cumberland sought retribution the length of the Great Glen for it. Perhaps we are too far secluded to trouble, aye? It must ha' been personal that Camden saw fit to come so far."

Carrick leaned back in his chair at the desk and steepled his fingers thoughtfully. ""ye, I s'pose it was at that." He nodded. "We must be wary, Geordie. The man threatened to return, and I am verra certain he will. He thinks me dead, and so he must continue to believe. It is my intention to make Ian the legal laird. He was no in the country during the rising and canna be blamed. I hope this will protect ye all, ken?"

"Aye, I do." Geordie nodded gravely. "Ye do what ye must, then. Ian is competent, and ye will be here to guide him."

"I will. And you as well," Carrick assured him. "Simply a legal precaution I should ha' done before Culloden, to be sure."

Concern on his face, Carrick returned to obtaining the status of the estate. "So, no much damage to anyone else," he restated with relief. "Good then. And the fold?" he inquired of his factor, a man with thorough knowledge and experience of Highland cattle. One of the best cattlemen in Scotland.

"Scattered in the hills," Geordie advised. "But none the worse for all we can tell. I ha' half the men out and about to be certain. The others are collecting the horses and stock. Yer stables will be full again soon. Yer Breamas and yer Solas are there now." He referred to Carrick and Cat's horses, respectively. "They're ready for ye whenever ye need them."

Cat had forgotten about the mare. Some memories were still vague or non-existent, creeping back in when stimulated at times by only a word.

"A fine job, Geordie, as ever," Carrick answered in approval. "I'll ride out then and inspect the result."

"Aye, Carrick." Geordie rubbed his grey-bearded chin. "All will be ready for the Falkirk trysts come the Summer. I must say, 'tis a good thing the barley was in before ye left." Geordie turned to the subject of the distillery. "Ye'll have no trouble there. We can begin the malting when ye're able."

"Excellent." Carrick nodded, calculating dates. "We begin when I return from Inverness. "I leave tomorrow. Make a list of necessaries, then."

"Aye." Geordie thought through what was needed. "It willna be much. We are well-supplied for the now. If ye'll excuse me." He rose stiffly and made to leave, casting a nod in Cat's direction. "I'd best be gettin' back to the tasks. Ye'll have the list tonight," he affirmed, as he slipped out the door and was gone.

"Well, lass." Carrick ran a hand through his hair and relaxed. The fear he had born for his people was lifted, and he felt a great need to inspect the estate to reassure himself. "Do ye fancy a ride?"

"Aye." Cat rose and moved toward the door. "I'll be a minute to change." Then, in a whisper, "I do wish I had my jeans," she said with a mischievous smile and went off to find suitable clothing.

"Nice to see you, too," Cat cooed to the white mare who nuzzled her affectionately. "I'm glad ye remember me."

"Of course, she would." Carrick reached round Cat to pat the gentle animal. "Ye spoiled her near to pieces," he teased. "But do ye recall how she came to ye, Cat?"

Cat beamed and turned to put her arms around Carrick's neck. "Aye, I do." She sparkled with the memory. "Ye gave her to me as a betrothal gift. The first horse I ever could call my own. I named her Solas, for Light. I've not forgotten."

Carrick held her close and kissed her tenderly on the forehead. "That was a proud day—the day ye accepted me. I was no certain ye'd have me, after all."

"Oh, aye?" Cat teased back. "How could a lass possibly resist a man on his knee in full Highland dress? I dinna believe it's possible."

Carrick laughed and hugged her closer. A demanding snort from behind him broke the embrace.

"Aye, Breamas, ye bit of mischief," Carrick said to the red gelding over his shoulder. "We're coming." Then to Cat, "Shall we go, *mo leannan*?"

"He's adorable!" Cat exclaimed, smoothing the shaggy red hair of the calf. "I'd forgotten how sweet Highland cattle are."

They had ridden up into the hills, awash in gold, purple, pink, and green—the hues of Highland wildflowers and flora. Coming upon a group of cattle, they dismounted to walk among them; Carrick checking each one for injuries or other issues as might arise.

"They seem sound enough," he commented, running a sure hand down the front leg of the calf's mother. "And aye, they are attractive beasts, and docile. Sturdy breed they are."

"I remember." Cat nodded as the calf brought his head up under her arm to snuggle. "They withstand the climate well and forage nearly anything, aye?"

"Ye remember well, Cat," he confirmed. "Everything seems well enough. Come." He led her to Solas and put out a hand to help her mount. "I wish to show ye something."

Carrick led the way through the braes and the small burns that rippled along the edges of the path. The heather was in bloom and cast a purple wave across the crags, mixed with the vibrant gold of gorse. The mellow fragrance of thyme rose from beneath the hooves of the horses as they made their way into a clearing within a thicket of pine. It opened to a magnificent waterfall rushing down the outcropping of granite into a pool so pure, Cat could actually smell the water.

"I wish I had a camera." Cat sighed, holding Carrick's shoulders as he helped her to dismount. "This is beyond words." She closed her eyes to absorb the scents and music of the waterfall.

"I knew ye would like it." Carrick twined his arm through hers and led her to a spot near the pool. He unrolled a blanket from under his arm and spread it neatly. "I thought we'd have a wee bite," he said, gesturing for her to sit.

Cat lowered herself and sat quietly, watching as Carrick went to Breamas and returned with a sack. He retrieved a bottle of wine, along with some bread and cheese, and placed them carefully before her.

"I know this place," Cat said softly, receiving the glass of wine Carrick offered. "This is where we were betrothed."

"Aye." Carrick nodded, clearly pleased with her memory. "It is. And it is also where I first met ye." He waited patently—hopefully—for her to recall.

Cat closed her eyes and let her mind fill with images of herself as a girl. Fourteen-years-old she was, chasing a lamb up the hillside. The frisky animal had been missing for a couple of days when she took it upon herself to search for it. She spied it, at last, near a stand of pine up the hill where her father's land abutted Laird MacDonell's pastures. She chased the lamb into the clearing and stumbled onto a clear pool fed by a waterfall.

"Are ye remembering?" Carrick asked tentatively, not wishing to interrupt her recollections.

Cat sighed contentedly. "Oh, aye," she answered with a laugh, her eyes full of humor. "I was chasing that daft lamb and near fell over ye. Ye were napping here by the pool and I didna see ye amongst the bracken."

Carrick laughed along with her. "Ye took me quite by surprise, and I wasna napping."

"No?" Cat poked at him. "Inspecting the grass, then?"

"Perhaps." He grinned, and pulled her into his arms. "But whatever I was doing, I ha' loved ye from that moment to this," he swore, as he kissed her onto her back. The sparkle of late afternoon sun, filtered through pine, showered them as Cat's memory broadened.

"I remember bathing here," she whispered, the sensuality and sudden need engulfing her.

"Would ye like to bathe now?" Carrick sat up and looked back at her.

"I was wishing for a shower only this morning." Cat turned her back to him. "This would be wonderful." She gestured toward the laces down her back. "Would ye mind?"

"Aye, if I can join ye." He began to loosen the

ties, and soon had them undone. Cat let the bodice fall into her lap as Carrick ran his hands up around her breasts, stroking them as he lightly kissed her shoulders.

"Now you." Cat turned suddenly and helped him off with his shirt. It always took her anew to see him this way—always as if it were the first time.

Quivering with desire, they undressed each other and slipped into the pool. Cat floated on her back, letting the golden curls of her hair flow and spread like fern in the water. She reveled in the bluest sky above—not a cloud in sight. Surely this was the closest one could be to heaven; this place of solitude with the purity of the water and sky. And Carrick with her, always by her side.

"Daydreaming?" Carrick broke her reverie, coming up beside her.

"I suppose." She turned to touch her toes to the bottom and stand before him, rivulets running down her shoulders and breasts. "I was thinking how perfect it is here. The elegant simplicity of nature."

"Well said," Carrick agreed, taking her hand and leading her toward the waterfall. "A shower my lady wishes, a shower she shall have."

Finding a natural step in the granite, Carrick helped Cat up and they stood behind the waterfall in a space that seemed designed for just this purpose.

Carrick knelt and drank the water flowing down her thighs as she gave herself up to the caresses of his tongue. He slowly, lovingly caressed her inner folds with his mouth and gentle fingers, spreading her to explore deeper. She ran her fingers through his wet hair, curled into gentle auburn waves by the fall's mist. She whispered his name over and again in a delicate building of passion.

When she could not endure another moment, she reached for his hands and urged him to stand. She tenderly guided him back against the granite wall behind him, the fall a curtain against her back.

As the mist surrounded them, Cat knelt and kissed his thighs, carefully avoiding his most private areas to heighten his arousal. A guttural sigh escaped Carrick and he managed to say, "Caitriona, no, ye mustn't…ye canna…*mo leannan…*"

Cat continued, despite his protests, licking, sucking, and kissing, until she took him fully into her mouth and deep into her throat.

Carrick could tolerate no more of this ecstatic torment and pulled her up to him, briskly turning her around against the granite wall. He deftly lifted her up and onto him, her legs instinctively wrapping around his waist, her arms tight around his neck as he filled her with his creamy juices—the coldness of the granite in contrast to their warm bodies intensifying the climax.

Sated, Carrick released her to stand, holding her tightly against him.

"Carrick." Still catching her breath and regaining her sense, Cat pointed to the curtain of water.

"Look! A rainbow!"

Carrick straightened, then pulled her more closely to him, holding her head against his chest. "A promise of God's protection," he said, the hope in his voice warming Cat's soul.

"Let it be so," she prayed. "Please, let it be true."

"Ye leave in the morning, then?" Hamish addressed Carrick from his place across the dining table. "Perhaps ye would be good enough to bring some medicines for me? That is, if ye can find them."

Carrick swallowed a bite of venison stew before answering. "Of course." He nodded. "We will do our best for ye, Hamish. I only hope we can find what ye need."

Glancing quickly at Molly, Hamish smiled. "Not a problem, Carrick. I consulted with Morag and sorted it out. And ye should have no difficulty locating laudanum."

"Good then." Carrick put down his fork. "Ye will be in good hands, mother," he said to Molly, who was listening intently.

"Oh, aye," she agreed. "Hamish and I will get along fine. We are old friends, after all." She shot a look at Hamish who appeared suddenly strained. "Isna that true, Hamish?"

"Aye, Molly," he hesitated briefly. He had a strange sensation of déjà vu—as though he had been at this table, sitting next to this woman, before. "Old friends, indeed."

"Is everything all right, grandda?" Olivia whispered on his other side as Molly and Carrick continued discussing what needed to be done while he was away. "Ye look odd."

"Not to worry, elf." Hamish squeezed her hand. "" bit of déjà vu is all."

"Seems to be going around." Olivia squeezed back. "I've had a good deal of it myself lately. I wonder what it means?"

"Probably nothing," he reassured her. "Eat up, Olivia. Ian will need ye strong when he wakes again."

"Aye, he will." She smiled softly. "The honey will truly work to heal his wounds?" Olivia had watched carefully when Hamish redressed Ian's ankles that afternoon. He had applied a salve of raw honey to the areas before wrapping them.

"Honey is a natural antibiotic, as I told ye," Hamish said. "Ye'll see how fast he heals now."

"What is an antibiotic?" Molly interrupted, a suspicious gleam in her eyes.

"Oh." Hamish was caught unaware, thinking her preoccupied with Carrick. "It's a - a medicine against infection, Molly."

"Something new from Edinburgh, I suppose?"

Her tone slightly sarcastic.

"Actually, Molly..." Hamish drew himself up in his chair. He knew he was being challenged. "Honey has been known to prevent and cure infection, among many other healing uses, for hundreds of years. Surely Morag knows that."

"Aye," Morag agreed from her place at the table's end. "Honey is a fine remedy. Just not always to hand, ye ken?"

"Oh." Molly sat back, chagrined. "Well then, we must take extra care of the hives." She cast her eyes back onto her plate and resumed eating in silence.

"Morag is going to teach me about herbs and remedies while ye are gone, Cat," Olivia broke the uncomfortable silence.

"A fine idea." Cat smiled at her sister. It would, she hoped, keep Olivia occupied and out of trouble for a time. "And I will try to find ye some paints and brushes if ye like."

"Oh, Cat!" Olivia cried happily. "That would be wonderful! There is so much to paint here."

Molly looked up at Cat quizzically. "My wee sister is an artist," Cat explained. "She came to us without supplies."

"A family of many talents," Molly commented carefully.

"I can show ye how to make yer paints and brushes," Morag put in. "Ye have all ye need right around ye, lass. Berries, flowers, the dyes of nature."

"I forgot about that," Olivia said, recalling her small knowledge of how such things had been made in this time. "It seems there will be a lot to teach me," she replied with enthusiasm.

"And so I shall." Morag patted her hand. "First thing tomorrow, aye?"

Oh aye, Molly thought. Something was not quite right here. The characters and stories matched, true. Everyone and everything looked the same. But it all felt - not wrong - just off somehow. As if you were looking in the glass, but the glass was slightly askew at an odd angle. Probably just weariness setting in, nothing more. It had been a difficult few days and everyone was exhausted. Just her imagination. Still...

They rode for several days, stopping at Inns when they could find one, sleeping under stars when they could not. The spring weather allowed for some comfort, despite the chill at night. Carrick kept a keen watch for signs of soldiers and, as much as possible, kept off the well-traveled roads to Inverness, riding instead through glens and forest. They followed streams which he knew eventually fed into the river Ness and provided camouflage from those who might recognize him.

On the second day, they made a small camp near a rushing burn as dusk began to create shadows in the clearing Carrick had chosen. The trees and shrubs provided enough cover to feel safely hidden. Situated on a small hill, they could see a crofter's cottage below with its chimney puffing into the clear evening sky.

They settled onto a granite outcropping to eat their dried meat and hard cheese— a tasty repast, if meager.

"I apologize for the cold fare," Carrick said, extending an oatcake to Cat, who eagerly took it. She was quite hungry after the long day of riding. "I dinna wish to build a cooking fire. It could attract attention to us."

"No matter..." Cat swallowed a piece of sharp Highland cheese. "The cheese is delicious. Molly really does a wonderful job making it. There are definite advantages to owning your own cattle." She smiled at him, his face fading in the shadows of the encroaching night.

"Aye, there are at that." Carrick leaned over and kissed her lightly on the cheek. "At least we can keep everyone fed through the hard times ye talk about. Do the bruises pain ye much?"

Cat put a hand to the cheekbone under her eye. It had been a nasty purple, but was quickly fading into an ugly yellow. "I hardly feel it at all now," she answered. "It would look better if I had some make-up to put on it."

"We'll see what we can find in Inverness. It doesna look that bad, Cat," Carrick assured her. "And it doesna matter how it looks. Only that it doesna cause ye pain. I swear, if I ever see that bastard again, I'll..."

"Nay, Carrick." She put a hand out to calm him. "No more violence, aye? Promise me? Best to just stay out of the way and mind our business."

Carrick laid back on the rock, his dinner finished. "I suppose yer right at that," he agreed with a sigh. He opened a small silver flask and took a swig of the whisky from his distillery. "Here, Cat." He handed it to her. "Have a wee dram. It will help ye sleep."

"Ye say that every night." She laughed and took a sip. The first time she tried it, she had coughed and sputtered it back out again. "At least I'm keeping it down now. I'm actually beginning to enjoy the taste. Grows on ye, doesn't it?"

"Oh, aye," Carrick answered, taking the flask back again and capping it. "Ye can taste the Highlands in it. The heather, the honey, the waters..."

"I can taste all of that when I kiss ye." Cat leaned forward and brushed his lips with her own. "I am learning to savour the whisky the same way I savour yer kisses."

Carrick's eyes filled with a glimmering mixture of love and passion, tender and intense at the same time. He pulled her quickly into his arms and kissed her more fervently.

"I was right to go and find ye," he whispered between breaths. "I will never let ye go, lass. Ye give me life and breath."

"I dinna wish to go anywhere without ye, Carrick," she replied. "Mayhap we should be off to our blankets the now? The sun rises early here."

"Aye," he answered, putting a hand up her skirt. "Let's off to the blankets where I can kiss ye properly."

It was very late when Cat heard something like an explosion and tortured cries of children in the distance. The moon had risen full above them, and the smell of gunpowder filled the air. She thought she had been dreaming when the sounds filtered into her dreams, but she quickly realized something was amiss.

She put out a hand to find Carrick missing from her side and abruptly sat up. Alarm shot fireworks through her stomach like molten liquid. Cat threw the blanket off and rose to her knees to look for Carrick. Surely the English were not this close? They had seen not a single sign of them so far. But then, perhaps she and Carrick had been begging fate to attempt the trip to Inverness so soon.

She narrowed her eyes and was able to make out Carrick lying on the granite outcrop where they had eaten their dinner a few hours before. Throwing her shawl around her, she made her way to him, stooping as low as she could so as not to be seen.

She heard every crackle of twigs and leaves underfoot amidst the horrible sounds coming from the small glen below. It seemed an eternity before she reached Carrick's side, shivering with a fear she had never experienced in her own time.

"What is it?" she whispered low.

"The sasunnach," Carrick whispered back. "Stay low, Cat. I dinna think we can be seen, but best to be safe all the same."

"How long have they been there?"

"I dinna ken. An hour perhaps? I woke to the voices. They dragged the family out…something about a fugitive of the rinsing and a tartan shawl in the croft. I couldna hear it all. They shot the husband—I assume it was the husband—and took him away with them. Then they fired the croft…"

Cat felt sick in her stomach as she watched the scene below. A woman with a small child and what appeared to be a teenaged boy, huddled together on the ground, looking up at the flames consuming their home. The poor woman was trying to calm the wailing child, while the boy stood frozen, their forms lit by the grotesque firelight.

"Are the soldiers gone? Can we go to them?" Cat asked. A desire to run down the hill to offer assistance overwhelmed her. Her solitary thought was a combination of compassion for the wretched family, and bitter revulsion for the sasunnach.

"Aye," Carrick answered as he rose from the rock and helped Cat up. "We'll go to them the now. But mind ye, Cat. Ye do as I say, ye hear? I needna tell ye…"

"No, ye needna tell me," she answered quietly, following him as they began their descent to the pitiful scene below.

They went in silence, Cat holding the hem of Carrick's shirt in front of her so as not to lose him or stumble on the uneven side of the hill. They slowly approached the woman who was attempting to rise from the ground, still holding the now quiet child in her arms. Her face was bathed in soot, silent tears, and despair.

"I'm Laird Carrick MacDonell of Ben Fhithich," he said in a tone meant to soothe. "This is my wife, Caitriona. We are here to help ye. What has happened here?"

"Ye are the Laird MacDonell?" She wiped the side of her face with the dirty sleeve of her blouse. Alarm suddenly froze her expression. "Ye must leave, Laird. Ye and yer lady must go from here, before ye bring more evil upon us."

"We want to help ye," Cat broke in. "We arena here to bring ye evil…"

The woman's face was white with terror. "Oh, aye, ye will!" she exclaimed. "They took away my Duncan for his part in the rising. Everyone kens the Laird was a Jacobite. They searched the house and found my old tartan shawl. I forgot it was even there, Laird! That's when they fired the croft and shot my

Duncan. If they find ye here, well…"

"Nay," Carrick put out a hand to steady her. "They have gone, lass. They have what they sought. And we must get ye and yer family to safety. I can well see ye have no one else to help ye."

"Sir," the boy broke in. He looked to be about fifteen, by Cat's reckoning. A boy in her own time, surely. But nearly a man in this. "I can well help me my mother, Laird. We dinna need yer help, I assure ye." He drew his lean body to stand even straighter, as if proud to take the role of man of the family.

Carrick let a small smile spread on his face in reply to the show of the boy's pride. "Aye, I havena doubt that ye can, lad. What is yer name?"

"Dougal, Laird," he answered, extending a hand in introduction.

"Dougal, then," Carrick answered, shaking the lad's hand. "Then humor me, Dougal. Get what ye can and take yer mother and… sister?"

Dougal nodded in affirmation.

"Get your things and take yer family to Ben Fhittich. Here is my *sgian dubhs*." He pulled the short knife from the hiding place in his hose. " Show it to anyone there and tell them I sent ye. Tell them it is my order to give ye food and shelter until I return from Inverness. Then we shall see what to do about yer father. Aye, lad?"

The boy's face lit with pride that the Laird himself had trusted him so. "Oh, aye, sir." Dougal nodded.

"As ye say, Laird."

"We canna impose…" the woman began.

"Aye, ye can and ye must," Carrick answered her. "What is yer name, good lady?"

"Mary Anderson, Laird."

"Well then, Mary. Young Dougal here will get ye safely to Ben Fhittich. The bairn needs food and shelter, as well, aye? Ye have no other remedy for it, do ye no?"

Mary considered for a moment and let out a sigh. "Aye, Laird. As ye say then."

"Good," Carrick ran his fingers through his hair, unruly in the gathering mist. He turned back to Dougal. "Come, lad. Let's see what we can make of this mess. Cat?" He looked back at her standing next to Mary. She had been silent through the exchange.

"Aye, Carrick," she answered. "I ken what to do here."

Carrick smiled and nodded at her before taking Dougal by the arm and leading him toward the croft. Perhaps there would be something, anything, this unfortunate family could salvage. For now and the foreseeable future, Ben Fhittich would be their home and sanctuary.

It had taken less than an hour to see the tattered

family on their way, Carrick giving final orders and warnings to Dougal to ensure their safe trip to Ben Fhithich.

The lad seemed competent enough and had a skill with the two horses they had managed to find after the sasunnach had released them from the shabby corral. Cat could only pray they would remain safe. She had no doubt they would find some small measure of security at Ben Fhithich. Molly would certainly see to it.

Finally viewing Inverness from the crest of a hill, Cat sucked in a stunned breath. "'Tis nothing like the Inverness of my time," she commented. "Not that I would have expected it to be, but surely I though it would be more developed than this! Most of the houses are veritable huts!" She waved her hand across the vista to indicate the small houses with thatched roofs.

"Aye," Carrick agreed. "I was in yer Inverness," he said, allowing Breamus his head to graze in the tender grass. "It is still a major port, but the people are poor. And ye see there?" He pointed to an enormous heap of rubble in the distance. "That is what is left of Fort George. They built it incorporating parts of the old castle."

"What happened to it?" Cat asked. She had been to Inverness Castle in her time, but it had been rebuilt in 1836 and was red sand stone.

"The Jacobites blew it up," he answered, matter

of factly. "Ironic though," he continued, shaking his head. "A French officer - L'Epine, I believe his name was, directed the placement of the explosives and they went off prematurely. He was killed in the explosion."

"I guess he wasna that good at his job then," Cat remarked. "At least it isn't a fortress now. Lucky for us."

"Aye," he agreed. "Let's on to town, then," he said, pulling the reins in and urging Breamus down the hill. "And mind ye," he added, "We must be even more watchful than before, aye?"

`"Aye, Carrick," Cat nodded her assent, the chilling warning making her flesh prickle.

"What is it, Cat? I can see yer troubled." He signaled Breamus to stop and turned to Cat, who appeared strained.

"Oh, nothing." She rubbed her arms to chase away the chill. "I just feel overwhelmed at times. I am living the history I learned about in my time. It's a verra odd experience."

"So it must be," Carrick agreed. "Yer time was a shock to me as well. I wonder, do we ever become accustomed to it?"

"I dinna ken," she answered somberly. "But I do wonder if my coming back here with ye—well, I have changed some history already. Perhaps Ian would not have been injured, Anne would still be alive, if I had stayed in my own time. Perhaps I should have..."

"Cat," Carrick attempted to soothe her concerns. "We can never ken if yer coming caused those things to happen, aye? How could we ever ken it? If ye were not meant to be here for some reason, I think ye would not have been sent back. Mayhap there is something good to come of it, ye ken? Ye must think of it as a good thing. Yer knowledge of the future canna be but useful. And yer grandda's skill as a doctor will only serve to help in the days to come, aye? I can tell ye those things for a certainty. Events will unfold as they must and we may see the answer, or we may not. But it does ye no good to believe it bad."

"Aye, Carrick." Cat did her best to smile at him. "Ye are right. I will do my best to make it a good thing, to contribute in a positive way in all things." She brushed away a stray lock of hair the breeze had lifted. "Do ye think we will ever go back to my time?"

"I dinna ken, Cat," he answered, casting his eyes to the cloudless sky. "Do ye miss it so much?"

"Some things I miss, but I'd rather be with ye, no matter where," she assured him. "As long as I do no harm."

He put his hand out to her shoulder in affection and reassurance. "Nay, Cat," he said gently. "Ye could never do that. It's not in ye to do harm."

"But maybe I will without meaning to," she answered.

"Nay, never." He squeezed her shoulder. "Let's on to town, aye? Think of the good ye will do for the family and clan. Ye are their Lady now, as before. Only good can come of that," he said as they began their descent from the hill into Inverness.

Olivia sat in the garden, one iPod earbud tucked discreetly in her ear. She had placed it strategically under her hair, bushy from the lack of conditioner in this time. Everyone was busy with their chores and she sorely needed a break from Morag's tutoring on herbs, so she snuck out to a secluded spot to relax and listen to music. She was sketching a nice grouping of Foxglove when she dropped her pad, startled at an unfamiliar sound.

"What the…?" She turned to see an equally startled Ian behind her, leaning on padded crutches. "Oh!" She breathed a sigh of relief. "It's you. What are ye doing out here?"

Ian gingerly lowered himself to sit on the bench beside her. "Practicing with the crutches yer grandda gave me," he answered, obviously proud of his progress. "Do ye mind if I sit with ye for a bit?"

'Uh – no, not at all." Olivia put her hand to her ear, trying to figure a way to get rid of the earbud before he noticed it. "Ye're doing verra well with those, Ian. I dinna expect to see ye up and around so quickly. It isna too painful, I hope."

""A bit," he said with a small grimace. "But worth it to sit in the garden with ye."

"That's verra flattering." Olivia put her hand up under her hair to retrieve the earbud. It caught in a tangle and she couldn't free it.

"What is it, Olivia?" He looked at her oddly. "Is something caught in yer hair? Do ye need help?" He reached a hand to offer her assistance.

"No!" She grabbed his wrist to stop him. "It's fine. Just a twig or something from when I was lying on the grass…"

"A twig? Then what is this?" Ian lifted the wire that was hanging over her shoulder and began to pull on it gently. It caused the iPod to peek out from the skirt pocket where she had secreted it.

"Leave it be!" Olivia pulled the wire from his hand and the earbud dropped from her hair. "It's nothing, I told ye," she reprimanded, quickly pushing it all back into her skirt and accidentally disconnecting the earbuds from the unit.

"Aye, it's summat." Ian's curiosity was fierce now. "What is it? I havna seen anything like it. Some new contraption from Edinburgh? Do let me see it."

"I canna!' she exclaimed, slapping her hand over the pocket. In her anxiety to hide it, her hand slapped too hard, the pressure hitting the on button and causing music to play over the built-in speakers. "Oh, shit!" she cursed as she fumbled in her pocket to turn the thing off.

Ian reached over and grabbed her hand away. "Now I ken for certain 'tis summat. Is that music I hear? Let me see it, please." He firmly pulled her hand from the pocket, the hand containing the iPod and the disconnected earbuds. Carrie Underwood's voice filled the space, "I took a Louisville slugger to both headlights…"

"What is this thing?" Ian was fascinated and stunned, his mouth gaping as he turned the iPod over and over to examine it. "What's a *Louisville slugger*? And ye attack cheating men in Edinburgh? Isna it easier just to leave them?"

"Give it back, Ian. I'm not supposed to have it!" Olivia jumped up and stood before Ian, trying to wrest it from his hand. "My grandda is going to kill me! Please!"

Ian grabbed her wrist, keeping her at bay and held the iPod behind him. "Nay, Olivia. Not until ye explain what this is. Calm down, lass. Sit down and tell me. I willna tell yer grandda, I promise ye."

Having no choice but to do as he said, Olivia sat back down beside him and heaved a sigh in resignation.

"All right, Ian," she began, dropping her accent. "But you won't believe me. Damn!"

"Mayhap I will. Ye don't ken that until I hear the truth." He smiled at her as the song ended and the iPod went silent. Ian brought it from behind his back and examined it closely. "Where does the music come from? How does it work? Where did ye get it?"

"Okay, Ian." Olivia took a deep breath and

looked him square in the eye. "I'm from the future," she began in earnest. "I'm from 2010, and that is called an iPod. You put your music on it so you can listen to it whenever you like."

"From the future ye say? 2010?" Ian laughed at her. " Are ye mad, Olivia? Have ye a fever or summat?"He reached his hand to her forehead to check.

"No, Ian. Just listen. You said you wanted the truth, so listen."

"Right then. Go on." Ian sat back against the bench and folded his arms, iPod tightly clenched in his fist. "Tell me."

Olivia went on for some time, telling Ian all that had happened and what led up to this point.

Ian sat quietly throughout the telling, making faces at certain parts of the tale, leaning forward in intense concentration at others. When she finished, Olivia sat back and waited for his judgment.

"Well?" she said at last, the silence was disturbing.

"I suppose it could be true," Ian said slowly. "Morag truly sent Carrick through time to find Jenny and bring her home? Amazing. Who wouldha thought?" He relaxed a little, seeming to accept all that she had told him.

"Yes, Ian." Olivia placed her hand on his. "I wouldn't lie about it. It has been a very difficult time for us all. And you must keep this knowledge between us. I beg you."

"Oh, aye, I will," he promised emphatically. "But I will talk with Morag, if ye dinna mind. Just to be certain, aye?"

"Fine," Olivia spat. "You won't believe me until you do, so go ahead. Can I have my iPod back now, please?"

"Well..." Ian smiled devilishly. "Ye can, if ye play some more tunes for me."

Laughing, Olivia took the iPod and turned it on. "Want to hear the Beatles?" she asked.

Chapter Thirteen

Despite the awful incident with Mary and Dougal, and the burning of their croft, the trip to Inverness had been successful. No one had recognized Carrick as they went about their business, at least not openly.

They remained in town only long enough to purchase what they needed and from merchants who did not know him. Working in haste, they managed to leave within a few hours and head back the way they had come.

They arrived at the Invergarry Inn without incident and, feeling a sense of relief and relative comfort, were able to enjoy a hot meal and welcome by Carrick's friend, and the Inn's owner, John Anderson.

"The lobsterbacks havena returned, Laird," John told him as he joined them for a pint over a savory beef pie. "We set a watch all over the glen for them. Some of the crofter's bairns are runners to alert the folk should they return."

"Do they ken I'm alive?' Carrick asked between bites. "Camden is vicious and will cause suffering to all should he think ye hide me."

"Aye," John answered with a pull on his ale. "Everyone kens it. But they are loyal to ye, Carrick, and willna breathe a word of yer presence. Ye've done good for yer people and they dinna forget it. No need to worry on that, I assure ye. Ye must excuse me..." He stood at the sound of an arriving coach outside. "It seems we have a guest."

He gave a slight bow to Cat, who nodded in response as John turned toward the door at the end of the room.

As he reached for the door, a force threw it open from the other side, and a woman in expensive finery blew through with an air of importance. John stepped back quickly in astonishment

Carrick dropped his fork at the sight of her and cursed.

"Fiona! Hell's teeth!"

"Who is it?" Cat leaned over to whisper.

"Yer bloody, fukit mother!"

Cat blanched at his use of the profanity. She had never heard Carrick utter that particular word, and it shocked something deep within her.

She felt nausea rising and her head began to spin wildly. Vivid memories of this hateful woman washed over her like a bucket of ice. She suddenly couldn't draw a breath and gripped the table to right herself before she fainted.

"Well, look who's here." The garishly attired and painted woman sauntered to their table and glared at Cat. "If it isn't the Laird and Lady themselves. A bit dirty and ragged for such high positions, aren't you?" She spat the venomous words at them. "Have the mighty fallen on such hard times? You Jacobites got what you deserved, I say. Get me a chair, Carrick," she commanded. "Try being a gentleman for once in your life."

"Get it yerself, ye cursed cow," he refused, and picked up his fork to resume eating. "Ye're no welcome here ye *buidseach.*"

"Now, Carrick," she said sweetly as she pulled up a chair and sat. "Is that any way to speak to a lady? And if you are going to call me a witch, you could at least not use that vulgar Gaelic. And after I worked so very hard to rid myself of that filthy Highland accent. Besides…" She let out a sigh, "French or English are so much less common."

"The only lady in this room is my wife." He laid down his fork and glared at her in disgust. "And in any language, ye are common and still a witch and worse."

The flamed-haired Fiona threw back her head and laughed—a throaty cacophony that resounded to the rafters. Despite her forty-five years, she was still a beauty, the only good thing she had passed on to her daughters.

"You always did have a sense of humor, Carrick." She leaned over and patted Cat, who had been silent. "And my darling daughter. Not pregnant yet, are you? Either you're barren or, can it be? Your husband doesn't enjoy the company of women?"

Cat began to rise in fury, but Carrick grabbed her arm to stop her. "Nay, Cat." He pulled her down to sit. His eyes said leave it be, so she kept her peace and looked at her plate.

"What do ye want, Fiona?" Carrick said calmly, not wishing to fuel the woman. "Why have ye come here after all these years away? Did the Frenchman tire of yer poison?"

"He's dead," she said nonchalantly, settling back into her chair. "A year now," she continued, removing her gloves a finger at a time. "The ungrateful pig barely left me a stipend. About the same time dearest William died, making me a widow." She looked at Cat as she referred to her late father, Fiona's abandoned husband. She reached out a hand to Cat in mock sympathy. "I came as soon as I heard, dear."

Cat turned her head away in refusal and said nothing. She fervently groped for memories of her father's death and, once retrieved, tears sprang as though hearing of it for the first time.

She recalled how much she had loved Laird William—what a wonderful, doting father he had been. She also vividly remembered the torment and insufferable pain Fiona's leaving had caused him. William had been broken for years after, and was never able to love another woman.

He had allowed Hamish to take the younger Olivia with him to Edinburgh, to educate her and raise her away from the scandal. That, too, had broken his heart.

William's only true companion at his death had been Cat who, even though married, continued to care for him. Her marriage had been one of the few consolations of her father's life. She kept her face turned to the wall so as not to encourage more of Fiona's malice.

"Why do ye come now, Fiona?" Carrick was fighting the ire rising in him, but he had to know.

"There is nothing for ye here. And William's estate went to Cat. Ye should go back to the hole ye crawled out from."

"Cat, is it now?" She looked at Cat with a wry smile. "Using your middle name, eh? Well, why not? I went by Lorraine in France. More sophisticated than the Fiona my da hung on me. How is the old turd, anyway? I heard he lives with you now, along with that changeling child I birthed."

"Leave her be, Fiona." Carrick's voice was a low, threatening growl. "Can ye no see the lass is distressed by yer appearance? Must ye do her to death as ye did William, and most likely yer Vicomte as well? Must we murder all ye ken?"

"I take it by your non-response that the old bastard is well." She ignored his insult and rose to leave. "Well, I shall see soon enough. I sent word to Beinn Fhithich of my arrival. And we'll just see who owns what. I am William's widow, after all. The prick never would give me a divorce so I could marry the Vicomte," she said with a menacing gleam in her eye. "The English are not well-disposed toward handing over estates to Jacobites these days. I will see you at Beinn Fhithich. Till then..." She gathered her heavy silk skirts and, with nose held high, strode aristocratically out of the Inn.

"She just threatened to turn you over to the English!" Cat exclaimed in alarm the moment the woman was gone. "What are we going to do, Carrick? Oh, my God!"

"Fiona has always been full of bluster," he assured her as if it was not important. "My guess is that she's bluffing. Bullies usually do, and she doesn't really want all that land or the house. She just wants money. Ye pay her off and she'll slink away."

"I hope yer right. But what about grandda and Olivia?" She stiffened, suddenly remembering Fiona's reference to Hamish. "They don't even know who she is! We'd better get on to Beinn Fhithich and warn them…"

"Well, who wouldha kent Fiona MacHendrie would ever show her face here again?" John said as he returned to the room. "I just gave her lodgings for the night. She willna spread trouble at Beinn Fhithich for a day, at least."

"Thank ye, John." Carrick stood and extended a hand to Cat. "We'll be on our way, then," he said, handing John payment for their meal. "Fine hospitality, as always."

"A pleasure, Laird," John answered as Carrick led Cat out to their tethered horses, fresh and ready to ride. He helped Cat mount, and they began the climb up the glen to home.

"Carrick?" Cat broke the silence. "What about grandda and Olivia?"

Carrick was hesitant to share his thoughts on the matter. He was fearful that Cat would think he had lost his mind.

"Well..." he began. "Do ye recall when I first told ye the story of Fiona? I told ye I thought it possible yer grandda and Olivia were reincarnated, too?"

"Aye, I recall," Cat answered slowly.

"I do think it possible, Cat." He pulled Breamus to a halt and looked at her squarely, compassion in his eyes. "I didna tell ye. I didna want to cause ye pain until I was forced to. But it is time ye kent it." He steeled himself for her coming emotions. "Before we traveled here, yer grandda and I made inquiries. We discovered that Jenny's - yer - sister and grandda, died in Edinburgh over a year ago. We dinna ken how, just that they did."

Wrenching grief filled Cat as memories of her sister and grandda in this time surfaced. "Oh, no!" she cried out, sobs seizing her and tears beginning to pour.

"I'm so sorry." Carrick dismounted and came to her, reaching his arms up to lift her down into them. Enveloping her closely, he whispered into her hair, "I'm so sorry, Cat. I'm so verra sorry."

He held her for a long time, letting her spill her grief into his chest until she could cry no more. Slowly, she gathered herself and pulled away from him. Looking up into his worried face she said, "You really do believe they are the same souls?" She wiped her face with the edge of her shawl. "But that would mean..." she sniffled, trying to digest the idea and think it through.

"It would mean they arena dead. They are here with us now, and we must protect them from Fiona."

"But they dinna recall any past lifetimes," she gently argued.

"They may well do when Fiona arrives at the house," he answered ominously. "And I've a notion it willna be a pleasant recollection. Let's on to home," he said, lifting her back onto Solas. "And let's make haste at that, aye?"

"Aye," Cat agreed, resolute to prevent the evil that was Fiona from doing further damage.

"We're glad yer back in one piece." Hamish clasped Carrick heartily on the shoulder. "No too bad a trip, I trust? Mary Anderson and Dougal arrived a few days back. Molly gave them one of the cottages yonder, and put Mary to work in the kitchen. A fine cook, she is. And young Dougal has a way with the cattle. Geordie had seen to him." Hamish shook his head as he updated Carrick on the family. "Nasty business, that," he said in disgust.

"Aye, Hamish," Carrick replied. "Thank ye for yer kind help in it. We'll be seeing to what we can do about the husband, aye?"

"Aye," Hamish agreed as the two went off into the parlor to discuss what must be done.

"I'm off to find Olivia," Cat said from behind them as she hurried toward the garden, leaving the men to talk of the business.

"Good to see ye safely back," Hamish commented, sitting in the chair he had come to think of as his.

"Thank ye, Hamish," he answered. "I did what I could for the list ye gave me. The goods are to be delivered by end of the week next." Carrick was debating how to bring up the subject of Fiona. "I do have a thing to s ay to ye, Hamish…"

"Carrick!' Cat exclaimed as she entered the parlor with agitation. "Ye are no going to believe what the wee sprite has done now. Ye too, grandda."

Olivia stood behind her sister looking shamed and nervous. Ian appeared puzzled at all the fuss, and made his way to the sofa where he sat and laid the crutches on the floor beside him.

"Well, what have ye done, elf?" Hamish asked Olivia gently, not wishing to condemn her before hearing it out.

Olivia stood silently, her gaze fixed on the floor. Guilt poured from her and filled the room.

"Since Olivia won't deign to tell ye, I will," Cat began. "I was in the kitchen where Ian was sitting, and overhead him humming a verra familiar tune. Ye do ken *I Want to Hold Yer Hand*, the Beatles song, do ye no?"

"Aye..." Hamish answered cautiously..

"Where do ye think Ian heard that tune, grand-da?" Cat put her hands on her hips, clearly displeased. "Our Olivia brought her iPod with her! Can ye believe it? Did ye no ban the bringing of modern items?"

Hamish nodded, carefully thinking it over. "I did," he said at last. "Olivia," he rose and began to pace the room. "What have ye done, lass? I told ye the reasons for it, and ye did it despite me. What were ye thinking?"

Slowly, Olivia raised her head to meet her grandda's disappointed eyes. "I wasna thinking, grandda. I suppose I only wanted to have my music with me. I'm so sorry. But it did no harm, really," she argued. "Ian promised not to tell anyone about it. And he so enjoyed it, didn't ye, Ian?"

Ian shifted uncomfortably in his seat. "Oh, aye, indeed," he agreed readily. "I did swear not to tell, Hamish. I won't tell—ever. The music is unlike anything I ever heard and..."

"There's a reason it's unlike anything ye ever head, brother," Carrick broke in firmly. "'Tis no from our time, ye ken? If anyone kent about this, Olivia could be accused of magic. Ye do realize it, do ye no?"

"No!" Ian protested, realization dawning. "I didna think of it. Truly, Carrick, I will no say a word to a soul!"

"And ye, elf?" Hamish asked Olivia, who was now standing next to Ian in a sort of unified front. "Ye ken the history here."

"Oh, aye, grandda." She nodded vigorously. "I ken it. No to anyone, I swear."

"Do ye have anything else we should ken, Olivia?" Cat asked, waiting apprehensively for the answer.

"No!" Olivia said staunchly. "Only what ye ken about. The lighters and the flashlight. That's all. I swear!"

"What are those?" Ian asked, interested in what other gadgets she had brought from the future. "May I see them?"

Hamish sighed in resignation. "Are, ye may. *In private,*" he emphasized. "Then hide them away, Olivia. Ye put yerself and us all in danger should they be found."

Uh - well - there is one last little thing." Olivia went pink again. "My ghillies."

Hamish took a long, patient breath, and exhaled it slowly. "Yer ghillies, Olivia? Why in heaven would ye bring yer dancing shoes? Ye ken ladies dinna Highland dance here."

"Aye, grandda, I ken." Olivia lifted her chin to defend herself. "But ye ken how I love to dance, and I plan to compete when we go home..."

"Go home?" Cat asked incredulously. "Are ye mad? Can ye no see where ye are? 'Tis no a holiday we are on. How do ye think we will go home?"

"I just thought that maybe we would find a way…somehow," Olivia sputtered with the realization that their situation could be permanent. "I thought perhaps Morag could…"

"Morag told ye herself she has no the power any longer," Hamish reminded her. "Nay, lass. This is home now. Ye must get used to it, aye?"

Olivia's eyes began to mist as she tried to smile at Hamish. "Aye, grandda. Okay."

"*Okay*?" Ian repeated in question. "What does *okay* mean?"

"I'll tell ye later," Olivia murmured to him, recovering her emotions.

"Hide it all away, sprite. Please," Hamish implored her a final time.

Cat sighed at Hamish's verdict. "Grandda, ye ken how she is," she protested. "Ye ken she willna be able to help herself…"

"Nay, Caitriona," Hamish answered, taking her hand and leading her to the door. "We will trust her to keep her word this once." He motioned to Olivia to join them. "Come along, sprite. Let's find a safe place for yer things and appease yer sister, aye?"

"Aye, grandda." Olivia gave Ian a shrug and followed them out of the parlor.

"Right, then," Carrick said to his brother. "With

all of this, I hadna chance to say how good it is to see ye walking about."

"Did ye really travel through time to the future?" he asked Carrick, ignoring the remark on his health. "What was it like?"

"Verra interesting," Carrick said thoughtfully. "They have machines ye fly in, and things called automobiles which ye ride in and move on their own power. No horses or carriages. And boxes called televisions where ye can watch moving pictures that talk and...well, I can tell ye all of it later. Mind ye, dinna tell mother, aye?"

Ian put his hand over his mouth indicating his silence on the matter. "She'll nay hear it from me, I assure ye, Carrick." Ian's eyes were wide at the thought of what his brother had described.

"So then, if ye are fit enough, I will need yer help with some things, Ian. Come into the study with me, aye?"

"Aye," Ian beamed and reached for his crutches in order to follow Carrick, who was nearly to the door. "Anything I can do to help, Carrick," he said, and begun humming the Beatles tune again in perfect pitch.

"Aye, Nessa?" Carrick acknowledged the housekeeper standing in the door of his study. He had spent the last three hours going over estate business with Ian. "What is it?"

"Well, Laird," Nessa answered tentatively. "There is someone here to see ye-

"I don't need an introduction to my own family," Fiona interrupted and charged past her into the room. "You can go now," she spat at Nessa and waved her away. "The laird knows who I am."

Fiona abruptly sat herself down in a leather chair and glared at Ian. "You're grown since last I saw you. You *are* the brother, aren't you?"

Ian, who could not recall the woman, stared back in silence and awe. He had never seen such a flamboyant woman before. He merely nodded in assent.

"What are ye doing here, Fiona?" Carrick began to rise from behind the desk. "I thought ye were lodging at the Inn."

"I was." She sighed with a pout. "But I changed my mind. I was anxious to see my dear da and the rest of you. It's been so very long."

"I'm quite certain ye were," Carrick replied sarcastically. "That's why ye stayed away—what is it, Fiona? Nigh fifteen years? What makes ye think ye're welcome here?"

"Fetch me a brandy, boy," she ordered Ian. "And be quick. I'm parched. This Highland climate is most unnerving. And tell my da and your mother I have arrived while you're at it."

Ian grabbed his crutches and quickly left the

room. He didn't know who the woman was, but the malicious tone she used all but chased him out. He was happy to get as far away from her as he could.

"What's wrong with him? Is he a cripple?" Fiona turned back on Carrick. "Bad breeding, I suppose. You Highlanders, always marrying your cousins..."

"Enough, Fiona," bellowed Carrick, leaning over the desk at her. "I'll have none of your vitriol under my roof. Ian was injured defending yer own daughter against the sasunnach you love so bloody much. Now shut yer vile gob. Ye have no right to be here. State yer business and get out. Now."

"No need to be so rude, Carrick," Fiona scolded with a smile. "I'm sure your mother would not approve of your treating a guest so. Where is Molly? I'd like to pay my respects. We are old friends, you know."

"Ye ended that friendship when ye left Laird William." Carrick was seething and trying to gain control of his temper. He would not let this woman undo him. "I doubt my mother would want to see ye. Now, I say again, state yer business."

Fiona settled more deeply into her chair. "I already did," she stated flatly. "I came to see my family. Won't your brother get them, or do I have to go and find them myself?"

"No need." A furious Cat entered and stood squarely in front of Fiona. "I thought we were well rid of ye, Fiona. I want ye out of my house this minute."

"Now, Caitriona." Fiona slowly rose to face her. "You wouldn't throw your own mother out? I have nowhere to go, my dear. Surely you aren't that cruel?"

"As cruel as ye, ye mean?" Cat stiffened in righteous anger. "As cruel as when ye abandoned yer family for a French Vicomte? Oh aye, I am. 'Tis in my genes. Just watch me..."

"In your what?" Fiona asked, confused by the word *genes*.

"I inherited it from ye, Fiona." Cat leaned closer to Fiona's face, itching to smack her. "Get out of my house!" Cat raised her arm as if to hit her.

"Caitriona!" Hamish stood in the doorway. "None of that, lass. Ye must no strike yer mother, regardless of what she has done in the past."

Hamish had been informed of Fiona's presence and quickly recalled the story Carrick had told him. He instructed Ian to fetch Molly and Olivia to the parlor, and went on to meet the notorious woman alone.

"Let's go into the parlor," Hamish commanded in his gentle way.

Cat lowered her hand and pushed past Hamish without comment. Fiona quickly did the same, not daring to look at Hamish.

"Ye cleared the room, Hamish," Carrick said, joining him as they followed a ways behind the women. "Well done."

"We shall see, Carrick," replied Hamish with a shake of his head.

Cat was seated on the sofa, arms folded over her chest, glaring pointedly at Fiona. Fiona had settled herself into an opposite chair and assumed a casual air.

"Well, da," Fiona greeted Hamish with a careless tone. "You're looking fit for your age. I thought you'd be long dead by now."

"Ye dinna need to jab at me, Fiona," Hamish answered as he moved to stand near the mantle.

Carrick joined Cat on the sofa and listened intently.

"I wasn't jabbing, da..." Fiona began.

"Aye, ye were," Hamish cut her short. "And I demand ye be respectful to all in this house while ye're present. D'ye hear me, lass?"

Fiona lowered her eyes to the floor, not in shame, but in defiance. "If you wish it," she muttered.

"What is yer business here at this time, Fiona?" Hamish questioned. He stood firmly by the fireplace, a stern look on him.

"She wants my inheritance," Cat broke in. "She means to take us to court for Laird William's estate and turn Carrick into the sasunnach."

"I merely wished to see my family..."

"Bollocks!" Cat interrupted with vehemence.

"That's not what ye said at the Inn. Ye threatened Carrick."

"Is it true, Fiona?" Hamish watched Fiona for signs of discomfort to prove her lie. As he did, a vague image came into his mind of a fire-haired child in his arms. A willful, spoilt child who did as she pleased, and was often disciplined to no avail.

The memory was vivid and odd—he had never had a daughter in 2010. He shook off the image and began again. "Is that yer intent?"

"I only want what is rightfully mine," Fiona answered insolently. "I am Laird William's rightful widow. Everyone knows it."

"Nay, Fiona. Ye surrendered that right when ye left him and yer bairns." Hamish's vision was flooding with images of this woman at various times of her life. Child, adolescent, and the mother abandoning her daughters and husband.

Had he truly lived that life as her father? Was he really the reincarnation of Hamish MacAllan as Carrick suggested? If not, then what? He had never considered himself psychic. He'd never had a supernatural experience outside of the travel to 1746, although he did believe in the unexplainable. Could it be true? Was this truly his daughter in a past life?

The possible truth of it nearly unnerved him. Composing his thoughts back into logic, he said. "So now ye come to the family ye hated and left to ask hospitality, do ye? I am most ashamed of ye, daughter." *Where had that come from? Daughter?*

The word hung in the air between them, and Cat stared at Hamish in astonishment. What is going on here? she wondered. Odd that Hamish would play the part so well. He was never a good actor or liar. Either someone had coached him very thoroughly, or… could it be true?

"I have a wee proposition for ye, Fiona," Carrick interjected. "With yer permission, Caitriona," he said, seeking her approval before continuing. Cat merely shrugged, too numb to verbalize a response.

"Aye, then." He leaned forward, hands clasped in front of him. "There are caretakers living in *Taigh MacHendrie*. Ye may abide there for a wee time, provided ye pay yer daughter, Caitriona, fair rent. Ye'd be responsible for yer own expenses and board. Perhaps six moths? Or do ye need more time to find a new husband, being a woman of yer age, ye ken?"

Fiona reddened against the insult. "Pay my own daughter to lodge in a house I rightfully own? Are you mad, Carrick? And where do you expect me to get the money to pay her at any rate?"

"I doubt the noble Vicomte left ye as abject as ye claim." Carrick calmly leaned back into the sofa. "I'm quite certain he paid ye what yer services were worth to him. Nay, ye shallna have complete charity from yer daughters, I will see to that. 'Tis charitable enough as I offer it. Do ye no like it, ye may go back to France and see what charity ye may find there – if there is any left for ye, which I doubr, or ye wouldna be troubling us."

"And you, Caitriona?" Fiona was furious. "Do you agree with this plan? And you as well, da?" She looked from one to the other, seeking support.

"I do," Cat said simply.

"And I, Fiona," Hamish finally managed to say. He was steadily recovering from his visions, and looking stronger by the second. "It is best for all concerned."

Realizing she was in no position to argue the point further, Fiona sighed deeply and put up her hands.

"Fine then," she agreed disparagingly. "As you wish. When may I move into the house?"

"There is a stipulation first, Fiona." Carrick was all business. "Ye willna go to the courts, nor will ye be unkind or bring harm to anyone on these lands. If ye canna agree, ye will leave, never to return. I dinna believe ye can hold to it though. Ye canna uncurl a sow's tail, can ye now?"

Fiona was sick of his demands, but saw the futility of non-acquiescence. "I agree," she said curtly and sat back in her chair to rest her chin on the back of her hand. "May I have a brandy now that we have concluded the business portion of my visit?"

"Oh, my God!" Olivia exclaimed from the doorway. She was white as a cloud and looked about to faint. "It's you!" She pointed at Fiona as she collapsed to the floor.

"Olivia!" Cat cried, running to kneel at her sister's side.

Hamish and Carrick quickly joined her; Hamish looked back to Fiona in anguish."See what ye've done to her, Fiona! Do ye see what good yer coming has brought?" Then to Carrick, "Can ye take up to her bed, Carrick? I will tend to her there, away from this madness."

"Aye, Hamish," Carrick answered as he lifted the unconscious Olivia into his arms and started for the door.

"Fiona," he addressed her, looking over his shoulder. "Be gone when I return. Ye may move into *Taigh MacHendrie* in the morning. I will notify the staff to make ready for yer arrival. See to it, Ian," he directed his brother and left.

"Ye're a bloody hateful viper," Cat cursed Fiona as she rose to follow Carrick. "I wish to never lay eyes on ye again. How dare ye?" she said as she left the room. "How dare ye come back?"

Fiona sat in stunned silence. She hadn't seen Olivia since the girl was six-years-old and hadn't expected her to be such a beauty. "Was that…?" she asked Hamish.

"Aye, Fiona."' he answered softly. "Yer changeling child. Olivia is her name. And she grew into a fine woman without ye. Do as Carrick says, Fiona. I warn ye, he will no tolerate yer games and lies. Tread carefully, daughter." Leaving the warning behind for Fiona to contemplate, he went to care for Olivia.

Ian sat frozen. He had never seen such a spectacle in his life and was speechless in its wake. Slowly, deliberately, he began to reach for his crutches so that he could carry out Carrick's directives.

"Fiona MacHendrie!" Molly entered the room and planted herself firmly in front of Fiona. "I couldn't believe it was true. So, now ye come crawling like the snake ye are—back to the verra folk ye betrayed. Ye always did have a nerve, woman."

Molly put her hands on her hips indignantly and glared at the woman who had once been her best friend. "And I am told ye want Caitriona's inheritance to boot. Well, ye never did have any shame."

Fiona put up her hand to stop the tirade. "Enough, Molly," she said, tired from the battles. "I'm leaving immediately. My business here is concluded." Fiona rose and stepped past Molly, who refused to budge. "I'll not trouble you further," she swore as she walked toward the door. "Nice to see you, too."

Fiona went into the foyer and let herself out. She strode arrogantly to her waiting carriage and was assisted into it by the driver. Molly followed to be certain Fiona was truly going. She stood in the portico and watched the carriage drive down the hill as a flock of ravens flew directly over the departing coach—their shadows cast ominously on its rooftop.

Olivia was sitting up on her bed, back against the pile of pillows Cat had arranged for her. She had awakened as soon as Carrick laid her down.

"How do ye feel now?" Hamish asked, taking her pulse. "Any light-headedness or wooziness, perhaps?"

"No, grandda," she answered, putting a hand to her head. "Just a slight headache. Who was that woman?"

"Who do ye think she was?" Cat asked anxiously, sitting on the bed beside her sister. "Do ye recall anything?"

"Aye," Olivia answered slowly. "I remember coming into the room and seeing her. Then it was as though my vision was gone, and I was only seeing flashes of things...almost like memories. Wait! I saw myself as a child with that woman! Oh, my God. Oh, no!" screamed Olivia. "No! No! It isn't true...!"

Olivia jumped from the bed, wresting her hand from Hamish. "Do ye think it's true—what Morag told us?" She asked them in an agitated, high-pitched voice.

She looked from Carrick to Cat, then back to Hamish as she paced the room like a wounded animal. "She said that families reincarnate together. That we are the reincarnations of Jenny's family? But it can't be!"

Cat went over and put her arms around Olivia, holding her tight. "Who knows, baby? Who knows what is true. Do ye feel it's true?" she asked, rocking her gently to comfort her.

Olivia began to cry, tears spilling onto Cat's

sleeve. "Aye," she sniffled, looking up at her. "Aye, I do. I'm the other Olivia—Olivia MacHendrie," she said, composing herself a bit. "I saw it. And that horrid woman was my mother!"

"And mine," Cat said compassionately. "I have already dealt with her twice now. I ken yer feelings toward her well, Olivia. She's an evil one. I had hoped to protect us all from her. I had no idea ye were involved as well."

"Ahem," Hamish cleared his throat to beg their attention. "I think perhaps— well—it may be that she was my daughter as well as yer mother," he volunteered tentatively.

All eyes turned on Hamish in wonder. Had the immensely reasonable doctor actually had a supernatural experience?

"Ye too, grandda?" Cat managed, her face paling at the confession.

"Aye, Hamish," Carrick finally broke in. "I thought ye looked a wee bit pale for a moment when ye addressed her as *daughter*."

"Ye have the right of it, Carrick," Hamish answered, running a hand through his grey hair. "As Olivia, I had the visions, too. Powerful visions from somewhere deep in my bones. Aye, I believe it's true," he said firmly.

"Wonderful," Cat replied, letting go of Olivia, who sank into a chair. "What do we do now?" she asked to no one in particular, but turning instinctively to Carrick.

"We keep our agreement to her. She may live in *Taigh MacHendrie* for six months. That will give us time to devise a plan for dealing with the *buidseach.* In the now, we take joy that the family is united—by reincarnation or otherwise, aye?"

"Agreed," Cat went to her husband's side and hugged his arm. "Strange it may be, but we are together. That is all that matters."

"A united front!" Olivia exclaimed, rising to her feet and hugging Hamish.

"Aye, elf," Hamish hugged her in turn, then stopped abruptly and drew slightly back. "I always wondered where I got the idea to call ye elf or fey."Realization dawned on his features. "From that damned Fiona, who called ye a changeling."

Hamish reddened and softened his voice. "I apologize to ye, Olivia. I'll no call ye that again, I promise."

"No, grandda." She smiled back at him, the love rising in her eyes. "It doesna matter. I ken ye always said it with love. Dinna stop, please. I am what I am."

"And what ye are is mine," Hamish cupped her face and put a light kissed on her cheek. "As are ye all," he said to his family standing around him. "Fiona can never change that."

"So there ye are," Molly was bending over a tray laden with brandy, tea, and scones, readying them to be served. "Are ye well now, Olivia?" she asked. She had lately developed an affection for the girl and took an interest in her well-being. "May I pour ye a wee dram?"

Giving Molly a quick hug, she proceeded to the sofa and sighed. "Aye, Molly. I'm fine. Just a bit of a shock to see Fiona, ye ken?" she answered. "And a dram would be welcome, thank ye."

The rest of the family filed into the parlor and made themselves comfortable. One by one, each helped themselves to the tea tray, and they sat companionably enjoying their snacks, trying to avoid the topic on everyone's minds.

"Is she gone?" Ian asked from the doorway.

"Aye, Ian," Molly answered him. "Do come in and refresh yerself."

Ian made his way to a chair and laid the crutches down. As he did, Olivia sprang up, fixed a plate and cup, and brought it to him. "Here ye are," she said, presenting it to him. "I hope ye enjoy it, Ian. I made the scones my self this morning." She beamed with delight and accomplishment.

"Ye made these?" Cat was taken aback. "Ye've never cooked a thing in yer life!"

"I ken it," Olivia answered, smiling proudly at her sister. "I thought it was time I learnt." Then to Ian, "How did I do?"

Ian swallowed a bite and looked up at her. "Oh, aye, they're wonderful, Olivia," he complimented her. "A fine job, lass."

"I'm verra proud of ye, sprite," Hamish put in. "Ye'll make a fine cook, ye keep practicing this way."

Olivia smiled and sat down on the footstool in front of Ian. "Thank ye—all of ye. But mostly Molly. She taught me. Now," she continued. With the crisis past, she was quickly becoming her old, outspoken self. "Do ye think we can get Morag to cast a banishing spell on Fiona?"

Molly sputtered her tea at the remark and dabbed her chin with a napkin. "Olivia!" she reproved. "Whatever in the world…?"

"Well, Morag is a witch," Olivia went on thoughtlessly. "Maybe she could rid us of Fiona…"

"Olivia!" Molly reprimanded. "Ye mustna speak that way about Morag. 'Tis a dangerous thing to call a person!" Molly looked about to choke.

"Molly's right," Cat added with a look that said *remember where you are*. "Morag is simply a midwife—a wise woman, Olivia. I'm certain she doesna cast spells and is no witch."

Chastised, Olivia realized her error and backtracked. "Aye, Cat. Ye're right. I dinna ken what I was thinking."

"It's fine, Olivia." Carrick took a sip of his whisky and looked over to Ian. "Did ye get word to *Taigh MacHendrie* of Fiona's arrival?"

"Aye, Carrick," his brother replied. "Geordie said he would be going there any road, so he agreed to take word. Mind ye, he wasna best pleased to hear she was come back."

"I imagine few in the glen will be," Carrick answered, a chill creeping over him. "Best brace ourselves for a verra long six months."

Chapter Fourteen

"Where have ye been all morn?" Ian seated himself next to Olivia on the garden bench. "I've been looking for ye everywhere. I shouldha realized ye'd be in yer favorite spot.'

Olivia looked up at him, shading her eyes from the brilliant sun. "Aye, Ian." She smiled back at him with affection. "I'm taking a wee rest from the baking. I've been helping Molly since dawn." She gave a small yawn and stretched her arms over her head. "And what are ye up to?"

"I was helping Carrick with tables for the *ceidhli* tonight," Ian said proudly. "I did it without the crutches!"

"Oh, Ian!" She threw her arms around his neck with joyful abandon. "I'm so proud of ye!" Then she drew back, her face creased with concern. "Are ye all right? Are ye sure ye should be doing such vigorous work so soon? Are ye in pain?"

"Nay, Olivia." He laughed. "I'm fine, I assure ye. Dinna fash. I willna risk a setback, I promise. Besides..." He cast her an impish smile. "I am saving myself to dance with the most beautiful lass in the glen tonight."

"Ah, Ian. Ye flatter me so." She cast her eyes to

the ground as she blushed. Her heart beat wildly when Ian was near. It always had. She always had men's attention, but somehow Ian's was different. Courtly, respectful, and a true gentleman. She felt safe though oddly nervous with him.

Ian, a bit anxious himself, gently took her hand in his and stroked the back of it, as if touching a fragile piece of porcelain. They sat in silence for a few moments, neither of them knowing what to say next. Finally, Ian worked up his nerve and began softly.

"Olivia," he said, looking into her violet eyes. "I ken this may be a delicate question. Ye dinna have to answer if ye dinna like, aye?"

"It's okay, Ian," she answered, her hand pressing his. "Go on."

"Okay means 'tis good, aye?"

Olivia gave a little giggle. "Aye, Ian. It means it's good."

Sitting up a bit straighter and giving her hands a light squeeze, he continued.

"Well. then. Um. Do ye truly believe ye are Olivia MacHendrie reincarnated?" He studied her face carefully as he waited for the answer. Various emotions crossed her expression. Thoughtfulness, puzzlement, a bit of confusion, then finally confidence.

"Aye," she said at last with a self-assured tenor. "Aye, I do. I believe it. I wasna sure at first, if I was imagining what I saw, but as time goes by, I remember more and more. Bits and pieces. And things begin to make more sense, do ye ken?"

Ian nodded and took her other hand into his free one so that he now held both. He drew them to his chest and hugged them. "I understand," he said.

"Do ye believe me?" she asked.

"I do," he answered. He raised her hand to kiss the back of it. "I believe it all. It was rather incredible at the first, but I do the now. Although, I confess that I do feel pain at the thought of Fiona as yer mother. Ye poor, wee lass."

Tears began to pool in Olivia's eyes. "Aye." Her voice broke a bit. "'Tis unfortunate, that. Well…" She cleared her throat and held her head higher. "What can ye do? It is what it is, after all. We make the best of it, I suppose. And look at the wonderful family we have, Ian. With all of ye to love me, what is Fiona to that?"

"'Tis true, ye ken," Ian leaned closer and looked deeply into those violet eyes. The bonny eyes that were so like the lavender that grew on the braes. He was lost when he looked into them and his head skirled—like the pipes played on an Easter morn at sunrise. Surely she was part fey to enchant him so.

"Ye are loved beyond all else," Ian continued. "Ye are wanted and treasured, especially by me." He could feel her pulse begin to race under his fingers. "Ye are my own treasure brought by the faery Queen herself. And I must always cherish such a gift, aye?"

Olivia had never been spoken to by a man this

way and was unsure how to react. "Aye, I suppose..." she managed, her entire body beginning to feel limp and moist. Her own feelings for Ian were rapidly rising within her, engulfing her.

"I cherish ye, my fey lass," Ian whispered as he leaned even closer. "I love ye, Olivia. With all of my heart," he said and lightly kissed her trembling lips—a kiss as tender as the wings of a moth.

Taken by surprise, Olivia timidly returned the kiss. Ian deepened it further, tasting the outline of her lips with his velvet tongue. He slowly enfolded her into his strong arms as she melted into the embrace, eager to drown in the pool of love he offered.

Her mouth responded to the caress of his and she found herself wanting more. She sampled the slight saltiness of his mouth as his tongue entwined hers in a tentatively sweet dance.

Ian stroked her long blonde hair with a free hand and broke the kiss slowly. "Yer hair is as I imagined it would be," he said, catching his breath and putting his forehead to hers. "'Tis like the silky moss of yon glade, or the lace of a fine spider's web. I am well and truly caught within yer web, Olivia."

Olivia slid her fingers under Ian's chin, and lifted his freckled face to meet her gaze. His amber eyes were misted, and he glowed in the morning's golden light.

"Ian," she began. "Ye are in my heart as well," she assured him. "But we mustna..."

"Mustna?" he protested. "Do ye no love me in return?"

"Aye, I do. I love ye, Ian," she answered. She had long ago realized her heart belonged to Ian, but had not put words to it until that moment. A nagging in her mind, however, caused her to pull her arms away and rest her hands in her lap.

"I love ye more than anything. Ye are the world to me," she said, touching his cheek with her finger as she spoke. "But Cat and Carrick wouldna approve," she said sadly. "And what of yer mum and my grand-da? Have ye no thought of it?"

Ian took her hand from his cheek, turned it up, and kissed the palm. "Of course I have," he replied, and held her hand in both of his. "I have already spo-ken with my mum and yer grandda, both."

Olivia sat back, stunned at the news. "Ye have?" she gasped. "What did they say?"

"My mum was over the moon." Ian smiled broadly. "She loves ye as her verra own. And yer grandda, well, he gave us his blessing as long as it was what ye wished. He said, 'If my elf loves ye, ye may have my consent, Ian.'" Ian glowed with pride as he waited for her response.

"And Cat…?" Olivia could not believe he had done all of this without a word to her. She was not offended in the least, she was overwhelmed. Never had she thought anyone would care enough for her to secure her grandda's permission.

"Cat will approve," Ian interrupted. "Ye will

see. So then, Olivia..." Ian began as he lowered himself to his knees on the ground before her.

"Do ye mean...?"

"Aye, Olivia," he said, bringing her hand to his lips once again. "Will ye marry me, be my wife, the mother of my bairns, my best friend? I will cherish and protect ye forever, I swear it. Only say aye?"

"Ian, I..." Olivia sputtered. "I had no idea of yer feelings until this moment. I..."

"Do ye love me, lass?" Ian stopped her. "If ye do, say aye quickly and end my misery."

Olivia threw her arms around him with a great sob, tears streaming. "Oh, aye, Ian!" she cried. "Aye, Ian. Forever."

Ian held her tight; as if afraid he would lose her. "Why are ye weeping, *mo brèagha*?"

"Joy," Olivia answered, sitting back on the ground to look at him and wipe her eyes. "Joy that I never thought would be mine. And here ye are." She sniffled.

"And here I am - and here ye are. My faery princess come to save me that night," he said. It had been several months since he had awakened in horrific pain to find her by his side—his personal angel.

Taking something from his waistcoat, he said, "This was my grandmother's. My mum gave it to me this morning." Ian took her hand and slipped a simple silver ring engraved with knots on her finger.

"I wish this were rubies, or emeralds, for that is what ye deserve. Accept this humble token of my love for ye, and a promise to be with ye always, aye?"

Olivia stared at the elegant ring encircling her finger, and her eyes moistened once more. "Aye, Ian," she whispered. "I am honored. I will be yer wife and give ye bairns. I will be at yer side the now and always."

"We will announce the betrothal tonight, aye?" Ian watched her admire the ring, unbridled happiness bursting within him.

"Aye, Ian," she leaned over and kissed him quickly. "We shall announce it tonight. Oh, Ian, I am so verra happy," she said, kissing him more thoroughly.

Boy, is Cat going to be surprised. And not a little pissed off.

She smiled to herself as they held each other in the passion of their newly acknowledged love.

Cat stood before the armoire mirror adjusting her green velvet bodice and its laces. She always had difficulty getting them to lace up the front equally and stay in place.

"Lace it from the bottom, and from the outside," Olivia said from behind her. "It lies better that way and laces more evenly."

"Oh," Cat said, unlacing them to start again. "I guess ye would ken it, what with wearing an Aboyne for dance and all."

Cat referred to the Aboyne costume Olivia wore as a Highland dancer. A velvet vest with a petaled hem and laces up the front. "This is so similar to the Aboyne, but that won't come as a dance costume until the 1950's, "she commented. "Amazing how accurate they were when they designed it, aye? Especially since Aboyne is so far from here. I guess they wore it all over Scotland, not just in Aboyne."

"Aye, it seems ye're right about that," Olivia agreed, reaching out to help Cat lace it up. The small silver ring on her third finger gleamed, but she wasn't about to bring it up. Not yet.

"I wrestled with getting it right for a long time. Don't feel bad. It's a bit tricky. Are ye looking forward to the party tonight?"

Cat stood still while Olivia did her up. "It should be a nice break for everyone after all the troubles. They could use a bit of fun, I think."

"I ken I could use some fun." Olivia finished the lacing. "There ye are," she said and plopped down on the bed, carefully hiding her ring hand within the other. She could have taken the ring off, but she couldn't bear to have it off her finger for an instant. "Generous of ye and Carrick to do it for everyone."

"They did help with putting the new roof on the barn, after all," Cat smiled. "I've never seen anything like it. Neighbors and crofters working together to do the job. A real community and camaraderie, ye ken? Unlike our time where everyone keeps to themselves and does only for themselves."

"True," she agreed. "Will there be dancing, d'ye think?" Olivia's eyes gleamed.

"Olivia…" Cat began to warn her sister. The look in her eyes spelled trouble. "No Highland dancing, ye hear? Promise me ye won't sneak it in. Ye'll scandalize the whole of the glen."

"I won't," Olivia promised half-heartedly. "But Jenny Douglas…"

"Never ye mind Jenny Douglas. She won't be around for another hundred-fifty years at least," Cat reproved. "There's no need for ye to change the history of Highland dancing so ye can be the first woman to do it and break the male barrier, ye understand? No surprises tonight, aye?"

"Aye, Cat," Olivia still had that mischievous sparkle. Cat would certainly be surprised, but with the betrothal. Although the idea of Highland dancing did appeal…

"I understand," she lied. "So, do ye think Fiona will dare to come?" She shifted the subject away from herself. "She wasna invited."

"Fiona would dare to do anything, even if we havena seen her in several weeks," Cat sat to put on her hose and slippers. "We should plan to see her just in case."

"Ye're right," Olivia agreed. She rose from the bed and swiftly reached the bedroom door. "I'll see ye later, then?"

"Aye. Later then." Cat nodded, slipping the second hose over her calf and up onto her thigh. "Mind yerself."

"Oh, aye," Olivia chirped. "That I'll do."

Why do I have a bad feeling about this? Cat thought, then cast it aside to finish dressing.

The *ceidhli* began at dusk, the crofters and neighbors arriving as they could by horseback or their own two legs. Each brought a bit of something to contribute—a jug of whisky, a dish from an old family receipt, a slab of bacon from their smokehouse.

The tables had been set between the house and the newly roofed barn, and were draped in linens and bed sheets, surrounded by every available chair from the house and outbuildings. Carrick and Dougal had earlier laid long wooden panels on the ground, forming a perfunctory dance floor with an area for whichever musicians in the glen would care to play. Cat and Mary set torches around the perimeter and up the walk to light the way.

No longer able to wear their colorful tartans, the folk still managed to appear in brightly colored garb of every variety, although the men were heard to grumble about the *triubhas* they now were forced to wear instead of kilts.

Ever frugal, some of the women had chosen to dye their tartans a dark color, so they could still be worn as shawls and wraps. Not a single soul was pleased with it, but no one wished to beg the English's attention.

In an area near the barn, a side of venison roasted on a spit and on another, a side of Carrick's best Highland beef. The tables bowed heavily with smoked meats and fish, apples and pasties.

Near the makeshift dance floor, a fiddler struck up a strathspey. A few couples began a country dance, flowing in and out and behind each other in lilting steps and figures.

Everywhere geniality and good humor prevailed. Tankards and tumblers of ale and whisky flowed freely from Beinn Fhithich's own alehouse and distillery.

"Have ye seen Olivia?" Cat asked Ian, grabbing his arm and pulling him to her as he walked by. "I've no seen her at all tonight."

Ian's grin struck Cat as mischievous. "Oh, aye, Cat," he replied, pulling his arm away. "She'll be out in a bit. She had to tend to something."

Cat folded her arms and stared hard at Ian. "Tend to something?" She frowned. "What might that be, Ian? She isna up to one of her surprises, is she now?"

"Sorry, Cat," Ian said over his shoulder as he turned to make a hasty retreat. "I dinna ken, honest." He gave a shrug and hurried into the crowd, so that Cat couldn't question him further.

Exasperated, Cat stood with arms crossed, staring after him.

"What is it, *mo cridhe*?" Carrick asked as he placed his arms around her from behind. "Yer wee sister giving ye fits again?"

"Aye." Cat nodded and wrapped her hand around one of his arms. "She's up to something. I can feel it. And it's never a good thing when she is."

"Dinna worry about her, Cat." Carrick turned her to face him. "Olivia will do what she will. Ye canna be watching her like a child. Come," he pulled her by the hand to the dance floor. "Let's have a dance and ye can forget yer cares, aye?"

"I suppose." Cat smiled up at him. He always did know how to wipe away her worries.

They joined the other couples in a romantic waltz and after a turn about the floor, Cat began to feel the stress ease away. By the time the dance was over, Cat was laughing with Carrick and ready to sit and enjoy some food. Carrick led her to a table and seated her next to Molly and Hamish, then went to bring her a plate.

As they sat eating venison, beef, and samples of neighbors' dishes, they talked and enjoyed the balmy weather and a starry sky.

The fiddler began to play again, accompanied by a bodhran. After the first few notes, Hamish and Cat's eyes met in alarm.

"The *Sean Triubhas*?" Cat whispered to Hamish.

"I'm afraid so," Hamish answered, apprehension thick in his voice. He began to rise from the table along with Cat, but it was too late.

Olivia stood in the center of the dance floor wearing a great kilt wrapped around her waist, belted, and the plaid draped and pinned over her right shoulder. A dark blue velvet bodice completed the thrown-together Highland costume.

With a defiant confidence, she danced the steps of the *Sean Triubhas,* a dance that meant "Old Trousers," and told the story of the prohibition of the kilt and the subsequent wearing of *trewes,* or trousers. And when the dance became freer and faster, the story of the Highlanders' right to wear the kilt again after the Act of Proscription was repealed.

"These people willna see this dance come into fashion for thirty years yet," Cat commented to Hamish.

She could hear the shocked murmurs around her. The crowd sounded their stunned amazement at a woman wearing a kilt, let alone show her legs in such a fashion. They voiced their outrage that a woman would dance so in public.

But there were also remarks of awe that she

would have the courage to do it at all. And how very well she performed it! The power, the stamina, the grace!

Cat and Hamish stood silently watching as Olivia finished the dance with an enormous leap and bowed.

The crowd immediately broke into wild cheering, whistling, and clapping. In the end, her would-be detractors gave whole-hearted and, in some instances, grudging approval for what she had done. Olivia may have begun the dance in scandal, but she ended it with acclaim.

Ian stepped to her side as the drummer did a quick roll, calling for silence.

"Dear family and good friends," Ian began, now that he had their attention. "A hearty welcome to ye all this fine night of joy and celebration. Please charge your glasses!"

"What is he talking about?" Cat whispered to Carrick and Hamish, standing on either side of her. "What are they up to now?"

"I dinna ken," Carrick answered. "But I think we are about to find out."

"Tonight," Ian continued, looking at Olivia, obviously enthralled with her, "Olivia and I ask that ye join us in raising a glass to our betrothal. Olivia MacHendrie has done me the honor of accepting my proposal of marriage. I ask ye to be upstanding for my betrothed. To Olivia!" Ian raised his tumbler to her as she blushed a deep scarlet.

The guests responded in resounding *Slaintes, Ayes,* and various acclimations that astounded Cat, Carrick, and Hamish.

"Did ye ken about this?" Cat turned to Hamish.

"Aye, I did." Hamish raised his tumbler toward the happy couple. "He asked my blessing this morning, but I had no idea he would act so quickly. Ah well, Cat. Be happy for yer wee sister. 'Tis time she has a man in her life."

"And you?" She turned to Carrick who gave a shrug and a shake of his head.

"Nay, Cat," he answered. "But I canna say I am no well pleased. They are a fine match to my way of thinking."

Cat let out a long sigh and resigned herself. "Well then," she said, taking each by an arm. "Let's go and congratulate them. I supposed ye're both right. I just wish she had confided in me is all. That girl..." Cat trailed off as the three made their way to Olivia and Ian, who were busy accepting congratulations from everyone.

Finally, the crowd thinned and Olivia broke through to hug Cat's neck. "I'm so verra happy, Cat!" she exclaimed. "Can ye believe it? Isn't it wonderful?"

Cat loosened Olivia's hold on her and gazed at the bliss in her younger sister's alabaster face. She could not deny Olivia the very happiness that had brought her and Carrick—all of them for that matter—

to this place and time.

"We will talk later, aye?" Cat hugged Olivia tightly. "I want to hear it all, sprite. I am so glad that ye found yer true love. He *is* yer love, is he no?"

Olivia pulled away and gave Cat an enormous, contented smile. "Oh aye, Cat." She beamed. "He is that and more. And I will tell ye everything and we can plan the wedding together, you and I!"

Cat hadn't thought as far as the wedding. Realization dawned quickly and she said, "I supposed we must, at that!" She laughed with delight. "We'll begin in the morning, aye?"

"Oh, aye!" Olivia grabbed both of her sister's hands with enthusiasm. "And ye must play the violin for it, please?"

"Well, we'll see..."

"So the Queen of the Fey found a consort, did she?" Fiona's sarcasm cut through the air like a broadsword as she edged her way in to stand next to the sisters. "I can't for the life of me understand the boy—and he is a boy—but," she said, taking a sip from her tumbler and raising it to Olivia, "to each their own."

"Now, Fiona…" Cat began, but Olivia cut her off.

"You filthy witch," Olivia spat, taking a step closer to the smirking woman. "How dare ye come here and spread yer shite around decent folk? How dare ye come at all, uninvited and unwelcome as ye are?"

Olivia was turning red with a rage that Cat had never witnessed in her sister. She grabbed Olivia's arm to pull her away as she rapidly scanned the crowd for Carrick and Ian.

"Come away, Olivia." Cat pulled on her arm. "Dinna listen to her. She just wants to ruin it for ye, and ye willna allow her the satisfaction…"

"That's right, Cat," Fiona laughed, a high-pitched cackle that reminded Cat of the Wizard of Oz. "Protect your baby sister. Just like old times, isn't it?"

"Nay, Fiona," Carrick said from behind the woman. A hush fell over the guests as they witnessed the escalating scene. Every single soul knew who Fiona was, and not a one would speak for her.

"Nay. In old times, ye wouldha run off with some rich gent and be gone," Carrick said, taking Fiona's arm and pulling her up in front of him to meet her eyes, loathing streaking through his own eyes like lightening. "Ye spread yer hatred while living on yer daughter's mercy. I suggest ye leave immediately. Ye havena right to be here, and today of all days. Get ye gone, Fiona."

Fiona set her jaw and glowered at him in defiance. "I will leave when I wish," she said through clenched teeth.

"I'll see to her." Ian was suddenly at Carrick's side. His face was granite and his broad shoulders set for a fight. "Ye'll leave with me now, Fiona, if I have to carry ye."

Seeing that she would not get anywhere with her games this night, Fiona shrugged, handed Carrick her tumbler, and eyed Cat and Olivia.

"All right then." She sighed prettily. "I only wanted to congratulate my daughter on her upcoming nuptials. Let me know when you begin planning the wedding," she said over her arrogant shoulder as she turned to join Ian. "Every bride needs a mother's hand, after all," she tossed out as Ian led her down the hill to her carriage.

"I think ye'd best get out of that kilt," Cat said gently, but firmly, to Olivia. "Who kens the trouble Fiona will make of yer dancing tonight, let alone wearing tartan."

Olivia's eyes widened in fear. "Ye dinna think she'd go to the sasunnach, do ye?"

Cat put her arm around her sister's shoulders and began leading her toward the house at a brisk pace.

"I dinna ken, but we canna take the chance. I do wish ye hadna given us reason to worry. But it's done now, so let's make the best of it, aye?"

"Aye," Olivia agreed meekly as they hurried up the stairs. "I'm so sorry, Cat. I dinna think of it. I assure ye," she said, turning to look her sister in the eye, contrition etched on her face. "I willna be so foolish again. I swear."

"I do hope ye mean it." Cat smiled to reassure her. "Let's get ye changed and back to the *ceidhli*. It is yer betrothal party, after all." Cat patted Olivia's shoulder with affection and encouragement.

I hope she's learned her lesson, Cat thought. God alone knew what would come of Olivia's exhibition this night. Perhaps her betrothal to Ian would turn out to be the best thing possible for Olivia. Perhaps he could keep a hand on her. But she doubted it.

Chapter Fifteen

Am I interrupting ye?" Cat asked Carrick as she seated herself near his desk. "I saw Geordie leaving yer study and thought it may be a good time to talk, seeing as we couldna last night."

Carrick stretched his arms out in front of him and smiled. "Nay, *mo leannan*. Ye arena interrupting. I received word that Duncan Anderson willna be released from prison, so Mary, Dougal, and wee Marie will be with us for a time, it seems. Geordie is off to begin the malting at the distillery. I'll be going up there later myself. 'Twas an excellent *ceidhli*, aye?"

"It was," Cat agreed. "I am sorry to hear about Duncan, but glad his family will be safe with us. Carrick," she changed the subject. "I am a wee bit worried. Olivia's stunt may have consequences."

"Ah." Carrick sighed knowingly. "Ye're thinking of Fiona."

"I am. She has more ammunition against us now. If she cares to use it."

"Aye, she does." Carrick sat back and considered the situation. "But if she truly has nowhere to go, why turn traitor to the charity we have provided her?"

Cat laughed wryly and let her accent slip a bit. "Are you kidding?" she argued. "Because it's her nature to destroy and betray, that's why! For no other reason than she just can't help herself! God, I wish I knew for certain what she is up to."

"Well, now…" Carrick gave her a sly grin. "That's where ye have underestimated me, Cat."

Cat leaned toward him in surprise. "What? What have you done? Tell me."

"Cat," he began, a hint of reproval in his voice. "Ye ken how we have the lookouts throughout the glen? To alert everyone to the coming of soldiers, aye?"

"Aye…" Cat nodded, getting her accent back under control. "I do."

"Well, do ye actually think I'd allow Fiona to live on the land without setting a lookout on her as well?" Carrick smiled proudly and stood up to lean on his desk conspiratorially.

"I shouldha thought…"

"Aye, ye shouldha," Carrick said as he came to pull Cat out of her chair and embrace her. "Now go to Olivia and Molly, and begin the wedding plans. The sooner we have done with it, the better, aye?"

Cat kissed his cheek and turned to go. "Aye. I see yer point. One more thing though. I wanted to give *Taigh MacHendrie* to Olivia and Ian as a wedding gift.

How do we get Fiona out? "

"A noble gesture, to be sure. But for the now, we don't." He kissed the top of her head. "We will find a way soon, I promise. In the meanwhile, Fiona will do no harm here, I assure ye."

"All right then," she answered. "I love ye, ye brilliant man."

"I love ye, too, clever wife." He laughed as she left the room. He wouldn't worry Cat with the news that Fiona had left for the present English stronghold of Inverness that morning.

Chapter Sixteen

"May I introduce myself?" the tall, dark-haired man addressed Fiona as he lifted her hand to his lips. "I am Captain Caldwell Camden, Second in Command at Fort Augustus."

Fiona gave the younger man her most flirtatious smile and held her head a bit higher. "Second in Command, you say?" she answered him, retrieving her hand to quickly snap her fan open and cool herself.

"Indeed." Camden offered an arm to lead her to a quieter spot on the terrace and away from the musicians in the ballroom. "I've only been posted here for a few months or so. Fascinating place, Inverness."

" A dung heap, more like" she retorted, the disdain clear in her manner. "I often wish I had stayed in France among civilized people. But then, what can you do when family duty calls? I am Lorraine Binoche, by the by. *Comtesse* Binoche," she lied. She had taken the title and name without marrying the Vicomte, knowing that no one in Scotland was likely to question it these days.

Besides, the Vicomte always called her his Vicomtess, which she loosely translated as Comtesse. Better than the proper and less impressive address of Lady.

And she had been known by her middle name, Lorraine. to hide her true MacHendrie identity, and thus disguise her Highland origins.

Camden smiled wickedly, and appraised her full length. "Oh, I know who you are," he said. "You are staying with Lord and Lady Braden, are you not?"

"I am." Fiona folded her fan shut. "We met years ago at the French Court when Lord Braden was Ambassador."

"I see." Camden nodded and turned to look at the garden. "And you are from...?"

"Edinburgh, originally," Fiona quickly put in. "Nasty business, this Jacobite rising. I suppose you are helping to arrest the Highland rebels?"

"Now, Comtesse." His eyes gleamed mischievously. "You well know I can not divulge my orders. I am here to help keep order, shall we say?"

Fiona looked closer at the handsome officer. Younger than her, but not too young for a diversion. He was a fine and fit man with well-defined English features, and striking eyes that assessed everything around him. He could be interesting, she thought. Didn't she hear someone mention that he was an English Lord?

"Of course, you are correct," Fiona agreed. "You are Lord Camden, isn't that so? I thought I heard someone..."

"Oh, that." He cut her off with a wave of his

hand. "True, true. But no matter titles, eh? Come, Comtesse. Tell me how such a beautiful and sophisticated woman came to be in Inverness, especially in such troubled times. Surely there must be an interesting story to it?" He seated himself on the bench nearby and patted it for Fiona to join him. She seated herself at the other end, but he swiftly closed the distance between them.

"What is the family duty which brings you to Inverness, Comtesse?" Camden leaned toward her, heat obvious in his eyes as he met her gaze. "Nothing too serious, I hope."

He put a strong hand on her wrist. The gesture of familiarity sent sparks up her arm and into her head, nearly making her gasp as she tried to restrain the sudden surge of sensuality it ignited.

"No," she managed through a hitch in her breath. "A minor thing, really." She composed herself quickly and waved a hand in the air as if to dispel the matter. "An elderly father, you see."

"Your father is in Inverness?" Camden removed his hand and put it on his thigh His firm and well-shaped thigh. "I would have thought an elderly gentleman would not remain in the Highlands during the rising. None too safe for the frail…"

"He's in Edinburgh," Fiona interrupted quickly. She did not want to give the solider clues to her true identity. Fun was fun, but in the current climate, the truth could imprison, or even kill.

"My father is a well-respected physician there,

and requested I come and see to his household. He is unwell, but not an idiot. Nor is he political," she quickly added.

Camden gave her a sly smile with a tinge of something like suspicion. "Why did you not sail straight to Edinburgh, then? Why Inverness?"

Fiona stood, suddenly not wishing to answer more questions. Lifting her chin, she snapped open her fan and glared at the captain. "The only ship on which I could book passage sailed to Inverness. Besides," she softened her tone," Lord Braden was insistent on my visit. Seeing that my father was not at death's own door, I decided a bit of amusement would not be amiss before I assume the drudgeries of tending the aged. Is that enough information for you, Captain?"

She turned away to leave. Perhaps a liaison with the young captain would not best serve her after all. He was too keen on knowing her secrets, learning her business. She took two steps toward the open doors and tossed over her shoulder, "Good night then, Captain. Another time, perhaps?"

"Come now, Comtesse." Camden was at her side instantly, and put out a hand to stop her retreat. "I meant no offense. Do forgive me."

He laid a gentle hand on her arm and said apologetically, "I'm afraid my duties have caused me to forget my manners among polite society. I should not have pried into your affairs so. "

Fiona pulled her arm away and allowed a slow smile of condescension to lighten her expression. Perhaps the game wasn't over yet, she thought. She had the upper hand now.

"My dear Captain, you are forgiven *this time* I can well imagine how dealing with the Highland ruffians can cause one to lose their - shall we say - *savoir faire*?" She put out her hand to signal an end to the encounter. "Until we meet again, Captain. It' has been most charming."

Camden took and quickly kissed her hand, before she pulled it away and turned to go.

"Comtesse," he said. "When will that be? May I call upon you?" He was a bit too eager and Fiona read him perfectly.

"Of course, you may," she said with a quick glance over her shoulder. "But keep in mind that I leave soon and have much to do. *Au revoir*, Captain…," she trilled as she glided through the doors.

"I will see you again, Comtesse. Very soon," he called after her.

"Perhaps," she called back nonchalantly. If you are man enough, she thought and went to find her coachman.

Hamish had been working all morning in the little room off the kitchen he had designated as his surgery. He had stocked the shelves with various herbs and supplies, and with Morag's expertise and guidance, had collected and prepared herbs and other remedies.

She had been an invaluable source of 18th century medicines, some of which, he was not entirely surprised to find, had their accepted uses in 21st century medicine.

There were some he had been aware of, such as foxglove as the source of modern-day digitalis - a common medicine which regulated heartbeat. Of course, willow bark, he had always known, was the source of aspirin. But he was surprised at the efficacy of feverfew and comfrey when used properly.

This morning he was checking the inventory of the laudanum which Carrick had brought him from Inverness. With tales of increasing violence by English soldiers throughout the Highlands, he wanted to be certain he could deal with any contingency should it come to Beinn Fhithich. He prayed it would not be necessary, but he knew his history and was not wiling to take the matter on faith.

"Have ye a moment, Hamish?" Molly's soft voice came from behind him. "May I come in?"

He turned toward her and smiled. He was fond of Molly. She was a kind and gentle woman, if a bit suspicious of him. Try as he had though, he did not recall her from the past. Odd, since memories of his former life had been returning at a gradual and steady pace.

"Of course, my dear," he said as he pulled a chair over for her. "Do sit down. What is the matter? Ye look troubled this morning."

"I'm afraid I've a wee cut from pruning the roses, Hamish." She held out her thumb so he could examine it. "'Tis a tiny thing and I shouldna be troubling ye with it. All the same, ye did warn me about infection, aye? I canna afford to be ill, what with the wedding and…"

She looked embarrassed as Hamish took her hand and turned it over to gently pull away the small bit of cloth she had wrapped around it.

"No a wee thing, Molly," he said gently as he dabbed droplets of the still oozing blood. "Ye've cut it fair deep. Ye were right to come, lass. Hold yer hand up to help stop the bleeding while I get my things, aye?"

Molly quickly did as he requested, her face going a bit pale. "It willna need to be stitched, will it, Hamish?"

Recognizing her fright, he put a hand on her shoulder. "Nay, Molly. I'll just cleanse it and wrap it. That should do it. Ye look pale, lass. Would ye care for a wee dram to help steady ye?"

"Oh, no, not first thing in the morning! But thank ye just the same. Ouu!" She flinched at the sting of alcohol Hamish applied to the wound. "That stings like a hornet!"

"I'm sorry at that," Hamish apologized as he

finished cleaning the cut and began to apply a small dressing. "But it needs be done. As ye say, ye need no be ill these days. How is the wedding coming?"

Molly sat a little straighter in the chair and creased her forehead. "Well, Olivia is doing most of the planning. It is her wedding, after all. But she does have some verra strange thoughts on it all. Verra odd, indeed." She looked slyly at Hamish, as if he knew some truth he was keeping from her. "I suppose she got those ideas living in Edinburgh, eh, Hamish?"

"What kind of ideas might those be, Molly?" Hamish tried his best to keep a straight face. He already knew what she was referring to. Olivia had brought modern wedding planning with her and intended to implement it as much as possible.

"Well, for one thing," Molly began, "she wants Mary Anderson to make a wedding cake that has tiers sitting on upturned glasses. And flowers at the top of it. I never— "

"Oh, that." Hamish interrupted. "Aye, Edinburgh for certain," he lied to cover Olivia's modern flair for the dramatic.

"Ah, so I thought." Molly eyed him carefully, searching his face for clues of deception. "And then there is that strange tune that Ian whistles all the day. Ye ken the one, it goes like..." she attempted to hum *I Want to Hold Your Hand*. "Says it is their song, her s and Ian's'. She wants Cat to play it on the fiddle for the ceremony. Why, Father MacMurich will turn pink when he hears such a God-awful noise."

"Now, Molly," Hamish admonished, his eyes carefully fixed on the bandaging he was adjusting. "A harmless tune, surely? If the bairns have a song they enjoy together, why not let them have their day, aye? What's a simple tune, whether you and I find it pleasing or no?"

Molly sat back a little, thinking it over. "Right ye are then, Hamish," she agreed at last. "I suppose it does no harm. But the cake..."

"I'll talk with Olivia about the cake, Molly. Dinna worry. I'm sure the lass doesna wish to make it an ordeal for poor, wee Mary." Hamish patted her shoulder and led her to the door of the surgery. "Better now?" he asked.

Molly held up her injured hand and examined the bandage. Casting Hamish a suspicious glance, she said, "Oh aye. Better, indeed. Thank ye, Hamish. Oh, Morag" she addressed the witch as she opened the door. "I didna see ye there."

"'Tis fine, Molly," she answered, looking at the bandage on Molly's hand. "Are ye injured, lass?"

"Nay, a wee scratch at best. Hamish did a fine job of cleaning it," she said, slipping out the door. "I'll see ye later then, Morag?"

"Aye, Molly. Later." Then to Hamish, "Have ye a moment then, Hamish?"

Hamish nodded and gestured to the chair Molly had just vacated. "Always time for ye, Morag. Do sit. What can I do for ye this fine morn?" he said, closing the door. He was always cautious when speaking to Morag. She knew he was from the future, and he didn't wish to chance them being overheard.

"Well now, Hamish. I dinna ken it is me ye can help," the wizened woman said as she adjusted herself in the seat. "Olivia, more like."

Hamish let out an exasperated sigh. "Olivia? What has the lass done now? Are ye meaning to discuss her wedding ideas with me, too?"

Morag gave a croaking chuckle and waved a hand. "Nay, Hamish. Though I have heard some talk. Hardly dangerous, a wee song and a cake, aye? Well then, it is a concern that may interest ye that I've come about."

"Go on."

Morag pushed back a wisp of hair from her face and looked him in the eye. "Ye ken the wee music box the lass has? The one that plays the song young Ian loves so well?"

"Aye, Morag. I ken it well." Hamish sat. Something in her tone said that this couldn't be good.

"Well, Olivia, bless her, left it on my table yesterday. Forgot it, she said. Hamish, ye ken it well that ye canna afford to be careless. Ye wouldna wish people to ken ye are from the future - ye and Olivia and Caitriona. That I sent Carrick through time to find ye? We could all be arrested for such a thing. Even the mere rumor of it. Ye must speak to her, Hamish."

Hamish rose and began to pace the room. "Aye," he said at last. "I see yer point, Morag. It wouldna do. Wouldna do at all. I will speak to her, indeed. If she canna be careful, I shall take the thing and put it away. We canna take the chance…" Hamish stopped as the door opened. Molly stood in the doorway, white-faced and seething.

"I kent it!" she said, her chest heaving in fury. "I kent there was summat amiss with ye, the two of ye. And now I find ye all have been lying to me from the start! Who are ye, Hamish MacAllan? For ye are no the Hamish MacAllan that I kent all those years ago. The Hamish I dreamt about in my youth. The man who was my first love! He wouldha remembered me! He wouldna have treated me with such polite indifference. Who are ye, man?"

Morag gripped the edge of her chair, her face pale with the realization that Molly had heard the conversation. "Molly…I…" she began.

"Nay, Morag. You are in this up to yer scrawny old neck, ye are. I wish an answer from Hamish, no you." Molly turned back on Hamish to confront him again. "Well, Hamish?" she hissed, arms crossed over her chest, defiance in her eyes.

Hamish ran a hand through his hair and shot a helpless glance at Morag. "I suppose there's nothing for it," he said, watching as the witch shrugged in defeat.

"Well then, Molly," he began furtively, "ye're right. I dinna remember ye. I'm sorry at that. But the truth is…" he paused a moment to collect his thoughts. Every word he was about to say must be weighed and measured before he spoke them.

"It had better be the truth this time," Molly spat. "Do ye all think I'm that dumb or daft, that I didna notice yer private, secret meetings? And from the look of it, Ian seems to be involved as well. Though I havena yet figured that one. So go on, Hamish. Tell me the story. What have ye all been hiding from daft, wee Molly?"

"Ye arena daft, lass. I never thought ye were." Hamish gathered himself to begin again. "It was for yer own protection, I promise ye. Ye see, we are from the future, the three of us—Caitriona, Olivia, and me. We are from the year 2010."

Molly became ashen at the word 2010, and slowly seated herself in the other chair. "Go on," she encouraged. "This must be a fascinating tale. Do go on."

Having decided she looked strong enough to hear it, Hamish agreed. "All right then. Let me begin again," he said, checking the hallway outside and closing the door tightly. "It began with Jenny's death…"

Chapter Seventeen

"So ye truly dinna remember me?" Molly

asked, sitting in the parlor where they had removed to for the comfort of tea while Hamish filled her in. "But ye remember Fiona?"

"Aye," Hamish answered, shifting in his chair. "I dinna ken why. A mystery to be sure."

"And ye believe in this reincarnation thing, do ye?"

"How else to explain it, Molly? I recall Fiona and some other memories, as if it were yesterday. I am sorry..."

"It's fine, Hamish," Molly took a calming sip of her tea. "It was a teenage infatuation on my part. I am sorry I threw it at ye, ye dinna ken it—not ever. I never told ye. I was too timid back then. I'm embarrassed to have brought it up, ye being so much older than me at the time. Truly, it's nothing. I did love my husband, ye ken. And I forgot about it altogether when I met him. I didna mean to imply...well, I lost my temper with all yer secrecy is it."

"I thought the tale would distress ye, Molly. But ye seem to have taken it well enough. Are ye sure ye are all right?" Hamish watched her carefully.

"I'm not the wee girl everyone thinks I am," she retorted with a smile. "A strange story, to be sure. But better than left to wondering what devilment was going on. Mind ye, I dinna ken how much of it I believe, but I suppose it does explain some things, like Olivia's box that plays the tunes. Oh, aye, I have seen the thing, despite her attempts to hide it from me. I ken verra well the toy is no from Invergarry, and most likely no from Scotland, either. Time will out, I suppose. I will speak with Carrick, of course."

"Of course, Molly." Hamish relaxed at last. "And to the others, if ye like. But I would be careful..."

"I dinna plan to make a public announcement, Hamish," Molly chided him. "I realize what such knowledge could bring upon us. I wouldna hurt the family with it."

"Of course not," Hamish agreed.

"Well then," she said, rising and moving toward the door. "If that is the whole of it, I will go and speak with the others. Thank ye, Hamish, for finally telling me the truth."

Hamish rose and gave her a slight bow. "Ye're welcome, lass. I hope the knowledge doesna bring ye harm."

"Or any of us." She smiled and let herself out the door, leaving Hamish to contemplate the morning's events.

Good morning, Comtesse," the deep voice greeted her. Startled, Fiona turned to see the elegantly uniformed captain alighting from a fit and shiny chestnut horse. "You look well, I must say," he said as he walked slowly over to her.

"Captain Camden," Fiona tossed her red curls under her wide-brimmed hat and opened her parasol to shade herself. "What the devil are you doing here?"

"I am here to see you, Comtesse," he said as he gave a slight bow. "You did not respond to my messages, so I thought I would see if you were ill, or..."

Fiona quickly composed herself. She had not answered his many messages that had arrived over the last week since their initial meeting. She was unsure how she wanted to proceed with him, if at all. Besides, if she decided she did want something from him, best to leave him wondering, thus increasing his ardor.

"I have been quite busy, Captain Camden," she said saucily. "My many social obligations, you see. And I am leaving in another week to help my poor, dear father in Edinburgh."

"Ah yes, the poor father. Ill isn't he?" Camden responded, a tinge of sarcasm in his tone. "He mustn't be that ill if you are still in Inverness."

Fiona drew her back straight and eyed him sharply. "That is none of your affair, Captain." She turned to continue past him.

Camden reached out and gently grabbed her elbow. "So, it is," he said, backing down a bit. "I nearly forgot my manners; I was hurt by your ignoring my invitations. I do apologize. Allow me to take you to lunch?"

Fiona wrested her elbow away slowly, teasingly. "Very well, Captain. I accept."

"There is a nice little place a few blocks from here. Would you care to walk with me? I promise interesting conversation and decent food." Camden extended his arm to her.

Fiona smiled ferally. A bit of male attention would not come amiss. After all, the company she had been keeping was rather old and boring, if not politically important.

"I should be delighted," she said, hooking her arm through his. "Lead on, then."

"Wonderful, Olivia. Just wonderful!" Cat said as she rounded up behind her sister, who sat in the garden on her usual bench. "Ye've really done it now!"

Olivia looked up from her book. "What now, Cat? Did I do something wrong…again?"

"Oh, aye, something wrong." Cat plopped down on the bench beside her and put her head in her hands. "Molly kens…"

"Molly kens? How much?" How is it my fault?" Olivia put down the book and turned to Cat, apprehension in her expression.

Cat took a breath. It wasn't entirely Olivia's fault, after all. Molly had been suspicious of them for a very long time now. Maybe from the start.

"Yer iPod heightened her suspicions."

"She saw it? Oh no. I thought I hid it well."

"Apparently not. Then she overhead Grandda and Morag talking about ye having left the damned thing on Morag's table the other day. Oh well…" She sighed deeply and tried to relax. "It mayna matter anyway. She doesna seem that upset by it all. I'm no even certain how much she believes."

"I'm so sorry, Cat." Olivia put a hand out to touch her sister's arm. "I really did think I had it hidden well. I guess I just forgot."

"It's fine, Olivia." Cat was calmer now and smiled at her. "I'm just worried about what we are heading into, ye ken, the Clearances and all. If people thought something was amiss with us here, we could lose their support in the coming days."

"I understand," Olivia assured her. "Well, it's a bit of a relief, anyway. Not having to hide the truth from Molly is a good ting, I think."

"Ye're probably right," Cat answered, playing with a lock of her long curls. "It does make things easier without having to always be so careful, looking over yer shoulder before ye speak to make sure she isna around. Okay then, sprite." Cat decided to change to a lighter subject. "Tell me what yer latest wedding plans are. I hope ye havna added anything too strange."

Olivia laughed—a light, tinkling sound. "No, nothing strange. Ye'll be happy to ken I've decided on a traditional wedding, concurrent with the time we are in. A real 1746 wedding." Olive smiled proudly, and Cat let out a huge sigh of relief.

"You are Scottish, a re you not?" Camden asked Fiona. "You speak well-born English, but with your father in Edinburgh, I assume you are Scots."

"Lowland Scots, which makes us Loyalists, Captain. I assure you, I have no sympathies for the Jacobites," Fiona told him. The charming captain had the authority to arrest her if he suspected she was a Highlander. These days, all Highlanders were suspected of being, if not outright Jacobite, at least supportive of them. But playing with fire was nothing new to Fiona. It was dangerously exciting, in fact. She softened her approach as she listened to the captain go on.

"I was not questioning your loyalty, Comtesse. Only your origins," he assured her. "Are you enjoying the duck?" Camden poured more champagne into the tall flute in front of Fiona's plate. "For a small town, this hotel does a rather nice job of it."

"Understood, Captain. I apologize if I took it amiss. The rising has made Loyalists, such as myself, a bit testy. And yes, the duck is not bad at all. "

Fiona wiped her sly smile with a crisp linen napkin, careful not to stain it with the red lip rouge she wore. She looked up coquettishly from her darkened lashes and whispered, "Who would imagine a Scottish *duck* could be so - uh - sensual?" She licked a small corner of her lip in innuendo.

Camden grinned at her remark. "If you mean the fowl, Comtesse, quite so. If you mean me, I need not remind you that I am not Scots." He lifted his champagne glass to her and took a sip, a wicked gleam in his eye.

Touché, Captain." Having finished her main course, Fiona was toying with a small plate of chocolates. She delicately chose one and examined it. "Such extravagance in such times as these."

She sighed and licked the long slender piece attentively. She cast her eyes upward as if in ecstatic bliss and sighed again. "I have missed the silky caress of chocolate on my tongue since I arrived here."

She put it farther into her mouth and drew it out again from between her red lips, then ran the length of it down her tongue with a knowing smile.

"It is so very—well—almost erotic. And Inverness leaves one so *parched*. Don't you agree, Captain?"

Camden cleared his throat. He was clearly fascinated with the way Fiona handled the stick of chocolate. He appeared, in fact, rather tortured by it.

"Yes—parched, indeed," he managed and reached out to grab her wrist which held the chocolate. "Comtesse, please," he looked into her eyes. "Do stop. You are making me quite—thirsty."

Camden leaned toward her to pour more champagne. "I am having a small soirée tomorrow evening. I was hoping you would attend."

Fiona put down the chocolate and folded her hands. "No more champagne, Captain. I'm afraid I must be getting back. And yes, I would enjoy attending your soirée. Where will it be?"

"I keep a townhome here in town for my personal use," he said with meaning. "I will send a carriage for you at seven, if that is satisfactory to you. Let me escort you home now, Comtesse."

Fiona agreed and they rose to go. They walked in silence most of the three blocks to the three-story manor in which she was visiting.

Camden walked her up onto the covered porch near the front door and quickly pulled her into the well-hidden alcove. He put his arms around her and kissed her, a slow, sultry kiss that seared her.

Fiona returned the kiss and felt a slight shiver

run down the young captain's arms. Delighted with the reaction she elicited, she deepened the kiss and felt his manhood rise long, thick, and hard below.

"I must go in," Fiona said breathily, breaking the contact. "Tomorrow night then, Captain."

Camden's eyes held a fire that Fiona recognized. "Tomorrow night, Comtesse," he said as Fiona brushed her hand across the front of his crotch, lightly teasing the member within.

Camden quickly recovered, tipped his hat at her, and strode swiftly down the stairs to the street and his waiting horse.

Hmmm. Perhaps not such a boy after all. With a cock like that, he could be quite amusing. Quite amusing, indeed.

Fiona MacHendrie had found a temporary diversion in the Highlands that she loathed.

"Comtesse," Camden pressed her against the wallpapered entry wall after the other guests had gone. "I have been waiting all evening to be close to you again." He ran his hand down the back of her gown to show his intent. "I was hoping you felt the same after the kiss we shared yesterday."

"Why, Captain, surely that innocent kiss did not inspire this?" Fiona teased him, eyes sparkling with the thrill of the game they were playing.

Camden had been touching her thigh under the massive oak table all through the elegant dinner. Surrounded by important guests, the Commanding Officer of the garrison among them, it had been a perilous and tantalizing amusement. Now alone, the situation could turn serious and electrifying. It would intensify the players as well as the match. Fiona was at her best.

"Innocent kiss?" Camden pulled back to look deeply into her eyes. He smirked a bit as he ran his strong hands down her shoulders and arms. He gripped her wrists.

"My dear Comtesse, you are no innocent. I know the game you are playing."

"I play no games, Captain." Fiona laughed and tossed back her head. She twisted her wrists away from him, and then grabbed his forearms with an iron grip. "I know what I want, Camden, and I always get it"

"Do you, Fiona?" he asked. He leaned toward her and began to run his hot tongue along the side of her neck, causing Fiona to give a sharp gasp of pleasure. She let go his hands, and deftly ran her fingers along the inside of the waistband on his trousers.

"I did not give you leave to address me by my Christian name, Captain."

"Ah, Fiona." Camden sighed as he nipped her neck lower toward her décolletage. "You may get what you want, but I *take* what I want. That is the difference between us."

Lost in the pleasure of the chase, Fiona gave a little, lascivious laugh. "I suspect there is no difference between us, Caldwell," she retorted in a low and guttural tone. "Surely there are bedrooms in this manse of yours? Would you care to give me a tour?"

Camden broke the embrace and took her hand, leading her toward the sweeping staircase. "It would be a pleasure, Comtesse," he answered. "Allow me," he said, putting a foot on the lowest stair to lead her up.

"We shall see what I will allow," Fiona teased, and picked up her skirts to follow the deathly attractive captain.

"Oh, it's only ye, Cat. I thought it was Robbie Colson." Carrick looked up from his desk where he had been reading. "He is due here any moment. What is it, lass?" He laid down the sheaf of documents he was holding and sat back in his chair, arms folded behind his head.

Cat sat in front of the desk and leaned over it. "Ye ken that Fiona has gone to Inverness these past three weeks, do ye no?" She was a bit miffed that he had not told her before.

Carrick let out a long breath. He knew what was coming. "Aye, Cat. I kent it. I dinna wish to alarm ye with the knowing of it."

"But, Carrick, why? I mean, why did she go? I ran into Laurie, the housekeeper there. She told me Fiona left right after the *ceidhli*. And what is she up to? It canna be anything good where Fiona is concerned."

"I dinna ken, lass. I wouldha set a tail on her, but with the distilling season upon us, I couldna spare anyone for so long a time. We can only hope she doesna cause any grief." Carrick stood at the knock on the study door. "Ye'd best go, Cat. This is bound to end up in words exchanged."

"Robbie's been violating the stalking rules again, aye?" Cat rose to leave. "Best I go help with the laundry, then. Later, love."

"Aye, best ye be gone from here," he said, opening the door to allow her exit. "Later, indeed." He brushed a light kiss across her cheek. "Ah, do come in, Robbie, and have a seat."

"Good day to ye, Lady MacDonell." Robbie Colson nodded acknowledgment to Cat and took a chair. A wiry, scruffy looking man in his late thirties, he had a belligerent air about him.

"And a good day to ye as well, Robbie." Cat answered and closed the door behind her. Robbie breaking rules again. Carrick had looked concerned and not a little angry. Best to let him deal with it, she thought, having every confidence in her husband's ability to deal with the man. Laundry was calling.

"Thank ye for coming, Robbie," Carrick began as he seated himself behind the desk. "I have thing to discuss with ye."

Robbie sat casually in his chair. He appeared to be without a care, staring Carrick in the eye with a weasel smile.

"Aye, Laird. Ye ask me to come, I come. What is the thing ye wish to discuss?"

"Ye recall I've warned ye before—about the hunting on Beinn Fhithich lands, aye?"

Robbie folded his hands in his lap and grinned innocently. "Aye, Laird. I recall it."

"Then ye also recall I effected a rule on that. I have given all the tenants hunting rights. We all must eat and feed our families, aye? But I asked that none hunt the young deer, nor fish the young salmon, so as to conserve the resources here for all and future. Ye recall it, Robbie?" Carrick waited for the man to absorb his words. He watched as Robbie made a nearly imperceptible squirm in his chair and then repositioned himself.

"Oh, aye, I recall the rule. Yer point being…?"

"I have evidence that ye have been breaking that rule, Robbie." Carrick tried to sound measured and reasonable. He had to control his temper with this unpredictable man, but the estate and its tenants had to ensure the food sources it had in its game.

"I havena broken yer rules, Laird. Who says I have? Who accuses me? Bring him on!' Robbie s voice began to rise.

"I have several tenants who have seen ye taking the small salmon and stalking the young deer, then selling them to the sasunnach in Fort William for yer own profit." Carrick's voice began to rise at the man's denial. "Should it come to that, they are willing to give testimony."

Robbie rose in fury and slammed his fist on the desk. "By God, Laird, I havena done such a thing. Bring yer testimony. I have taken only what my family needs to survive, the same as any other."

"Sit ye down, Robbie," Carrick ordered. "Ye listen to me, now. I willna have ye selling Beinn Fhithich game to the bloody English, ye hear? Ye're a traitor to the land and yer Laird. Ye will stop it forthwith, Robbie, or I will be forced to evict ye for the good of all here. Is that clear?"

Robbie rose to his feet, blood in his eyes. He reached the door, thrust it open, and was halfway through it when he turned back.

"Ye are accusing the wrong man, Laird Carrick MacDonell. I'll see ye and yer precious

Beinn Fhithich brought low before ye evict Robbie Colson and his. I swear it!"

With that, Robbie stomped from the room. Carrick could hear the man's boots on the wooden floors as he made his way down the long hallway, and the slam of the front door as he left.

"May God save us from the likes of Robbie Colson," Carrick muttered to himself. But he knew there was worse to come.

Chapter Eighteen

"I am very glad your father could spare you for a few weeks, Fiona." Camden nuzzled closer against her back, coiling his body tight around her from behind. "It has given us time to know each other better."

Fiona gently pushed him off and turned toward him. She stretched her long arms overhead and yawned. Camden ran his fingers through her long red curls that spread out over the pillow.

"Yes," she agreed as she began to rise with the sheet wrapped around her naked curves. "But I must leave end of the week, and you must return to the garrison tomorrow, Caldwell. Let's not think of it just now. Let's dress and enjoy the day together, shall we?"

Fiona got out of the high bed and made her way to the dressing screen in the corner. She draped the sheet over the side and stepped behind it, not even a glimpse of her body in view.

"Fiona?" Camden called to her as he sat in the nearby chair and donned his clothing. He looked fit in his grey trousers and white ruffled shirt. A red waistcoat completed the ensemble, and his black hair gave a striking contrast to his white skin and black eyes. "There is something I would like to ask you..."

A knock at the door interrupted his train of

thought, and he went to answer it. A young kitchen maid in starched black and white linen entered, carrying an enormous silver tray.

"Good morning, m'lord." She attempted a curtsy. "Where may I set the tray, sir?"

Camden took the tray from the girl and dismissed her. "Thank you," he said. "That will do."

She quickly left and closed the door. Camden set the tray on a circular table in front of the fireplace between two overstuffed chairs.

"Come, Fiona," he called. "Breakfast has been brought. I believe you will enjoy this."

Fiona stepped from behind the screen, her hair swept up with curls hanging down the back to her mid-shoulders. The pale blue of her velvet bodice pushed her high breasts up, nearly peeking above the fine lace edging. She put her hands on her waist where the boning tightened and nipped just above the full dark blue jacquard skirt that flowed to her toes.

"The new gown fits quite well, Caldwell. I thank you again for the gift," she purred, moving closer for his inspection. He held out a glass of champagne mixed with orange juice and kissed her rouged lips.

"You look ravishing in my gift, Comtesse. And perhaps you will allow me to ravish you later, eh?" He tossed his should-length black hair with a shake of his head and placed a warm kiss on the top of her bosom.

Fiona gave a delighted laugh and sipped at her drink, adroitly spilling a few drops onto the top of her breast, as though his kiss had caused it.

Camden instantly took the hint and lapped the liquid, his eyes meeting hers as he did. Panther to tigress.

"Caldwell," she breathed, not taking her gaze from his. "Do you suppose we should eat a bit of something? I would so hate for you to lose your strength, my love."

Camden straightened himself and reached for a glass of his own. "Perhaps you are right, Fiona. Let's have a bite. Of food, this time?"

"Quite right.," Fiona laughed, and seated herself in one of the gold velvet chairs. Camden set down his glass and took up a plate of china.

"May I serve you, Comtesse?" He reached for the fork on the sausage platter, his eyes piercing her.

"Always, Caldwell," she commanded. "Serve me. You know my tastes by now." She sat back into the chair as though it was a throne put there for her regal use.

"I live to serve you, my glorious, exotic cat." Camden busied himself with plating the various items—fruit, pastry, egg, meat.

Fiona jolted at Camden calling her a cat. It shocked her sharply with the memory of her daughter, Caitriona, whom she had left behind in the detestable Highlands.

"Perhaps not a cat," she quickly corrected. "I

have an aversion to the name. Humor me in future, Camden."

"Of course, my darling," he acquiesced and handed her the china dish, laden with succulent choices. "And speaking of mine, Fiona. I still have that question to ask you, if I may?"

Certainly," she said between bites of a blueberry muffin. "What is it, Caldwell? You look so serious."

"We do get on rather well, do we not, Fiona?" he began as he sat in the chair opposite her. He leaned forward and folded his hands between his knees. "I do enjoy your company very much. I should hate for our friendship to end. Do you agree?"

"It has been an enjoyable diversion while I have been in Inverness," Fiona said pleasantly. "What are you getting at, Caldwell?"

"I realize the late Comte did not provide nearly enough - ah - resources for a woman of your tastes and stature. Would you consider becoming Lady Camden, Fiona? I could keep you quite comfortably, either here or in London. I also have a home in the country west of London, if you prefer."

Fiona sat back and gave a laugh at the thought. Seeing the expression on his face, she changed hers to match. "Why, Caldwell, you are serious, aren't you?"

"Very serious, Fiona. I do love you, you see. I know I haven't said as much, but I did rather think I showed it in the manner of my gifts and attention. It seems to be an incurable state that I find myself in."

He lowered his eyes to the floor and continued. "Neither of us desires a family, and we are well-suited in our interests and predilections. I think it would be a fine match."

"But Caldwell," she said, crossing her hands in her lap and adopting a gentler tone. "I am nearly fif-teen years your senior. What would your family say?"

"I have no family, Fiona. And I believe we have already proven the difference in age is not an issue. Oh, do say yes, Fiona."

He stood and moved toward her to take her hand. He pulled something out of his jacket pocket, placed it in her palm, and closed her fingers around it. "Say you will honor me by becoming Lady Camden."

Fiona opened her hand to find a magnificent diamond and ruby ring. "Camden!" she exclaimed. "It is a marvelous piece. It must be at least three carats of diamonds!"

"Four," he said plainly. "A family heirloom fit for a Comtesse. I realize you may not wish to give up your title, of course..."

"Lady suits me fine, Caldwell. Comtesse only seems to matter in France, after all." She looked from the ring to his eager face. "Yes, Lord Camden, I think it will be a most suitable match, indeed."

Camden pulled her to her feet and took the ring. He placed it on her finger, then pulled her into his arms where he kissed her deeply.

"I will make the arrangements so that we can marry before you go to Edinburgh."

"So fast?'

"Why not? Say that you will. Say please just once. Let me know you care?"

"I do as I please, I never say the word. You would do well to remember it, Camden," she flirted with him. She let out a small giggle as she looked at the ring again. "Oh,, all right. Please."

"Thank you, my love." He pulled her back into his arms. "You have made me a very happy man."

And you have made me very rich. This will be most rewarding and not a little entertaining.

"Cat? What are ye doing up here, lass?" Carrick put his arms up to help Cat alight from Solas. The patient mare stood quietly grazing, while Carrick helped her down to the ground beside him.

"I've brought ye some lunch, husband," she answered with a bright smile and shook out her skirts. "I have a wee bit of news for ye, and I thought I'd bring ye food while I delivered it." She reached back into the saddlebag for a cloth bag that contained their noon meal. She drew out a woolen blanket and tucked it under her arm before turning back to Carrick.

"Let's find a shady spot away from the malting house. I would have a thing to say to ye, if ye can spare the time."

"Always time for ye, Cat. There's a nice place over there, under the firs. Go on, and I'll just tell Geordie to take the noon break now, aye?"

Cat went to the place he had designated and laid out the blanket and food. When all was ready, she lowered herself to the blanket, soft and inviting with the sweet smelling grass underneath. She laid slices of cheese and bread on the linen napkins she had brought, and smiled again as Carrick came to join her.

"The malting's nearly done," Carrick informed her as he sat on the blanket and picked up the bread and cheese. "Mash will be next. Ye came at a good time, Cat. The men were getting hungry with the hot work." He took a bite and looked more closely at her. "Ye seem extra happy this day. The news must be good, aye?"

"Aye, it is," she said coyly, casting a sideways look at him. "At least, I hope you will think so."

"If it makes ye happy, Cat, then I am glad of it. Now, tell me. What could be so important as to bring ye this far up the glen?"

"Well…" she began, taking his hand in hers. "Ye're to be a papa, Carrick. Grandda just confirmed it this morning. In about five month's time." Her face radiated joy and light.

Carrick put down his food and swallowed

hard. "Are ye sure?" he croaked. His eyes misted and a glow suffused him. "Are ye quite sure, Cat?" He ran his free hand through his auburn hair, as if thinking it through.

"I hope ye are as happy as I about it, Carrick."

Carrick rose quickly with a grace belying his stature. He pulled Cat tightly into his arms and held her. "Beyond happy, Caitriona. A dream come true, to be sure. I never thought—"

"Ye never thought?" She pulled back to look into his proud face. "Because of when I was Jenny?"

"I suppose...summat like that. It just never occurred to me. It just doesna seem real."

"Well, it is verra real." Cat laughed and hugged him hard. "It's the best thing ever, Carrick! We will name him after ye!"

"Me?" The thought seemed to stun him. "A son? But we dinna ken what it will be. Any road, it is an enormous responsibility and oh..." A shadow crossed his face.

"What is it?" Cat stepped back and grabbed his arm in alarm. "What is it, Carrick?"

"I was just thinking - the poor bairn will be coming into verra bad times, no?" Cat could feel a small shiver rake down his body.

"Aye, perhaps," she agreed. "But we arena without resources, Carrick. We will raise a fine family no matter. I ken ye'd never let anything happen to us.

Ever."

Carrick's face brightened a little and he assumed a stronger countenance. "Aye, ye're right, Cat. I would defend and protect ye all to my last. I promise ye. I swear it to ye and the coming bairn."

Cat threw her arms around his neck and whispered, "Ye always have done, my love. And ye always will."

"Is the tea to yer liking, Lady Cat?" Mary stood near Cat's chair, awaiting her verdict. She had become a loyal and protective member of the household since Cat and Carrick had given them a home at Ben Fhithich. Carrick had even attempted, under the legal Laird Ian's signature, an appeal to obtain her Duncan's release from Fort Augustus. They had had no word as yet.

"Quite nice, Mary. I don't know how ye do it. I havena mastered the making of tea," Cat replied as she put the cup back into its saucer. "Go, now, Mary. Get some rest. We'll be fine, right Carrick?"

Carrick looked up from the book he was reading by the fire. "Aye, Mary. Go see to yer bairns— " He was cut short by the sound of the great front door slamming shut and quick footsteps coming toward the parlor. "What the...?"

"Hello, Carrick," crooned a rumpled Fiona from

the doorway. "Long time–

"Not long enough, Fiona. Do ye no have the good manners to knock before ye enter a person's house?" Carrick rose and tossed the book into his vacant chair. Then to Mary, "Go on to your bairns then, lass."

Mary began to step past Fiona who blocked her exit. "And you must be the wretched woman whom the gracious Laird saved from those nasty English soldiers." Fiona was enjoying taunting the woman. "And your husband in prison, too. Well, you heard the Laird. Go see to your poor children. Who knows how soon they will be fatherless, after all?" Fiona stepped out of Mary's way and let her pass.

"That was not necessary or kind, Fiona," Carrick grumbled at her, barely containing his temper. "Must ye always play the predator? Oh, aye, I forgot to whom I was speaking…" He took a few steps toward Fiona, who brushed past him and plopped herself down on the sofa.

"I've come to tell you that I will leave soon," she announced, looking Cat in the eye for a reaction.

"Ye're leaving?" Cat said evenly. "When? Where are ye going? Not that I care, only that ye'll be gone and away from here. None too soon, I might add."

Fiona gave a hearty laugh and picked up a biscuit from the plate on the table. "I am engaged to be married in two weeks time in Inverness. To an English Lord, I might add. I will not return here after that. I will leave next week. Oh, yes," she stopped and cocked her head at Cat. "Isn't Olivia's wedding this coming Saturday? Well, I shall leave on the Sunday then." She sat back and took a bite of her biscuit.

"I am quite sure, Fiona, that if ye care to leave sooner, Olivia wouldna be offended by yer absence," Cat spat at her.

Fiona rose with a flounce and started toward the door. "Don't worry, Caitriona. I will see to my motherly duties before I go."

Halfway out the door she turned to glance back at Carrick. "I hear you have an heir coming, Carrick. Well, good for you," she said with a smirk. "It will replace the one you forfeited at Culloden. See you at the wedding!" Her voice trailed away along with the clicking of her heels on the floorboards as she let herself out and was gone.

"She's going to marry an English Lord?" Cat said to Carrick from where she sat, straight as a pole in indignation and shock. "Now she's even more dangerous to us!" she cried in sudden realization.

Carrick hurried to her side and knelt beside her. "Dinna worry yerself, Cat. She canna harm us. I will see to it. I shouldha put a watch on her when she went to Inverness." He slapped his knee in consternation. "What was I thinking?"

Cat put a hand on his shoulder in reassurance. "Ye couldna possibly guess, Carrick. As long as she is gone from here, she canna do more injury. Just make certain she does go, aye?"

"Even if I have to take her to Inverness myself," he agreed.

It was going to be a very long week.

Chapter Nineteen

"What is it, Carrick?" Cat woke at the sound of the bedroom door closing. She sat up in the feather bed to glimpse Carrick in the night's gloom beginning to remove his clothes. "Are ye just coming to bed?"

"Aye," Carrick answered, a heavy tone in his voice as he shrugged off the trewes and pulled on a drawstring pajama pant. His muscled chest left bare in the late summer's eve. "I had news I had to tend to." He sounded as though he was burdened with something and wanted to talk.

"What news?" Cat asked as she put her feet over the side of the bed. She needed to wake a bit more in order to be attentive. "What happened?"

"Ye recall Robbie Colson? The crofter who violated the stalking rules? I spoke with him a time ago and gave him warning?" Carrick sat down beside her. "I had news tonight that he was seen in Inverness selling Beinn Fhithich venison to the garrison at Fort Augustus. There were several witnesses to the deed." His voice began to rise in anger mixed with betrayal and sorrow. "I'll no have it, Cat. He compromises the estate and everyone on it."

Carrick shook his head wearily. "I must evict him now. He's left me no choice." He softened his tone and hung his head. "He has a family, Cat..."

Cat let out a long breath and laid her hand on top of Carrick's "If ye evict him, well, do ye think he will do something vengeful? Like go to the English and tell them ye're alive? He could cause ye trouble there, Carrick. Ye could be arrested."

Carrick shook his head wearily. "Are, he could. But I'd rather me arrested than endanger the rest of the folk here. Any road, he will do as he likes, regardless I evict him or no. It must stop. Aye, I have thought it through."

Cat understood his sense of responsibility toward the people he cared for. She could not argue his point. At last, she said, "It will be all right then, love. Ye do what ye must. Ye canna allow one man's greed to put the rest in jeopardy. Ye're a good laird, Carrick. Good and honorable. He is responsible to his own family, and you yer own. Ye did give him warning, after all," she encouraged.

"True. All of it." Carrick gave her a small smile and lay back on the bed, pulling her down next to him. "Let's get some rest, aye? 'Twill be a long day tomorrow what with the wedding."

"Aye," she said, brushing a lock of his hair from his forehead. "I only pray it is a peaceful one."

"'Twas a beautiful ceremony, Olivia," Cat kissed her sister on the cheek as she handed her a glass of ale. The ceremony had just ended and the reception was about to begin. It was a scene reminiscent of the *ceidhli* with only minor changes.

An arbor had been set up at the front of the gathering. Olivia had twined hawthorne and various flowers though it—one of her "modern ideas," as Molly referred to them.

"Really, Cat?" Olivia chirped. "Did ye like it? Oh, Cat! I am so happy! I did think it was beautiful." Her eyes were filling with tears again and Cat quickly reached for the handkerchief she kept in her sleeve.

"Here, sprite," she offered it to Olivia. "Dab yer yes. Dab, not wipe, or ye'll ruin that expensive mascara Carrick brought ye from Inverness."

"Aye," Olivia agreed, carefully dabbing. "Thank ye for all yer help and for standing up for us. Ye and Carrick are the verra best."

"I'm proud of ye, Olivia," Cat answered, raising her tumbler of juice. "To ye and Ian. Long and happy lives together."

Olivia took a sip and gently pushed an edge of her ivory lace veil off her shoulder. "I hate to jinx this, but wasna Fiona supposed to be here?" she asked, searching the crowd.

"Aye," Cat answered, straightening the flower wreath on her sister's head. "She sent a note this morning that she has taken 'seriously ill.' Whatever that means."

"Well, what it does mean is that she willna be here causing her usual grief. Ah, here's Carrick. I should go and find Ian. If ye dinna mind, Cat."

"Not at all. Go. Find yer husband." Cat smiled lovingly at her as she walked away amid the well-wishers. *A beautiful bride, indeed. The sprite did it right for once, thank God.*

"I gave Father MacMurich the donation ye asked, Cat," Carrick said when he came to stand beside her. "And yer wee sister did nothing amiss this time. Yer grandda will be relieved."

Yer mother, too," Cat put in. "Poor Molly was a wreck worrying what else Olivia would ask for. Having no idea what our time is like, she could only imagine. And mind ye, yer mother has a large imagination as to what would come next."

"She must be feeling better then," Carrick agreed. "Speaking of mothers. Fiona is ill, is she?"

"Aye. So her note said... Oh, look. Grandda is about to lead Olivia for the first dance. I really do wish I had a camera." Cat sighed wistfully.

"Come then," Carrick took her tumbler and set it down on one of the tables. Taking her hand, he said, "Let's join them."

They watched as Hamish led Olivia around the makeshift dance floor for the few measures of a waltz, not dissimilar to the St. Bernard's Waltz that had brought Cat and Carrick together so long ago in Florida.

When they finished the waltz, Olivia nodded to Cat who went stand in front of the musicians. She lifted her violin as the singer, a tall, dark-haired man from one of the crofts, joined her. Cat had worked hard teaching him the song Olivia had chosen from 2010 entitled *Celtic Girl.*

She stuck up the initial notes and the man's lovely voice rang out:

"When you come to the end of your day
"nd you can't think of anyone to save your live
That could pull you through the big bad world

Then the chance is you never met a Celtic Girl"

"Woo hoo!" Ian yelped as he grabbed his new wife by the hand and pulled her to the dance floor where the two broke into an improvised country dance strathspey. Laughing together, Ian sang along,

"If you see a freckled face in your mind

And you just can't shake it cause you been daydream-in'

Of a head that's covered in curls

And the twinkle-eyed beauty of a Celtic Girl.

Soon, Carrick was singing along too as he gazed at Cat who was playing so hard that the strings on her bow were snapping and flying in the air.

"If she walks with the devil in her gait

And she'll dance for hours while her young man waits

And she tears when the bagpipes skirl

Then you know that you found yourself a Celtic Girl.

When you come to the end of your day

And you can't find anyone to save your life

Who can pull you through this big bad world

Then you know you better find yourself a Celtic Girl"

Everyone joined in the dance, including Hamish and Molly, laughing as they whirled under the canopy of arms held above them. When the music ended, a loud burst of applause, hoots, whistles, and yelps arose, engulfing every soul in the joy and merriment of the occasion. Hamish bowed to Molly gallantly, and Carrick beamed with pride at Cat. She bowed graciously and secured the violin in its case. She would play again later. But she was becoming hungry and the smell of venison was calling to her.

Carrick pulled out a chair for her as she set her plate on the table. "Thank ye," she said to him and focused on Molly. "I saw the two of ye dancing out there. Very spritely, ye were."

Molly blushed a bit and nodded, her eyes lowered under her lashes. "Aye. 'Tis been a time since I danced. ' Twas kind of Hamish to ask me."

"And ye danced it well, too, lass," Hamish put in. "It was— "

"Are ye Hamish MacAllan?" the boy interrupted at his side. "The *doctor* MacAllan?" He was a freckled teenager, not more than fifteen. He nervously extended a folded paper to Hamish. "For ye, sir."

Hamish took the note, a puzzled look on his face. "What the...?" He unfolded the paper and read it quickly. "From Fiona," he said at last. "She is worse and requests that I come to her. Now." He turned to the boy who seemed to be waiting for a response.

"She is worse? Ye are her page, are ye no?"

"Aye to both, sir." The boy nodded vigorously.

"Well, then." Hamish put his napkin on the table and rose. "Tell her I will be there forthwith."

He turned to the others and leaned over the back of his chair. "I will just get my bag and go. Hopefully, it will be nothing and I will return directly."

"Grandda!" Cat exclaimed. "She is just trying to spoil the wedding for everyone. She found a way to do it and it gets her the attention she wants. I think you should stay. Surely she can't be that ill."

"No, Cat," Hamish admonished. "I have a feeling about this. I will return as soon as I can."

Cat sighed in exasperation. "Well I hope you get back in time to see Olivia cut the cake."

"Aye, I will try." He turned to the boy who was waiting for him. "Lead on, lad. I am right behind ye."

Olivia's wedding was the talk of the glen for days. It had filled her with a happiness that set her and Ian to disappearing together at all times of the day. They seemed a couple deeply in love, and it warmed Cat to watch.

A week passed and Hamish had gone every day to tend to the sickly Fiona, whom he had diagnosed with measles. In an adult, it could be serious and quickly turn fatal.

For once, Fiona was not lying or milking the situation. She was simply too ill. There was little Hamish could do except offer supportive care—aspirin, rest, fluids, and a gentle hand for the miserable woman.

Fortunately, Olivia, Hamish, and Cat had been vaccinated in their own time. Especially Cat, who was pregnant with her first child, for whom it could have had serious consequences. Trying to explain vaccinations to Ian, Carrick, and Molly was a difficult task for Hamish as they had no real concept of bacteria or organisms. They did, however, understand the need for Fiona's quarantine and isolation from the rest of the glen.

Surprisingly, Fiona had been a relatively good patient. She was eager to be well and on her way back to Inverness, so she obeyed Hamish, if a little irritable at times. Her biggest concern was that her fiancé would worry as to her whereabouts, thinking her delayed in Edinburgh. Hamish assured her that if the man—whose name she had never divulged—truly loved her, he would understand. Fiona seemed to acquiesce to that reasoning.

And so, happy routine settled in at Ben Fhithich. It should have been a warning to them all.

"Ye're evicting me?" Robbie Colson growled between his clenched teeth as he took a step closer to Carrick. His entire countenance was threatening, but Carrick refused to give ground.

"Aye, Robbie. I warned ye time and again. These men here," he gestured to the four standing behind him, "are witnesses to yer selling Beinn Fhithich game to the English at Fort Augustus. Do ye dare deny it?"

Robbie's face was purple with rage. "I never… and ye are evicting me and…what about my wife? My bairns?"

"Yer sons are grown, Robbie. Aye, I am sorry for yer poor wife. But ye jeopardize the whole of the glen. We canna risk having ye here any longer. Ye have until tomorrow dusk to be gone." Carrick was the authority and he knew and projected it. "These men will see ye gone. Ye best move, Robbie. Ye have no minutes to spare." Carrick gave a glance at his men and turned to walk away.

"Ye'll regret this, Laird," Robbie yelled after him. "I'll see ye and yers suffer for what ye've done, I swear it. I curse ye all. Ye and yer bairns to come!"

Carrick kept walking up the hill to the house. His men would deal with Robbie, keep him under control and see him off the lands. But still, he hated curses. A superstitious part of him shivered. He shrugged it off and kept walking.

"I appreciate all you have done for me these last two weeks, da," Fiona said, actually humbled for a change. She sat, less imperially than usual in the grand parlor of Cat's former home *Taigh MacHendrie*, sipping tea.

"Yer welcome, Fiona." Hamish set down the cup and saucer he had been holding and looked firmly at her. "Ye should be fine, but dinna push it, aye? Ye still need yer rest. I'd not advise ye going off to Inverness for a few days yet."

Funny how her illness had subdued Fiona. She had softened a bit, and Hamish had begun to grow almost fond of her. His visits had brought back memories, not all bad, and stirred some paternal feelings from somewhere deep. Their discussions had become less self-involved and perilous on her part—more philosophical and intimate. She confided her past motives, experiences, and thoughts to him and it had opened a door that had stood between them.

"Yes, da," she answered him. "I will mind your orders. I don't plan to go until Friday next. Don't worry. I—"

The front door crashing open stopped her mid-sentence. She started to rise next to Hamish, who was already on his feet.

"Fiona!" a voice cried out, streaked with anger. "Fiona! Where are you?"

Fiona's face went white, and Hamish could see her begin to shake. In the parlor doorway stood an English officer in his red uniform, his face tight with fury.

"There you are, you duplicitous bitch!" he yelled at her. "Off to Edinburgh, eh? You lying, devious, whore…"

"Here now," Hamish broke in. "Ye have no right talking to a lady that way!"

"Lady?" He laughed maniacally. "This is a lady? Not on your life. And to think I nearly made her *my* Lady. My ancestors would have haunted me senseless for that."

He turned his hateful gaze from Fiona to Hamish, violence seething from every pore. "And who the devil are you, you Highland trash?"

Fiona abruptly sat. She looked about to faint, and Hamish was at her side in a flash, taking her wrist to check her pulse. He turned his grey head to look up at the sasunnach standing before him. His temper began to rise.

"I am her father, sir. And you are?"

"Her father?" Camden laughed again. "I pity you then. You bred a witch cat in that one. You should have drowned her at birth." He thought for a moment and began again. "You are the ailing father she was supposedly caring for in Edinburgh?"

Hamish straightened, satisfied that Fiona was stable. "I am her father. I was in Edinburgh. "He read the look on Fiona's face, one ripe with terror that said to play along. "I - uh - I came to Invergarry, because I had word Fiona was quite ill. I am a doctor, ye see."

Camden seemed to calm a bit at that, but took up pacing the parlor floor. "You, a sick man yourself, came all the way to the Highlands to care for your sick daughter? I don't believe you. I have a source that tells me you have been here for months."

He wheeled around to Fiona and raised an accusing finger. "That same source tells me that you are, in truth, Fiona MacHendrie, a Highlander. And that your daughter is Caitriona MacDonell who is married to the Laird Carrick MacDonell of Ben Fhithich. And Laird MacDonell did not die at Culloden, but is alive and well and running Beinn Fhithich this very day. How do you answer to that, Fiona?"

Fiona blanched again. "It is true, Caldwell. But,

let me explain…" her voice cracked.

"There is no explanation other than you are a lying whore," he spat back at her. "And as for the noble Laird, I have already set my men to find him. I will see him hanged, by God. And you?" He took a few steps toward Fiona, "You will rot here in the Highlands with your Jacobite family. I was in love with you, Fiona. How could you be so treacherous? I actually believed that you loved me in return."

"But, Caldwell. I did – I do – love you. Please, Caldwell…"

"Do not call me by my Christian name, woman!" he roared at her. "How dare you be so familiar? I shall never see you again. If I do, I will

see you hanged alongside your traitor son-in-law. Mark my words well, Fiona. You are dead to me."

With that declaration, Camden gave a final glare at Hamish. :" You should have let her die," he shot, and turned abruptly. His boots pounded hard on the entry floorboards. Hamish and Fiona held their breaths tight until they heard the door slam behind him.

When he found his voice again, Hamish cleared his throat and said, "I assume that was your fiancé?"

Fiona merely nodded and put her face into her hands. She began to quietly sob.

Hamish went to sit beside her, and put his hand out to her shoulder.

"Dinna worry, Fiona. It will be all right."

"No, da. It won't. He's ruthless. I've seen him." She looked up into his gentle face. "You must get word to Carrick immediately. He has been kind to me. You must warn him. I can't bear to see him hanged. Please, da. *Now*."

Hamish was on his feet in an instant. "Aye, I'll go. You will be all right?"

Fiona nodded and waved her hand, indicating that he should go. "Hurry, da. Please, hurry."

Hamish had rushed to Beinn Fhithich only to be told that Carrick and Cat were gone to the Invergarry Inn. Carrick had business with John, the Innkeeper and Cat wanted the respite and lunch.

Pray God they will be all right. Pray God the English haven't found them yet, he thought as he urged the horse faster. He was too old for this and unaccustomed to horseback. A part of him yearned for his beloved Jaguar. 1746 was definitely for young men, not a sixty-five-year-old retired doctor.

"Where's John?" her called to the stable boy as he quickly dismounted from the sweaty beast. His hair was wet with exertion and he wiped the drops from his forehead as he called again. "Have ye seen the

Laird, lad?"

"Aye," the boy finally answered, taking the reins of the horse from him. "In the dining room, sir."

Hamish headed as fast as he could toward the dining room, his mind fixed on getting to them with the warning. He saw them at a corner table with John and hurried over. He paused to catch his breath.

"Hamish?" Carrick immediately rose on seeing him enter and rushed to his side. "Are ye well, sir? What is it?"

"Grandda." Cat joined them. "Sit ye down. Ye look terrible." She put out a hand to guide him, but he pushed it away.

"Ye must…" He was breathing hard. "Ye must get away. The soldiers…"

"Soldiers?" Carrick cast a quizzical look at John standing beside him. "What soldiers? The watch dinna call alarm."

"The watch is probably dead," Hamish managed to gasp out. "They were at Fiona's. Caldwell Camden is – was – her fiancé. He is going to hang ye, Carrick. Get away now, and take Caitriona with ye."

"But, how did he find us? How did he ken it?" Carrick was already moving toward the door, Cat in tow.

"I think it was Robbie Colson told him," Hamish answered, following."Camden said he had a source. I canna think of anyone else."

"Damn the man!" Carrick swore as they made it into the courtyard. "John? I recall caves up the path yonder. Am I right?"

John nodded vigorously. "Aye, Carrick. Can ye find them, or shall I come?"

"Stay and keep the soldier's away best ye can. Come, Cat, we'll go to the caves until they are gone."

Cat held more tightly to his hand and stayed silent as they began to make their way up the rocky path, Hamish trailing along with them.

As they came to the side of a hill next to a rushing burn, they could hear the sounds of loud voices below them engaged in argument. The soldiers had arrived, it seemed. They continued to climb the path, now steep, in haste. The voices grew louder as Carrick ran his hands along the side of the cliff face, searching for an entrance to a cave.

"It's along here somewhere," he said, desperation growing in his voice, his manner. "Help me find the entrance."

Cat and Hamish joined him, pulling brush and shrubs away from the wall to find any sign of a cave. As the voices grew closer, their search grew more frantic.

"They're coming!" Cat cried. "Hurry!"

Carrick pulled back a thick expanse of gorse, bloodying his hand on the thorns. "Here it is!" He motioned to the others to follow him inside as he cleared an opening. "Ye, too, Hamish. Hurry!"

Hamish held back and shook his head. "No, Carrick. I will go back to the Inn. I will make sure the cave entrance is well-covered with the gorse, aye? I will come for ye when they have gone. Go now."

Carrick met Hamish's eyes in clear understanding of what must be done. "Aye," he muttered, then slapped his shoulder. "Good man. Be safe," he said and ducked into the cave behind Cat.

Hamish restored the foliage over the entrance as best he could, then set out back to the Inn below.

"Yer grandda has been a long time, now," Carrick said, tightening the makeshift bandage on his hand that Cat had torn from her petticoat. "The English must be very determined in their search to be such a while."

"Aye," Cat agreed, lifting her weary head from his shoulder. They had been sitting in the pitch black cave for hours. "It must be nearly morning by now." Her stomach gave a loud growl and she shifted next to him.

"Yer hungry," he acknowledged the rumble. "I'll peek out the entrance and see is it safe for us to go. Or me, at least. Ye and the babe need food." He rose carefully, so as not to jar her.

"Carrick! No!" Cat stood quickly and grabbed his arms. "Ye mustna go! What if they are still there? What if they catch ye? We—the babe and I—we need ye safe!"

Carrick kissed her quickly and moved toward the entrance. "I'll be safe, Cat. Dinna worry." And he was gone.

Cat sat anxiously awaiting his return. A million thoughts, all horrible, flew through her mind in vivid color. He would be hanged for certain, should they catch him. Weren't they rounding up and hanging every Jacobite they could find? And Carrick was Laird of an enormous estate. They'd want his lands, if nothing else.

A rustle in the brush made Cat stand abruptly and move back against the wall, deeper into the darkness. She held her breath lest they should find her.

"Cat?" Carrick's whispered voice called out. "'Tis safe, Cat. Come to me."

Cat slowly picked her way to him. She reached out her hand so that he could find her in the gloom. "They're gone?"

"Aye, they're gone. Come, Cat."

They made their way down the path toward the Inn, silent as they went. When they were almost there, Carrick stopped and turned to embrace her. Nuzzling her hair, he whispered, "There is a thing I'd say to ye, Caitriona."

Puzzled, she answered, "Go on, then."

"Ye love me no matter what, aye? And our bairn will be safe no matter, aye?"

"Aye, Carrick. Of course." She pulled back from him and stared intently into his eyes. Eyes that seemed to hold a mysterious burden. "What is it, for God's sake?" she insisted.

"Come, Cat." He turned and led her closer to the Inn.

"Oh, my God!" Cat cried, sinking to her knees in the dirt. "Oh, my God!"

Before her was the Inn with a parking lot full of shiny, modern automobiles.

Glossary

Bairn		Child
Ben or Beinn		Mountain
Beinn Fhithich	Ben Ee-heech	Raven Mountain
Burn		Creek or stream
Crag		Rock
Mo cridhe	Mow-cry- uh	My heart
Mo leannan	Mow-lawn en	My lover
Sasunnach	Sas-uh-nak	Derogatory term for the English in Scotland
Taigh MacHendrie	Tai MacHendrie	House MacHendrie

NOTE FROM THE AUTHOR

Invergarry Castle is real, but has been in ruins since Cumberland destroyed it in 1746. The ruins are featured on the cover of this book. It is one of the most beautiful places I have ever visited, and I go there every chance I get. You can visit the website at http://www.glengarry.net/castle.php

Invergarry Castle was the seat of the Chiefs of the MacDonells of Glengarry, a powerful branch of the Clan Donald, known as the Clan Ranald of Knoydart and Glengarry. Its situation on *Creagan an Fhithich - the Raven's Rock* - overlooking Loch Oich in the Great Glen, was a strategic one in the days of clan feuds and Jacobite risings.

This historic place needs stabilizing to preserve what is left of it. If you would like to donate to this worthy project, please go to

http://www.invergarrycastle.co.uk/

About the Author

Foery MacDonell is an award-winning, published author of historical romance. Her passion for literature and history led her into writing at the age of ten. Foery has honorary degrees in British Literature, Philosophy, Metaphysics, and Scottish History. She is a member of Romance Writers of America and Cactus Rose RWA.

A native Californian, Foery now lives in Las Vegas with her true-life Celtic Warrior and their Maine Coon cat, Guinness. Write to her at foery@moongypsy.com or visit her web site www.moongypsy.com

Also by Foery MacDonell

The Fool's Journey

From the mysterious monasteries of Tibet to the sweeping vistas of the Caribbean and its pirates, two people find their destinies in each other. The first novel in the Infinity Series, *The Fool's Journey* is an epic historical set in 18th century England and the Caribbean and spans the lifetime of Lady Catherine Bramwell and the three men who love her.

Lady Catherine: framed for the murder of her husband of an arranged marriage.

Jean-Philippe: the mysterious former English officer who wins her heart.

James: the loyal friend who loves her in silence

Artemus: the ex-pirate who wants to own her

CPSIA information can be obtained at www.ICGtesting.com
Printed in the USA
244757LV00006B/76/P

9 781449 538750